W9-BDM-307

His eyes widened when he saw her and the naked blade she held.

"Missed me?" he asked with a half smile. His gaze searched hers for the answer.

Her knife clattered to the floor; its blade rang against the stones. With a cry of "Sandor!" Tonia threw herself against him. The bulk of his body and the warmth that emanated from him soothed her fears.

Time stood still.

He did not speak, but his hand slid down her spine, exploring each hollow of her back. His touch was oddly soft and caressing. A delicious shudder heated her body. Tonia knew that she should fight against her growing desire to move closer to him. A lifetime of prudence counseled her to resist. It was not too late to turn away and put him back in his place. She was a chaste virgin dedicated to God; he was a wild, unpredictable Gypsy....

* * *

The Dark Knight
Harlequin Historical #612—June 2002

Praise for Tori Phillips's previous titles

One Knight in Venice
"...filled with intrigue, excitement, romance
and imaginative characters. Truly superb!"
—*Affaire de Coeur*

Lady of the Knight
"Ms. Phillips weaves an adventurous story...
a good, fast-paced read."
—*Romantic Times*

Three Dog Knight
"Readers will be held in thrall...a gem of a tale."
—*Romantic Times*

Midsummer's Knight
"...a fast paced plot...fully and funnily
Shakespearean...wonderfully written..."
—*Publishers Weekly* (starred review)

**DON'T MISS THESE OTHER
TITLES AVAILABLE NOW:**

#611 MY LADY'S PLEASURE
Julia Justiss

#613 THE COURTSHIP
Lynna Banning

#614 THE PERFECT WIFE
Mary Burton

THE DARK KNIGHT

Tori Phillips

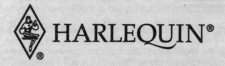

HARLEQUIN®

TORONTO • NEW YORK • LONDON
AMSTERDAM • PARIS • SYDNEY • HAMBURG
STOCKHOLM • ATHENS • TOKYO • MILAN • MADRID
PRAGUE • WARSAW • BUDAPEST • AUCKLAND

If you purchased this book without a cover you should be aware
that this book is stolen property. It was reported as "unsold and
destroyed" to the publisher, and neither the author nor the
publisher has received any payment for this "stripped book."

ISBN 0-373-29212-0

THE DARK KNIGHT

Copyright © 2002 by Mary W. Schaller

All rights reserved. Except for use in any review, the reproduction or
utilization of this work in whole or in part in any form by any electronic,
mechanical or other means, now known or hereafter invented, including
xerography, photocopying and recording, or in any information storage
or retrieval system, is forbidden without the written permission of the
publisher, Harlequin Enterprises Limited, 225 Duncan Mill Road,
Don Mills, Ontario, Canada M3B 3K9.

All characters in this book have no existence outside the imagination of
the author and have no relation whatsoever to anyone bearing the same
name or names. They are not even distantly inspired by any individual
known or unknown to the author, and all incidents are pure invention.

This edition published by arrangement with Harlequin Books S.A.

® and TM are trademarks of the publisher. Trademarks indicated with
® are registered in the United States Patent and Trademark Office, the
Canadian Trade Marks Office and in other countries.

Visit us at www.eHarlequin.com

Printed in U.S.A.

Available from Harlequin Historicals and
TORI PHILLIPS

Fool's Paradise #307
*Silent Knight #343
*Midsummer's Knight #415
*Three Dog Knight #438
*Lady of the Knight #476
*Halloween Knight #527
*One Knight in Venice #555
*The Dark Knight #612

*The Cavendish Chronicles

Please address questions and book requests to:
Harlequin Reader Service
U.S.: 3010 Walden Ave., P.O. Box 1325, Buffalo, NY 14269
Canadian: P.O. Box 609, Fort Erie, Ont. L2A 5X3

To my great-nephew,
Tyler Andrehsen,
Dinosaur Trainer, Pirate Captain
and Romance Hero-in-training!

Prologue

"Have I not here the best cards for the game to coin this easy match?"

—Shakespeare's *King John*

*The Gypsy Encampment on
Hampstead Heath outside of London
April 1553*

"Remember, Sandor, no blood is to be shed—not a drop when you kill the *gadji*." Uncle Gheorghe paused while he coughed up more green phlegm.

Sandor Matskella looked down at his hands, hands that were expected to snuff out the life of an unknown Christian woman somewhere in the north of England. "I am a horse master," he murmured. "What do I know of executions?" Now that he had learned the reason for his uncle's urgent summons, Sandor wished he had been too far away to have answered.

Uncle Gheorghe made a wry face. "Bah! It is of no consequence what you know or do not know. You are young, strong—and healthy. That is all that is necessary. As you see, I am not able to rise from my bed. You will do the deed in my place as the crown's executioner. You must—I have already spent the Constable's gold.''

"And he took our Demeo," snapped Aunt Mindra from her place by the fire. "That *gadjo* has thrown my boy into one of his deep pits in the Tower. He will hold Demeo among the rats to insure we keep our part of this contract." She spat into the flames. "May the dogs eat the Constable's heart and lick his blood."

Sandor shuddered at his aunt's curse. "What crime could a mere woman commit that the young English King requires her death?"

Uncle Gheorghe shrugged, then coughed up more phlegm. "Who knows? Who cares? It is enough that the death warrant is signed, sealed and delivered to me. Demeo is their hostage. The sooner you return from the north, the better it will be for him—and for all of us. Our people tread a slender rope here in England."

"I want my son back before he is polluted by those Englishmen or he dies of a fever in that foul place," Aunt Mindra snarled.

Sandor nodded, though he loathed the burden his uncle had placed on his shoulders. "I will leave within the hour," he answered in a low tone. "Young Demeo has the heart of a bear. He will return to your fireside as good as he was when he was torn from it." A little smile crossed Sandor's lips when he thought of his wily cousin. "I expect he will return with a wealth of winnings from the pockets of the *gadjo* who have the misfortune to guard him."

Uncle Gheorghe's eyes, dull with fever, glared at him. "It is no laughing matter when the Constable

himself delivers an order for an execution. Make haste
to this Hawksnest Castle in the north. Kill the old
woman and be done with it. But attend to every jot
and tittle of the warrant. No witnesses—it is to be a
secret execution. And no blood spilled. The Constable
was very clear on that particular point.''

''Why?'' Sandor furrowed his brow.

His uncle croaked a laugh. ''It is a *gadje* whim, I
expect. They employ the Rom to do their foul deeds
for them so there will be no blood on their soft white
hands. As to the woman, you can smother her but I
think the garrote is better. You have the strong hands
to do it properly.''

Sandor rubbed his palms together. What did he
know of killing? He had butchered a chicken or a pig
often enough, but never a human being. Certainly not
a woman. ''I will use the garrote,'' he answered, hoping that his face did not betray the revulsion in his
gut. ''The quicker the better—for her.''

''Mayhap she will be wearing a gold chain,'' Aunt
Mindra mused. ''Or pearl earrings. Bring me her jewelry to pay for my tears for my son.''

Her husband nodded. ''Aye, that is your right, Sandor. As her executioner, you are allowed a few priv-
ileges.''

The sour taste of bile rose in Sandor's throat. He
would give his finest mare and her colt to be free of
this onerous task, but his obligation to his mother's
brother overrode his reluctance. He balled his right
hand into a fist. ''I will take this woman's life
quickly, but I see no need to take her dignity as well.''

His aunt made a face. ''The condemned is a *gadji*,''
she said as if that one fact excused any wicked be-

havior on his part. "Since she is not a Rom, it does not matter what you do with her."

Uncle Gheorghe held out the warrant, written on stiff parchment. The official seal glistened like blood in the firelight. "Take this and keep it with you. If any man stops you on your journey, you will show him this and tell him you are on the King's business."

"Let us hope that man can read," muttered Sandor, who could not.

His uncle passed a small wooden box to him. A brass lock dangled from its clasp. "Once the woman is dead, cut out her heart, wrap it in cloth and lock it in this box together with a bit of her hair and a piece of her gown. That will be the proof that she is dead."

Sandor curled his lip. "What vile mind conceived this idea?"

His uncle sneered. "Good Christian men who sleep sound in their beds at night. The Constable was most insistent upon this last point."

"Demeo's life requires it," added Aunt Mindra.

Sandor took the box and pushed it deep in his canvas sack so that he wouldn't have to look at the thing any more than necessary. "You must have been paid well for this pretty piece of work," he dared to say out of the side of his mouth. When healthy, Uncle Gheorghe possessed a formidable temper.

"Not enough to insure my son's life," the older man growled. "Do your duty and be quick about it. The sooner you go, the sooner you return. So go!" He waved his nephew away from his bedside.

Before leaving the camp, Sandor paid a quick visit to his grandmother, the family's venerated *puridai*. He did not want to begin such a troubling journey without having his fortune read. Old Towla Lalow was the wisest woman Sandor had ever known. She greeted him with a smile when he lifted the flap of her bender tent.

"I knew you would come, my son," she said when he kissed her cheek.

He grinned at her. "Your cards told you this?"

She shook her head. "My heart," she replied, tapping her breast. Then she took her special deck of *tarocchi* cards from a burgundy velvet bag. Though the thick vellum cards were very old, their gilding still gleamed in the lantern's light. She shuffled her deck, then laid down the cards in a horseshoe pattern, while she sang to herself under her breath.

Sitting opposite her, Sandor waited patiently, despite his need for haste. Time with Towla was never wasted. When she had placed the spread of cards to her satisfaction, she studied them with deep concentration, adding lines to those the passing years had already etched on her face. The fire hissed in the charcoal brazier.

His grandmother pointed to the first card. "Here you are," she said with fondness.

Sandor snorted. "Prosto, the Fool? Aye, for I go on a fool's errand."

Towla shook her head. "Nay, your journey will be a most important one for you." Then she pointed to the second card. Two Lovers joined hands under a golden canopy.

Sandor only shook his head with a rueful grin. He was going north to kill, not to fall in love. However, he said nothing lest he insult his grandmother and her *tarocchi*.

Towla tapped the center card. Sandor sucked in his breath when he saw it was the grim figure of Death.

His grandmother chortled. "It is the card of great change. Does that frighten you, Sandor?"

He fidgeted. "Nothing frightens me except the devil."

His grandmother only broadened her smile. "You are wise to be wary of change, my son, and yet, do not hide from it."

He cleared his throat. "What do you see?"

"You will help others who would never help you," she began.

He snorted. "That describes every *gadjo* I have ever trained a horse for."

"You were born lucky in many things, but not in all," she continued.

Sandor nodded. His parents had died in an outbreak of the sweating sickness when he was a child, yet he had survived unscathed. He had a gift for training horses, almost as if he knew their thoughts, yet now he was commanded to take up his uncle's employment and become a killer. How was that lucky?

Towla touched the Hermit, the fourth card of the spread. "Your journey will be one inside of you as well as on the road. Use this time wisely to read your soul."

"And the change that you speak of?" he asked, pointing to the card bearing the black figure holding a scythe.

"Ah!" Towla's eyes twinkled in the firelight. She pointed to the Lovers. "You will have a friend who is an enemy. You will find life holding hands with death. And—" she tapped the Fool "—you will make a decision that will alter your path forever—if you dare to risk it."

"Is the risk worth the effort?" he asked, discomforted by her predictions.

She swept up the cards into a neat pile before he had a chance to look at the fifth card in the spread—the one that foretold the outcome. "That is your decision to make, not mine," she replied. "Come closer and let me kiss you, Sandor, for we never know when we kiss for the last time."

"Grandmother, your talk is none too cheerful," he said as he kissed her.

"Then smile for me," she commanded. "Ah, your smile would beguile the very angels from their clouds." She kissed him on each cheek. "*Baxtalo drom!* May your road be lucky."

"And may I soon return to you," he whispered. He started to rise, but she put her hand on his sleeve.

"Where does Gheorghe send you?"

He sighed. "To the mountains north of here, to a place called Hawksnest. It is a castle, I think."

Towla considered his destination. "Sounds cold. Wrap up warmly. Take extra food—and a sheepskin. Methinks you will need them anon, for your journey will be longer than you expect. Whom do you execute for the boy King's pleasure?"

Sandor cleared his throat. "It is a noblewoman, though why, I do not know."

A tiny smile curled his grandmother's lips. "And her name?"

"Lady Gastonia Cavendish."

Chapter One

Hawksnest Castle in the Pennine Mountains

Tonia Cavendish huddled as close to the dying embers of her cell's meager fire as she dared. The feeble heat barely warmed her fingers numbed by the icy wind whistling through the tiny arrow slit high in one wall, her only source of daylight. At home in Northumberland, her father would be overseeing the spring planting on the family's estate. Did Sir Guy Cavendish have any inkling that his eldest daughter was not safely in the little house of prayer she had established near the Scottish border? Instead, Tonia shivered inside a dark prison, high in the mountains that ran like a bony spine down England's length.

Was it a week ago that she had been brought to this ruined ancient fortress, or ten days? Time seemed to have stood still since the moment she and her band of pious young women had been torn from their prayers, taken by night to York, and tried for the crime of treason against the crown. Tonia would have considered the charges to be ludicrous except for the fact that her stern judges had sentenced her to death.

She had been given no chance to defend herself, or to call upon her family for aid. Within the hour of her sentencing, she had been driven through the streets of York, bound and gagged inside a dark coach. After a day and night of nonstop travel, she found herself here at the end of the earth. Her four guards, rough, swearing men, told her nothing, and they begrudged her the crusts of bread and sticks for her fire. If she was to die, why didn't they just leave her to starve or freeze to death and be done with it? They said she must wait. So she spent her days and most of her nights in prayer—waiting and shivering.

At the end of the hall, beyond the stone-cold room that was her cell, the men kept a cheerful fire going in the guardroom. Tonia could smell the oak and hickory smoke and see the light of the high flames dance on the wall opposite the barred window in her door. Other savory smells taunted her: meat roasting on the spit and hot chestnuts popping on the hearth just out of sight of her little icy hell.

Tonia tried to forgive her captors as she knew she should, but sometimes the hunger that gnawed her empty stomach sent all her good Christian thoughts flying like the snowflakes that occasionally fluttered through her pathetic window. Huddling deeper in the woolen cloak that the guards had allowed her to keep, she prayed to her patron, Saint Michael, for deliverance.

Tonia shook herself awake; she had dozed off frequently during the past few days. She feared that if she slept, she would freeze to death. Outside, the pewter-gray sky had changed to a darker hue. Then she noticed that the voices in the guardroom spoke in louder and more animated tones. Flexing her aching joints, Tonia rose from her hearthside pallet and crept to the door. Pressing her cheek against the rough wood, she peered through the bars but could see nothing except the stone wall opposite, the turn of the corridor and dim shadows beyond. The voices told her that two, possibly three of her guards were conversing with someone new.

The stranger's voice, deeper than the others and lower in tone, spoke with a foreign accent, though Tonia could not make out the words he said to the men. A sudden trembling overtook her. She remembered the story she had heard as a child that the late King Henry VIII had sent to France for a special headsman when he had executed his second wife, Anne Boleyn. Had Tonia's own headsman finally arrived? She pressed her chapped knuckles against her lips to keep her fear from crying out. She would not give those louts at the end of the hall the pleasure of witnessing her distress.

The conversation ceased abruptly with a clatter and several bawdy jests. Then Tonia heard their footsteps recede. The silence that followed frightened her far more than the lewd suggestions and taunts her captors had thrown at her during her captivity. The suffocating stillness engulfed her. Her ears tingled with the strain to hear something—anything. The light of the guards' fire that mocked her chilled body slowly burned down, leaving the end of the hall in near-darkness for the first time since her arrival.

While there was still a lone spark in her own hearth, Tonia picked her way across the uneven flagstone floor to her pallet. "Good Saint Michael," she prayed aloud, not caring if any unfriendly mortal also heard her, ''send me your strength for I am very weak and sore afraid.''

The last ember winked out in a thin plume of curling smoke. Tonia pulled her cloak tighter around her. A new thought knifed through her. Suppose the guards had abandoned her! They may have received word to return from whence they came, and to leave Tonia to her fate in the bowels of this isolated mountain fastness. She choked back a sob. She must be strong to the end—and a bitter cold end it was likely to be.

It gave her little comfort to think that she would die a martyr for daring to open a Catholic nunnery within the boundaries of her Protestant homeland, currently racked with religious dissension in the name of the sickly young King Edward VI. Her father had warned her of her folly, but Tonia thought that by living so far from London, she and her followers would be safe from the stern laws against popery. And what of the others who had been arrested with Tonia? Had Lucy, Agatha, Margaret and little Nan suffered the same fate as she? Were their deaths on her soul? ''Pray forgive me, sisters,'' she whispered into the darkness.

A noise awoke Tonia with a start. Angry with herself for falling to sleep again in the middle of her prayers, she blamed the lack of food for making her light-headed. Again she heard the noise that had disturbed her slumber. Someone had returned to the guards' room. She was not alone! A sudden gladness overwhelmed her before her common sense prevailed. Whomever was bustling around out there had not come to free her, or he would have done so immediately. This unseen person was either a new jailer, perhaps one skilled in torture—or her executioner.

Through the barred window she saw a light move toward her. Her stomach growled with a bleak anticipation of food. A man's heavy tread echoed down the narrow corridor; his armament jingled as he walked. Then a dark form blotted out the light on the other side of the door.

Her heart nearly jumping out of her breast in fear, Tonia pulled herself erect. She would face this stranger on her feet rather than huddling on her knees. After all, she was a Cavendish, one of England's greatest families. She would not dishonor the Cavendish's sterling reputation for bravery—no matter what the next few moments might bring.

A key rattled in the door's lock. Tonia's teeth chattered. Clenching her jaw, she squared her shoulders. She would be bold, like the great wolf that was the Cavendish family emblem. Squealing in protest, the door swung open on its rusty hinges.

Tonia sucked in her breath.

The man in the doorway appeared huge. His dark cape covered his broad shoulders, making him look as if he had just furled two large black wings. He had to duck his head to enter her cell. When he lifted his lantern higher, a small cry welled up inside Tonia. The man wore a black hood over half his face—an executioner's mask.

Even though her knees shook with terror and weakness from hunger, Tonia dropped a small curtsy before her fate.

"Good evening, my Lord of Death," she said in a steady voice. "I have been expecting you."

The man took a step toward her then stopped and

lifted his lantern higher still. Behind the slits in his mask, Tonia saw a pair of dark blue eyes glitter in the candle's light.

Now that the worst had happened, she felt almost giddy with relief. "Come in, sir, and close the door quickly behind you. I fear you are causing a draft, and I am chilled enough as it is."

He stood still like a large shadow.

Tonia stepped more into the pool of light cast by the lantern. Giving him a smile, she hoped that her lips did not tremble. "I pray you, my lord, do not linger but close the door. My time grows shorter by the minute and I prefer not to freeze to death in the meanwhile."

Giving Tonia the briefest of nods, the hooded man turned and shut the door as if he were a guest in her father's house instead of a rough minion of the crown. Then he placed the lantern on the small plank table that constituted the cell's main piece of furniture.

"You are Lady Gastonia Cavendish?" he asked in a low tone. Had the man not been a headsman, his voice could have belonged to a minstrel.

She inclined her head. "I am. And who, sir, are you?"

He shook his head, and half turned away from her. "My name is not important."

Judging from the sound of his voice, Tonia deduced that the man was young, perhaps near to her own age of three-and-twenty. She smiled again. "You fear that I would curse you with my last breath if I knew your identity?" When he did not reply, she suspected that she had hit the core of truth. "Have no fear, Master Death. My last words will be for God alone, I assure you."

The headsman strode to the fireplace and stared at the heap of cooling ashes on the hearth. "Why did they not give you more wood before they left?"

Taken aback by his question, Tonia shrugged. "Why should they waste fuel—or food—on one who will be dead by dawn?" She hid her hands in the folds of her cloak so that he would not see them trembling. She wasn't sure how much longer she could keep up her veneer of courage.

He glanced at her over his shoulder. "You have not eaten?"

Tonia sank down on the only stool. "Not since last evening at this time. I fear that you arrived just before my midday meal."

"'Tis no way to treat a lady," he muttered, more to himself than to her.

Tonia detected a chivalry that she had not expected from so dire a visitor. "My jailers did not consider me a lady, but only a common criminal awaiting my appointment with death." When he said nothing in response to this, she pushed her boldness a little further. "I pray you, sir, could you fetch me a cup of clean water before we proceed to more serious matters? My throat is parched. I would bless your name, if I knew it, for such a little kindness."

He muttered something that sounded like an oath under his breath, but Tonia did not recognize the language. Then he turned on his heel. Without a word to her or a backward glance, he flung open the door, strode through it and banged it shut behind him. At least he had left his lantern. Tonia stretched out her fingers to its flickering heat while she wondered what would happen next.

* * *

Once he had rounded the corner of the hall, Sandor ripped off his hood and mopped his sweating face with his sleeve. Why hadn't one of those *gadje* guards warned him that his intended victim was young and exceedingly beautiful, instead of the old crone he had expected? He pressed his burning forehead against the rough stone wall to cool his skin, though nothing could temper the flame that had ignited him the moment his lantern's light had fallen upon Lady Gastonia.

Tall and slim like a willow in a summer meadow; her every movement like a dance. Bright blue eyes like precious sapphires set against the white silk of her skin. And her hair! Sandor groaned to himself. A man would be in paradise if he could lose himself within that raven cascade; her disheveled appearance from her captivity only made her more enticing. And what unexpected courage lodged in her heart! She had curtsied to him as if he were the finest lord of the land even though she had recognized him for what he was—the instrument of her death.

Sandor clenched his large hands. This beautiful *gadji* had been sent to tempt his soul. Pushing that thought, and more lusty ones, to the back of his mind, Sandor replaced the hood over his head. Then he lifted the water skin from the peg on the guardroom wall and threw its strap over his shoulder. Loading one arm with a stack of split logs and kindling, he swept up his travel pack and an abandoned cup with his free hand. Taking a deep breath for fortification, he returned to the lady's cell. Before pushing open the door, he peered through the little window.

Lady Gastonia still sat on the stool, though she had drawn his lantern closer to her. Its golden glow lit up her face. *Jaj!* She was even more beautiful than he had first thought. What madness had possessed the ministers of the King to seek the death of such a flower as this one? He pushed open the door, causing her to look up at him. She smiled, not like a woman knowledgeable of the world, but like an innocent child—and yet no child had such lush lips so full of delightful promise. He kicked the door shut behind him.

Her finely arched brows drew up. "You come better provisioned than I had hoped, sir."

Her voice was silver, rippling like the music of a lover's lute. He swallowed the knot in his throat. "I have traveled three nights and four days in the saddle since London, my lady," he said as he dumped the firewood on the hearth stone. "I am cold, tired and hungry." Hungry for her, as well as the bread and cheese that he had in his sack.

She folded her hands in her lap. "I fear this place does not offer many comforts."

You are here and that is a comfort. Sandor shook off this dangerous thought. The lady was marked for death, not life. He hunkered down before the fireplace and arranged the logs and brush. Then he thrust a twig into the lantern's flame. When it ignited, he touched it to the dry kindling. Flames leapt at his command. Sandor was aware that the bewitching *gadji* moved her stool a little closer to the fire. He could feel the heat of her body behind him even through the fur-lined cloak that he wore.

"My grateful thanks to you, *Monsieur de Mort*," she murmured. She lifted the skirts of her simple gray gown so that the fire could warm her feet and ankles.

Sandor dared to look at her again, though her

beauty made his tongue stick to the roof of his mouth. "You speak French?" he blurted out.

"*Oui,*" she replied, then continued in that language. "My mother was born in the Loire Valley. From birth, my sisters and I learned both French and English."

He wet his dry lips. "I was born in a field outside of Paris one winter's morn when my family camped there for the season," he replied in French.

Again she lifted her dainty brows, and her jewel eyes widened. "You were born in a tent?"

He chuckled. "*Oui,* and my first cradle was our wagon horse's collar."

"Then you were like the infant Jesu?" Her voice held wonderment.

He shook his head. "*Non,* we believe it is good luck for newborns to sleep in such a bed. Horses are our life. That is the way of the Rom." He fed another log to the fire.

She half cocked her head, then asked in English, "Pray, what is a Rom? I am not familiar with that word in either language."

Sandor lifted the water skin off his shoulder, uncorked it and poured some of its liquid into the chipped clay cup. Why should he be afraid to tell her? After all, he was here to kill her, wasn't he? Her opinion, one way or the other, was of no importance to him. She was only a *gadji.*

He handed the cup to her. "The Rom are my people," he said as she gulped down the water. "That is what we call ourselves." He poured more into her cup. "You…that is…Christians have called us many different names, some of them are not fit for a lady's ears." He took a deep breath. Why was his heart beating so fast? "The French thought that we came over the sea from Egypt because our skin is darker, our hair is black and we speak in a strange tongue."

"Egypt!" The lady's eyes shone. "A friend of my family's is a merchant who travels over the Mediterranean Sea. Jobe has often told us wondrous tales of that ancient country. How I have longed to go there! Tell me, are there truly beasts that have large mouths full of fearsome teeth and scales so thick that arrows bounce off them?"

Sandor could not help but smile at her enthusiasm. He shrugged. "I do not know, my lady. I have never been to Egypt. Nor has any member of my clan, yet we are called Egyptians. But here in England, the Rom are known as Gypsies."

The lady regarded him over the cup's rim. "You are a Gypsy, then?"

He nodded, watching for her reaction. She surprised him by smiling.

"I have never met a Gypsy before, but I have heard of your people."

"No doubt," Sandor muttered. He could well imagine what good *gadje* parents would tell their delectable daughters about the evil Gypsies.

"When I was little, my mother taught me a poem— a silly little rhyme." She put the half-empty cup on the table, and then recited, "'If you enjoy having futures foretold,/Watch out for your pennies, your silver and gold.'"

Sandor gave her a rueful look, then completed the doggerel that he too had learned as a child in France. "'These ragged tramps, full of futures to tell,/Bear little but the words of the fortunes they sell.'"

She held out her hand, palm up. "Can you read my fortune?"

It is death. Aloud, he replied, "Nay, my lady. My grandmother has that skill—I do not. I am a trainer of horses."

She furrowed her brows. "Methought you were the headsman."

Sandor looked away from her—her beautiful eyes could pierce his thin defenses. He opened his sack and took out several cloth-wrapped items. "I am that as well—for the moment."

She gasped aloud. When he looked at her, he saw that she had turned a shade paler.

"Do not be alarmed, Lady Gastonia. I will be gentle when I...uh...take you."

She uttered a high, brittle laugh. "You will kill me with kindness?"

He clenched his jaw before answering. "I do what I am bound to do, my lady. I bear weighty responsibilities that are not of my own choosing. Believe me when I tell you that I am no murderer. Merely a servant of the crown."

He unwrapped strips of dry smoked meat, then paused. It went against the Rom's strict rule of *marime* to eat with a *gadji*. Everyone knew that the non-Rom were polluted with evil. His food would be defiled if this beautiful lady even touched it. Yet she was starving. Brusquely he offered a piece to her.

With only a brief hesitation, she accepted it and gingerly tasted it. "'Tis good!" She sounded surprised—and pleased.

"My grandmother always said that food seasoned with hunger tastes the best." He took a large bite from his piece. "I assure you, my lady, I would not poison you. 'Tis not in the death warrant."

She swallowed the food, then asked, "Have you my warrant with you?"

"Aye." He regarded her out of the corner of his eye slit. "Can you read?"

She nodded. "If the penmanship is not cramped and the wording is in a language I know."

Sandor wiped his hands on his leather breeches before he extracted the thick parchment from his shirt. The King's official seal swung from a red ribbon at the bottom. He handed it to her. "Then read your fate, if you so desire," he said, wishing he had that learning.

Lady Gastonia pulled the lantern closer to her, then pored over the words. Warming his backside by the fire, Sandor watched her. He liked the way the lantern's light caught the reddish highlights in her dark hair. Her lips moved as she read, and Sandor fantasized her whispering his name while they made love. He could almost taste the honey of her kisses. He yearned to feel the satin of her milky skin against his own swarthy one. His loins began to throb.

Sandor shifted his position, in part to hide his growing arousal. Though the laws of the *kris* forbade it, he had made love to *gadje* women in his reckless youth, and they had moaned with pleasure at his touch. He looked down at his hands. He brushed the knotted thong of the garrote hitched in his belt.

She has bewitched me. Turning his back to her, he stared into the crackling flames. For a moment he had forgotten his pledge to his uncle and his responsibilities toward the family who had reared him after the death of his parents. His little cousin languished in the depths of the Tower at the King's pleasure until Sandor could bring proof of this lady's sudden demise. The sooner he did his job, the sooner Demeo would be free. He glanced over his shoulder at Lady Gastonia.

I can take her now, while she has her back to me. She would feel very little pain. It would be a quick death. I could be riding back to London before noon tomorrow. He pulled the garrote from his belt and looped it around his fingers.

Chapter Two

Sandor turned to face his victim. The knotted cord of the leather garrote bit into the flesh of his palms, just as it would bite deeply into the creamy skin of the lady's swanlike neck. He swallowed. A burst of sweat dampened his mask. He took a step toward her. Lady Gastonia shifted on her stool and the wooden crucifix that hung from her neck thumped against her tight bodice. Sandor stared at the tiny, outstretched figure on the cross—the same cross that had damned the Rom to wander the earth forever, or so the storytellers swore.

Sandor loosened his grip on the garrote. Even though she was a *gadji,* he knew that Lady Gastonia was a holy woman. Her plain garb and absence of jewelry proclaimed her piety. He could not kill her without allowing her the chance to make her amends to God, though he could not imagine what sin she could possibly have committed. He did not want to have her unshriven spirit haunt him the remaining years of his life.

Just then, the lady looked up at him. The expression in the depths of her azure eyes melted away his murderous intent. *Forgive me, lady.*

Then she laughed, though there was no mirth in the sound. "Did you know that my good judges have decreed that none of my blood shall be shed?"

Sandor suspected that they did not want her death to defile them any more than they already were. When he did not reply, she continued.

"When my father learns of my execution, the King and his minions can truthfully say that they did not spill my blood, yet I will be stone dead all the same." She shook her head. "Oh, the clever wit of the law-yerly mind! They split their words thinner than a cook can slice an onion. Aye, and weep the same tears without sorrow while doing it."

Behind his back, Sandor gripped the garrote. He said nothing since there was nothing he could tell her that would refute her clear-eyed deduction. He cleared his throat. Best to warn her to make herself ready to meet death. His hands shook.

She sipped more water from the cup then asked, "How will you do it? Kill me, that is?"

Sandor winced inwardly yet marveled at the candor of her question. He held up the knotted garrote. "With this, my lady."

Her mouth trembled just a little before she bit her lower lip. Then she asked, "Will it hurt much?"

I have no idea. Aloud, he spoke in the same voice he used to soothe a skittish colt. "They say 'tis quick."

She gave him a taut smile. "Who are 'they,' I won-der? And how do these wise men know such a thing? Has anyone come back from the dead to tell them?"

Sandor knelt before her so that they were eye-to-eye. He longed to take her hand in his. He hated the idea that she feared him. "I could wait until you sleep, then cover your face with my cloak."

She touched the furred edge of his cape. "How could I fall asleep knowing that I would never wake again in this world?"

He tore his gaze from hers. "I have no answer to that, my lady. I only know what I must do. I pray that you forgive me."

She touched the back of his hand. "Gentle Lord of Death, I have already forgiven you."

Sandor's skin burned under the light pressure of her fingers. A nerve throbbed at his temple. *Do the deed now and be gone for the sake of your soul!* He rose, towering over her. "Then, my lady, I must ask you to make your peace with God. I will give you a few moments alone."

He turned on his heel, anxious to flee from her before she unmanned him completely. Quick as a cat, she fell to her knees and clutched the hem of his cloak.

"Then my first prayer will be to you, *Monsieur de Mort.*"

Sandor's resolve shivered at the sight of the innocent beauty at his feet. He clenched his hands under the cover of his cape. "I am neither God nor the devil, my lady. Why pray to me?"

Tonia could not remember feeling so cold in her life. Her mouth had gone completely dry. Death was so close to her that she could smell the dark reaper's breath of decay over her shoulder. Mustering the last shred of her courage, she stared up at the powerful man who stood over her. Avoiding the sight of his large, long-fingered hands, she wished she could read his expression on the face that was hidden by his black hood.

"I beg you for one boon—a small one—before you snuff out my life."

He cleared his throat again. "What boon?"

She wet her lips. "I ask your generosity to allow me to live until dawn. I wish to admire the beauty of the sunrise one more time. 'Tis only a few more hours," she added. She smiled for additional effect, though she had no idea if he was moved or not. "Besides, I do not think you intended to begin your journey back to London when the night hours are only half-spent."

He said nothing, but looked over her head as if he sought some guidance from a ghost in the corner of her cell.

Grasping at this small hesitation, she added, "Methinks that my cold corpse would make poor company until the morning."

Continuing to stare at the far wall in stiff silence, he clenched and unclenched his hands. Tonia found this action alarming. She tightened her grip on his cape.

He moistened his lips. "You think that I…" He paused then snapped, "Are you offering me your body for my pleasure in exchange for a few more hours of life?"

With a gasp, Tonia let go of his cloak and sat back on her heels. She hadn't meant that at all. She shook her head, embarrassed to look at him and fearful that he might believe such a lewd thought. "I am a virgin, dedicated to our Lord. I do not know if you believe in God but…"

"I am no savage, Lady Gastonia," he rumbled

overhead. ''And I do believe in the same God as you, though I worship in a different manner.''

A sliver of relief pierced her terror. ''Then you should realize that I was not offering you my chastity as payment for my boon. If you require carnal pleasure, 'tis best that you strangle me now.'' She dared to look up at him to discover that he stared down at her. ''Do you think that I could greet my Lord God with the sin of impurity staining my soul?''

The executioner drew in a deep breath. His chest seemed to double its width. ''Nay, lady. You need have no fear of this...dirty Gypsy.'' He spat out the last two words. ''I have no intention to defile you.''

Tonia sighed inwardly, her mind spinning with a flicker of hope. If she could beg a few hours from him now, then she had a chance to beg a few more in the morning, and perhaps a few more after that, until she could devise some way to escape him altogether. ''I fear no Gypsy, Master Death, only the devil, and I do not think you are he.''

Though he remained silent, the man's shoulders relaxed their tense posture. Tonia took another deep breath, then continued. ''What are a few hours to you? Nothing, but they are a lifetime to me. In the name of the merciful God that both you and I serve, will you grant me my request?''

He rubbed his forehead, then he flicked his cape from her grasp. He strode to the cell's door before he answered her. ''I am not made of stone, my lady, and as you pointed out, the hour is late. I am tired and need to sleep. You may spend the rest of the night at your own leisure. I will not intrude until the sun climbs over yon mountain's crest.'' He flung open the door. A wintry gust of wind whipped through the small chamber, causing the lantern's light to flicker.

Tonia glanced at the fat candle glowing inside its glass house. "You have forgotten your light, *Monsieur de Mort.*"

One corner of his mouth twitched. "My people believe that a burning candle in the night keeps troublesome spirits at bay. I would not have your remaining hours—nor mine—be filled with disquiet. I bid you good-night, my lady."

Before she could thank him for this little kindness, the headsman whirled out the door, slammed and locked it behind him. Tonia sagged against the stool, weak with gratitude for her small reprieve. She cradled her head in the crook of her elbow and wept a few tears of relief. Though she tried to direct her mind toward spiritual matters, thoughts of the mysterious stranger intruded into her prayers.

Everything about the man intrigued her, beginning with his masked visage. Though she could not see most of his face, she thought that he must possess some good looks. His mouth belied his somber occupation, for his full lips looked as if they hovered perpetually on the edge of a smile. His profile, accented by the firelight, spoke of great inner strength. He moved his powerful body with the easy grace of a dancer. Yet Tonia sensed an air of isolation about him, as if he preferred to stand on the edges of a dance floor and observe the merrymaking of others. His eyes? They fascinated her. Turquoise blue behind his mask, they flashed his changing emotions like the suddenness of summer lightning. Had she detected a warmth simmering in their depths, a glimmer of compassion?

Tonia did not intend to fall asleep, but fatigue settled over her like a thick feather bed. In the midst of her musings of the virile, enigmatic man who lay just down the hall, she closed her eyes and drifted into oblivion.

The wind off the North Sea hurled sleet against the leaded glass panes of Snape Castle's high arched windows. Seeking greater warmth from the lashings of the spring storm, Lady Celeste Cavendish and her handsome husband, Sir Guy, had retreated to the small solar on the second floor where they played a lively game of piquant before the blazing fireplace.

Celeste fanned her cards. "Oh la la, *mon cher,* I have you now."

Guy said nothing but frowned at his hand. By his expression, his wife knew she had him by the tail. She always did whenever they played piquant.

An urgent knocking on the chamber door interrupted her gloating. Without waiting to be admitted, Master Bigelow, the family's chamberlain, threw open the door. A pale visage had replaced his normally ruddy complexion.

"Your pardon, my lord and lady, but Lady Lucy Talbott has just arrived and she is in great distress."

Celeste cocked her head. Lucy was one of the girls who had joined Tonia's venture into the religious life.

Folding his cards, Guy turned to his servant. "In this weather? Does her father accompany her?"

The chamberlain shook his head. "Nay, she comes alone save for some hireling lad of York. From the looks of them both, I would venture to say that they have been in the saddle since daybreak."

Celeste dropped her cards on the felt-topped gaming table. "*Ma foi,* Bigelow! Bring the child up here at once. She must be frozen. Take the boy to the kitchens. Mull some ale and bring a goodly bowl of pottage at once."

Guy rose, and his great height filled the small room. "In distress, you say?"

Halfway out the door, Bigelow paused. "Aye, my lord. Weeping and gibbering something about Lady Tonia."

Celeste's heart thumped within her breast. Had Scottish reivers swept down on Tonia's little convent and attacked the covey of women there? What about the serving men, Norton and Thompson? Hadn't they protected Tonia and her friends as they had been instructed?

"Don't stand a-gaping, man," Guy shouted. "Bring Lady Lucy here!"

Celeste gripped the arms of her chair, afraid to move lest she shatter into a thousand pieces. What had happened to Tonia, her beloved firstborn? Celeste closed her eyes and sent a silent, urgent prayer winging to heaven.

Guy paced the narrow confines of the chamber like a great caged bear. "This comes of folly—mine own," he berated himself. "I should have never let her move so far from home—nor have sanctioned her religious ideas."

Masking her growing fears, Celeste gave her husband a tiny smile. "You know that neither of us could ever deny Tonia anything. And her endeavor to retreat from this wicked world into a house dedicated to praising God was worthy." But Celeste had never fully understood why her beautiful daughter had chosen to pursue the celibate life when so many of the shire's bachelors had come wooing her.

Guy turned on his heel. "Mayhap the wicked world has followed her even there."

Celeste covered her breast with her hand to calm the rapid beating of her heart. Just then, Bigelow opened the door and ushered in Lady Lucy. The young woman, no more than seventeen years old, all but fell into Guy's outstretched arms.

"Oh, my lord, I am so sorry!" she wailed before her tears overwhelmed her.

Guy helped her to his chair, while Celeste draped her fur lap robe around the shivering girl. Lucy continued to cry in convulsive gulps. Putting her arms around the girl's thin shoulders, Celeste willed her strength to stem Lucy's grief. Deep circles, almost purple in color, stained the skin under her red, swollen eyes. Her light brown hair was windblown into tangles from her journey. The news she bore must be very dire indeed if Lucy had ventured out into this foul weather without even a head covering.

One of the kitchen maids arrived, bearing a large tray filled with several steaming bowls of food and drink. Celeste took one of the cups of hot ale, blew on it to cool it then held it to Lucy's quivering lips.

"Drink, sweetling, and take heart. You are safe with us."

Lucy slurped the brew, heedless of its scalding heat, until the cup was nearly empty before she leaned against the chair's back. Stroking the girl's brow, Celeste was further alarmed to discover that Lucy was running a fever.

Guy hunkered down before their guest so that his great height would be less intimidating. Taking

Lucy's trembling hand in his, he spoke to her in gentle tones. "Now, then, Lucy, what is amiss?"

The girl's eyes grew larger and fresh tears appeared in their corners. "They have taken Tonia away, my lord. Methinks they are going to…to…to execute her." She dissolved again into weeping.

Celeste felt hot and cold at the same time. A drumming hummed in her ears. *I cannot faint! Oh, my sweet Tonia!* She dug the nails of her fingers into her palms to keep from collapsing.

Though Guy's voice remained soft, a dreadful chill crept into his azure eyes. "Tell us who threatens to do this most foul deed, Lucy."

The girl wiped her nose on the tail of her hanging sleeve before replying, "The King's men, Lord Cavendish. They came to our house over a week ago in the dark of the night."

"Where were my men?"

Lucy hunched her shaking body deeper into the folds of the robe. "Norton and Thompson tried to stop them. They demanded to see the King's orders but the soldiers…oh, my lord, the soldiers killed them on the doorstep." She covered her mouth with her hand.

Guy compressed his lips into a thin line. "Are you sure they were minions of King Edward?"

Lucy nodded. "They wore the rose badge and the King's cipher on their surcoats."

Celeste and Guy exchanged quick glances. For decades the Cavendishes had feared just this sort of attack from the Tudor upstarts who had snatched the crown of England nearly seventy years ago. Someone must have discovered the family's secret of their Plantagenet blood and their remote claim to the throne through their descent from King Edward IV of blessed memory. Both King Henry VII and his son, Henry VIII, had spent their lifetimes wiping out the last known traces of the realm's lawful rulers. But to have visited their obsessive vengeance upon an innocent young woman was beyond perfidy—yet a craven trick well practiced by the uneasy Tudor kings.

Guy squeezed Lucy's hand. "What happened then?"

Lucy drew the furred robe tighter around her. "The soldiers bound us, even though Tonia fought them. Then they bundled us into a dark coach and drove off into the night." She grimaced. "Their hands were not gentle nor their tongues. They called us traitors, whores and a great deal of worse filth."

Anger at the indignities forced on her daughter and her companions replaced Celeste's fear. Striving to keep her boiling temper out of her voice, she asked, "Did those churls...touch you in an unmannerly way?"

Again Lucy shook her head. "They said they would ravish us if we did not obey their orders, but they never dared to carry out their threats."

Blue fire blazed in Guy's eyes. "Where did the knaves take you?"

"To York, though we did not know it at the time. The carriage's windows were covered with a heavy black cloth. We were blindfolded inside a mews before they led us into the courtroom."

"They convened a trial against you?" A muscle throbbed along Guy's jawline.

"Aye, my lord," the girl answered. "Three bearded men in black robes questioned each of us in turn. Hour upon hour they harangued us about our religious beliefs and our little nunnery. They wanted to know if we held allegiance to the Pope in Rome or to King Edward. They asked us if we read the Bible and what prayers we recited. They even asked us if we danced with the devil or practiced witchcraft. At one point, I fainted from hunger and thirst.''

Though Lucy's account was dire enough, Celeste felt a small relief that no mention had been made of the Cavendish's Plantagenet heritage. "Surely, 'tis no treason nor witchcraft to pray to God. What fault could they find in that?''

Lucy's voice sank into a hoarse whisper. "They accused us of being Catholics, of practicing an outlawed religion and going against the express decrees of the King.''

"And thereby you could be called traitors," Guy rumbled. "But *you* are free now. Why not our Tonia?''

At the mention of her friend's name, Lucy's eyes again filled with tears. "Alas, they convicted her, Sir Guy! They said that since she was the eldest one of us and because she came from a great family, they would make an example of her to discourage any other members of the nobility who had popish leanings. Those horrible judges condemned sweet Tonia as a traitor and sentenced her to death.''

Celeste sank into her chair, and ice encased her heart. "*Mon Dieu,* say 'tis a trick. 'Tis a lie.''

Lucy's tears spilled down her cheeks. "Not so, good lady. Afterward, the soldiers turned the rest of us out into the street without so much as a groat among us, but not Tonia. The last I saw of her, they led her through another door and I know not what they have done with her.''

Celeste swallowed down the lump in her throat. "I pray God that she still lives. They would not dare to execute the niece of the Earl of Thornbury—not without hearing an appeal for her defense."

Guy stood. "Young King Edward thinks he is doing God's will by cleaning out so-called popish heresies, but the conniving scullions who whisper in his ear know better. 'Tis earthly *power* they crave, and they seek to wrest it from the nobility by skullduggery, lies and intimidation. There is no gutter too low for them to wallow in."

"And Agatha, Margaret and little Nan? Where are they?" Celeste asked, though her thoughts rested only on her daughter's fate.

"We were taken in by Margaret's cousins who live in York, though that family gave us grudging hospitality, lest we infect them with our shame." Lucy drank the rest of her cooling ale. "They supplied us with enough coin to hire horses and escort to see us home. I came directly to you, Sir Guy. Mayhap, there is still time to save Tonia."

"If not, then I swear there will never be world enough or time to slake my vengeance," he muttered.

The tone of his voice and the look in his eyes frightened Celeste almost as much as her fear for Tonia. *If Guy is rash, I could lose both husband and child within the month.*

Leaving Celeste to care for Lucy, Guy sent messengers to the nearby homes of his son, Francis, and his nephew, Kitt, heir of the Earl of Thornbury. Guy chose not to involve his powerful older brother just yet until he knew further particulars of Tonia's whereabouts. What Guy needed now was the youth, strength and stamina of the younger Cavendish males.

He intended to be on the road to York by dawn's light. Based on Lucy's account of the time that had elapsed between her release and her arrival at Snape Castle, he reckoned eight days had passed since that farce of a trial. Time enough for Tonia's execution. He buried that possibility in the depths of his mind. She was still alive, he told himself, as he sharpened his sword. He would have received word by now if she were not.

If Tonia is indeed dead, falsely accused and even more falsely murdered, then God save the King—from me!

Chapter Three

The rattle of the key in the rusty lock of her cell door woke Tonia with a start. A thin stream of early morning sunlight filtered through the arrow loop window. Sitting up on the cold floor, Tonia massaged the crick in her neck where she had fallen asleep against the stool. A sudden rush of adrenaline shot through her. *'Tis morning and he's come for me!* She struggled to her feet before the executioner could open her door. She must present to him a cheerful face and as much bravado as she could muster.

When the man stepped inside her chamber, she saw that he still wore his black hooded mask though he had doffed his huge cape, making him look a little more human than an avenging dark angel. Despite the morning's chill air, the sleeves of his muslin shirt were rolled up to his elbows, revealing deeply tanned skin the color of acorns. Droplets of water dripped from his hands, indicating that he had just washed. Her gaze locked on to the slim dagger in a leather sheath that was strapped on his left forearm. She gulped.

Glossy black hair curled from under his hood and

a single golden loop winked in the light from his left earlobe. Around his neck, he sported a jaunty red neckerchief made from a piece of ragged silk that she had not noticed last night. The spot of bright color cheered Tonia a little, giving her the courage she desperately needed.

She swept him another low curtsy. "Good morrow, Master of Death."

He halted at her greeting. "Good morrow, my lady." He crossed his arms over his chest but said nothing more.

Does he expect an invitation to strangle me? Tonia's taut-strung nerves almost made her titter at the idea. *Two can play at this game.* She folded her hands in a pose of tranquillity that was at odds with her true feelings, and waited. For several eternal minutes the two stared at each other across the width of the small room.

Just when Tonia began to despair of this ploy, the executioner looked over her head at a spot on the bare wall and spoke. "'Tis daybreak, my lady," he informed her in a low gruff tone.

Please, dear Lord, soften this man's heart. Tonia feigned indifference. "Truly? I cannot tell. The window is too narrow and high for me to see out."

"The sun has risen over the mountain," he muttered, still not looking at her.

Methinks he is as nervous as I am. She gave him a little smile. "I long to see that glorious sight just once more."

He pointed to her window. "Stand on the stool and look for yourself."

Tonia took a deep breath. "Is there a walkway that faces east?"

He nodded once.

"Gentle headsman, pray escort me there that I may see the sun as a free person sees it and not through bars like a caged sparrow. 'Tis a little thing I ask."

He said nothing, nor did he move.

Tonia braced herself in case he should suddenly spring at her and choke her before she could evade him. She was a Cavendish and would not easily yield up her life no matter what that piece of royal parchment decreed.

When the silence between them had stretched to the breaking point, Tonia continued. "If you were me, wouldn't you desire one last taste of freedom?"

Finally he turned his masked face toward her and dropped his arms to his sides. "Aye, that I would." He swung the door wider. "Come, then, lady, and look your last, but walk softly, the walls of Hawksnest are old and crumble easily."

Now she laughed aloud. "You are afraid that I will fall and break my neck before you have the chance to do it?"

"The fall would frighten you, my lady" was his only reply. He held the door for her as if he were escorting her to a banquet instead of to her doom. As she passed him, he touched her elbow lightly. "To the left."

Her skin prickled at his touch.

It was after nightfall when Tonia had been brought to this ruined fortress. Since then, she had never been allowed to leave her cell. As she walked toward the spiral staircase at the far end of the corridor, her spirits grew lighter with each step. She had not realized how much she had missed the fresh air and the warming rays of the sun until this moment. Savoring the morning's light, she slowly mounted the winding stairs until they suddenly opened onto a parapet. As she stepped out onto the narrow walkway a strong arm around her waist checked her progress.

Her masked escort pointed to the deteriorating retainer wall, then kicked at the topmost stone. Without protest from the centuries-old mortar, the rock tumbled over the side. Tonia heard it bounce its way down—a long way down.

"'Tis dangerous, Lady Gastonia," he murmured behind her. His breath tickled her neck, causing the most unexpected sensation in the pit of her stomach. "Lean back on me."

Despite her distrust of him, Tonia laid her head against his chest and relaxed in the crook of his arm. Heat emanated from his body, warming her. His rapid heartbeat drummed in her ear; the feel of his hard muscles rippling under his shirt quickened her pulse. When his grip tightened around her, she shivered, though not from the cold wind. Laying her hand on his bare arm, she was aware of the quiet strength within him. He tensed under her fingers. Hastily she withdrew her hand and used it to shield her eyes as she looked out on the dawn's gilded-pink glory.

This side of the fortress hung over a deep ravine that cut between two mountains. The rising sun's beams turned a small stream at the base into a rivulet of molten gold. A thin curling mist rose from the water's surface. Bright blue colored the sky, with a puff or two of white clouds in the distance. A large hawk, his great wings spread wide, drifted on the updrafts in a lazy circle, searching for his breakfast. The day promised to be the most beautiful one that Tonia had ever beheld. She sighed.

"It pleases you?" he asked in a husky whisper.

"Aye," she murmured as her gaze drank in the beauty of nature.

They stood pressed together in silence for some time. Tonia wished that the moment would go on forever. She felt content and protected, an odd sensation since she was in the arms of the man who would kill her, perhaps even within this very hour.

Tentatively he fingered a tendril of her unbound hair that fluttered against her cheek. He smoothed it between his fingertips, before tucking it behind her ear.

"I wondered what it felt like," he explained in a hoarse whisper.

Tonia's skin tingled with pleasure where he touched the tips of her ears. A shiver of excitement rippled down her spine. She gave herself a little shake. These unexpected stirrings within her would never do—not now. She had to keep her wits sharp if she hoped to buy more time. Stretching on her toes, she ventured to peer over the edge of the unstable wall at the dizzying drop below them.

"What do you seek, my lady?"

Glancing over her shoulder, she held him in her steady gaze. With her heart thudding in her throat, she forced a smile. "I was wondering—where will you bury my body?"

Her guileless question struck him like a dash of ice water in the face. For a few precious moments, Sandor had almost succeeded in forgetting who he was and why he was standing on the edge of the world with a butterfly in his hands.

Behind his mask, he blinked. "I had not given

thought to that,'' he confessed with honesty. No one had said anything to him about disposing of her body—only cutting out her heart.

She turned in his arms so that she faced him. Sandor instinctively pulled her closer to him. The wall walk was far too narrow for much maneuvering. He looked down at her. The wind whipped her dark cloud of hair in all directions, making her seem almost otherworldly. Her lithe body molded against his. His blood, already heated by her presence, sizzled through his veins.

The lady cocked her head. ''The warrant plainly states that you are to bury me deeply in the ground.''

He couldn't help smiling at her, though his heart hung like a stone at her words. ''I am glad that one of us can read that paper. I dare not disobey the King's commands,'' he bantered.

Her lower lip trembled a little in the most provocative way. He was tempted to kiss it, but common sense and his lifelong discipline to distance himself from the unclean *gadji* stopped him. He was expected to kill her, and he had to keep reminding himself of that increasingly disagreeable fact.

She arched one raven's-wing brow. '''Tis a great shame that my time with you will be…ah…so short, for I could teach you your letters.''

Sandor would have liked that. Unlike the rest of his clan, he had always harbored a secret desire to read and write. And the beautiful *gadji* would have been a very pleasing teacher. *Banish such foolish woolgathering, Sandor! Remember that she is a walking dead person.*

He looked over her shoulders at the mountain peak on the far side of the valley. ''I am Rom. We have no need for schooling since there is no holy book for us to read.''

Lady Gastonia stared up at him with surprise in her sapphire eyes. ''You do not have the Bible?''

Her question amused him. ''Our storytellers say that in the beginning the Lord God handed out His laws to all the peoples of the world. The Jews in the Holy Land wrote down the laws on stone tablets, then later in the scrolls of their Torah. The Christians wrote God's words in their Bible. The Moors of the desert wrote their laws in the Koran, but the Rom?'' He shrugged with a wry grin. ''My people were, as always, very poor and they had no paper, so they wrote down God's laws on cabbage leaves. Unfortunately, a hungry donkey came along and ate up the leaves. That is why we have no book to read.''

She regarded him for a long moment then said, '''Tis a tale for children. It cannot possibly be true.''

He brushed the tip of her nose with his forefinger. He couldn't help himself. ''Who knows? But 'tis a good story all the same.''

She moistened her lips with the tip of her delicate pink tongue. ''I would love to hear more of your stories, *monsieur*. The day is still very young.''

He frowned. Why did she have to remind him of the time? He must be on his way to London before nightfall. His cousin's stay in the Tower's dank pit grew longer because of his procrastination. Sandor gritted his teeth.

He guided her toward the open archway that led back inside the fortress. ''We burn daylight, my lady. Your company has made me forgetful of my duty.''

She gasped as he pushed her down the dark stairway. ''You are going to…to do it now?''

He sighed heavily, his voice filled with anguish. "My will is not my own."

Spinning around, she placed her hands against his chest. Her warmth seeped through his cold skin, straight to his heart. He stopped in his tracks.

"One thought more before you snuff out my life," she said in a rush. "The day is cold, the ground probably frozen. No doubt 'twill take you several hours to dig a grave that is deep enough to hold me. If you allow me to sit by your side and keep you company, perchance your work will seem lighter and will take less time."

"You want to watch while I dig your grave?"

Swallowing, she nodded slowly. "Would you rather have my stiffening corpse by your side? Cold, grim comfort indeed for such tedious work. Let me live a little longer and I could talk with you, mayhap even sing you a song or two, though I must confess I have the voice of a raven, not a lark."

He rubbed the back of his neck while he pondered her latest request. How had things become so complicated? Yet, her argument had a point. Sandor most certainly preferred to keep her alive for as long as possible.

"By my troth, yours is a silver tongue, my lady. I feel sorry for your future husband—" He stopped when he realized that she would never have the chance to marry. "Forgive my foolish words. I must be light-headed from want of food."

She gave him a sweet smile. "There is nothing to forgive. I forswore the joys of marriage when I dedicated myself to God. I always expected to die a virgin—just not quite so soon as now." She stared down at her feet.

Appreciating the beauty of the woman before him, Sandor thought all chaste vows, no matter how religious, were a waste of the good God's gifts. Since he could not think of anything to say in reply, he merely guided her back toward her cell. She stopped at the door.

"In good Saint Michael's name, Master Headsman, tell me now what you intend to do with me so that I may prepare myself." Her shoulders shook a little.

He blew out his cheeks. "Break my fast—and yours if you have an appetite for it," he snapped more roughly than he had intended.

Gazing up at him, her eyes moist with a film of unshed tears, she said, "Aye, sir, I would be grateful to share another meal with you."

Not trusting himself to say anything else, Sandor pointed to her stool. After she crossed the tiny room and took her seat, he strode quickly down to the guardroom at the end of the passageway, grabbed up his saddle bag and wineskin, and returned to the lady's chamber before she had the sense to realize that he had left the door wide-open. Of course, there was no place she could go on foot unless she took it into her head to jump off the parapet, an idea that Sandor sincerely doubted. When he stepped though her doorway, he found her in silent prayer.

Respecting her private devotions, he busied himself with unwrapping the food he had bought at the village at the bottom of the mountain pass. Despite his attraction to this lady, his deep-seated prejudice toward all *gadje* caused him to separate her food from his. If she did not finish the wedge of cheese he cut for her or the chunk of the brown bread that he pulled from his loaf for her, he could never eat the leftovers himself. While he poured wine into her cup and watered it, he marveled at his peculiar situation—he could kill this *gadji* but not eat the food that she had touched lest she pollute him. When their simple breakfast was ready, he cleared his throat to attract her attention.

"Amen," she said aloud, then made the sign of the cross—a popish ritual that even Sandor knew had been forbidden by the King's religious laws. For this simple act, she had been condemned to death.

She smiled when she saw the food on the small table before her. "'Tis a feast," she murmured before biting into the hard cheddar.

With approval in his heart, Sandor watched her enjoy their small meal. "My grandmother always said that a good woman was one who ate a poor dish and praised it for its richness." Actually, old Towla Lalow had described this trait as belonging to a good *wife,* but Sandor saw no reason to mention that fact to his victim.

The lady laughed. "Methinks I would like your grandmother, for she sounds like a very wise woman."

"She is," he replied softly, remembering the puzzling fortune Towla had told him only a few days ago.

They ate the rest of their breakfast in a silence that was more companionable than strained. The lady's quietude impressed Sandor, for he knew that his wife, who had died in childbirth two years ago, would have chattered nonstop like a witless jay if she had faced the same fate that this lady faced. Remembering his loss, he again blessed God for taking his wife with quick, painless hands. For her sake, he would do the same for Lady Gastonia when the time came. He was relieved to see that the *gadji* left no scraps or crumbs.

Slinging his bag over his shoulder, he rose and beckoned to her. "Come, my lady, if you wish to watch me...work." He could not bring himself to name his macabre task.

With a heart-stopping smile she followed him out of her dark prison.

Fortified by the food and buoyed by her reprieve, Tonia almost skipped along the uneven paving stones as the executioner led her into the sunshine. Crossing the bare courtyard, she glanced back at the place wherein she had spent the past week. The dilapidation of the mountain fortress surprised her. The wing that housed her cell was the only section of Hawksnest that still had four standing walls. The second and third levels of the fortification had long since tumbled down the sides of the ravine. Until now, Tonia had thought she had been kept in a more substantial building. From its air of desolation, she guessed that Hawksnest had not been used for well over a hundred years, perhaps longer.

She nodded to herself. Considering the precise directions of her death warrant, the King and his overzealous minions intended that her execution would not only be done in secret, but that she would virtually disappear from the face of the earth—her resting place unknown, unmarked and unmourned. She knotted her brows together in a frown. 'Twas meant to be a cruel punishment for her family as well as for herself. How could men who professed to love God do something so pitiless as send her to eternity without the comfort of shriving her soul? Their perfidy was doubly damned for forcing her dear parents to grieve her unknown fate for the rest of their lives.

She cast a quick glance at the tall man who walked ahead of her. Perhaps he would send a message to her father. Then Tonia remembered that the headsman could not write. Perhaps he would allow her to send a last letter to her family, telling them where they could find her grave. She chewed on her lower lip. Since her too-intriguing executioner couldn't read, he didn't know that her grave was to be unmarked. She decided that she would not enlighten him; in fact, she would do exactly the opposite.

Just then, he veered to the left toward what remained of the stable block. He whistled and a soft whinny answered him. Glancing over his shoulder to Tonia, he smiled at her beneath the ominous black mask.

"'Tis Baxtalo, my horse," he explained, his tone much more lighthearted. "He must be wondering what happened to me."

Tonia stopped outside the stable while the man disappeared through the dark doorway. She heard him speak a strange language to his mount. Tonia gave a quick look around the now-empty courtyard. Ahead of her, she saw the yawning portal that led to the outside world—and freedom. Her instinct to run almost overwhelmed her until her common sense prevailed. If she bolted now, he could easily catch her, especially when she had no idea of the lay of the land beyond the fortress's walls. The executioner might decide that she was too much trouble and kill her on the spot. Tonia's best hope for her life was to stretch out the time as long as possible, as well as win her executioner's trust and goodwill.

Hearing the horse's hooves scrape against the stones, Tonia looked back toward the stable. Grinning with pleasure, the man led out a spirited gray stallion with charcoal mane and tail. At Snape Castle, Tonia had grown up riding the best horses that her father could buy, and she recognized a good animal when she saw one. In fact, the quality of the headsman's mount surprised her. The execution business must pay exceedingly well, she thought. Then she remembered that the man had said that he was not an executioner.

He guided his horse toward Tonia. "Are you afraid of this one, my lady?" he asked in a solicitous tone.

Smiling, Tonia shook her head and approached the horse with her hand out, palm up. "Nay, *monsieur*. I love horses and yours is particularly fine." She gave him a sidelong glance. "I wonder where you got him." She recalled that Gypsies were reputed to be sly horse thieves.

He caressed the horse's velvety nose and patted its neck with obvious pride of ownership. "I have raised him from birth. He was a gift to me from his dam. That is why I call him Baxtalo. It means 'lucky' in my language."

The sleek animal sniffed Tonia, then allowed her to pet him. She admired his confirmation. *He's in excellent condition. I wonder if he would allow me to sit on his back after he's gotten used to me.* Baxtalo could be her savior.

While Tonia mused on the fresh possibilities that the horse offered, his owner returned to the stable. When he emerged, Tonia saw that he carried a short-handled shovel over one shoulder. The headman's mouth had reverted to its usual serious expression.

When he drew near to her, his blue eyes hardened to ice behind the slits of his mask.

''Come, Lady Gastonia, show me where you would like your grave.''

Chapter Four

Though his brief words chilled her to the marrow, Tonia kept her smile fixed on her lips. "My family and friends call me Tonia."

Amazement replaced the headsman's grimmer look. A cynical grin curled his full lips. "You think I am a friend, my lady?" he asked in a gruff tone.

"They say that a gentle death is a good friend to be desired, and you have promised to be gentle." Tonia prayed that he did not see how much she shook under her cape.

He stared at her for a moment, then took up Baxtalo's reins. "The day grows older," he muttered as he started toward the main gate.

"And more beautiful, methinks," she replied, following him.

He didn't look back at her but plodded through the archway. Tonia's heart soared as she left the walls of her prison behind her. Beyond the gate, a broad, rock-strewn meadow sloped down to the stream that they had seen from the wall walk. Though the remains of last summer's grass were brown and brittle underfoot, Tonia thought it the most splendid piece of earth she had ever seen. After watering his horse, the headsman turned the animal loose to forage. Then he looked at her.

He swept his arm in a graceful arc, like the lord of the forest that grew on the far side of the stream. "Well, my lady…er…Tonia, where pleases you?"

A hundred miles north of here at the very least. She skipped down the gentle hillside until she stood before him. Turning, she looked back up at the ruined fortress. Even in the bright sunlight, it exuded a dark, forbidding air. She certainly did not want to be buried within its looming shadow. Closer to the stream, she saw a hillock that overlooked the deep valley below them. She wondered if the dead were able to admire the beauty of their final surroundings.

"There." She pointed to the sunlit spot.

He nodded. Without a word, he walked over to the mound, braced his legs apart for balance on the slope and struck the earth with his shovel. He muttered something under his breath. Tonia joined him.

"Still yet frozen." He pushed the shovel down with his foot. A few clods of dark earth broke free.

Tonia concealed her glee. She sent a quick prayer of thanksgiving to Saint Michael. The executioner's spade loosened another small clod or two. At this snail's pace, it would take him a week to dig a grave that would be deep enough to hold her—and if the weather again turned cold, that time could stretch out even longer.

Masking her joy at this unexpected turn of events, Tonia pretended to be crestfallen. "'Tis not very promising, is it?" She prodded one of the dirt clods with the squared toe of her shoe.

The large man merely grunted as he attempted to

wrest another shovelful of earth from the hillside. Gathering her cape around her, Tonia perched on a low stone that protruded from the ground. In silence, she watched him labor.

After a quarter of an hour, he had managed to scrape off the top layer of sod roughly in the contour of a grave. Though the shape did little to comfort Tonia, the frozen earth below encouraged her hope for a long reprieve. Pausing, the headsman mopped his perspiring lower face with the sleeve of his padded woolen jerkin.

Tonia took a breath. ''Methinks 'twould be more comfortable for you if you removed your mask,'' she suggested.

He shook his head, wiped his palms on the thighs of his brown leather breeches and then returned to his task.

Tonia pushed her windblown hair out of her face. ''I give you my word of honor that I will not haunt you—afterward.''

Avoiding her gaze, he again shook his head.

Tonia rubbed her shoulders. Even though the sun shone, the wind kept the air chill. She rose and sauntered over to inspect his progress. Happily he was less than a foot down at one end.

She cocked her head. '''Twill take some time, methinks, for I wish to be buried deeply in the earth.''

He jammed the shovel's head into the dirt until it stood upright, quivering on its own. He glared at her. ''*I* will say when 'tis deep enough.''

Tonia refused to back away. Instead she assumed an injured expression. ''Agreed, *Monsieur de Mort,* but I tell you truly, I had a nightmare of the wolves and wild boars feasting on my bones.'' She did not need to feign her revulsion at this thought.

He looked down at the shallow hole. ''I give you my word. You will rest in peace, my lady.''

She inclined her head in a small gesture of thanks. ''The day is yet young and the sun still warms his rays. Come, let us walk in yon forest and allow the earth to…ah…soften a bit.'' She held out her hand to him.

He bent his head and studied his work. ''I have promises to keep,'' he muttered.

Tonia swallowed, knowing exactly what he meant. ''Aye, 'tis true, but you have also given me a promise—to plant my body deeply in this earth. Yet the ground is not ready for such a great hole. Let us walk awhile and enjoy the day while the sun does its task.''

She held her breath. A walk would give her more time to win the man's trust. If she intended to escape on his horse, he had to permit her more freedom of movement.

The executioner wiped the dirt from his hands, then nodded. He looked across the rickety bridge that spanned the stream in front of the fortress. ''What do we do on this walk?'' he asked in an odd, husky tone.

A spiral of fear shot through Tonia. She hoped that he didn't intend to ravish her within the hidden recesses of the trees. After all, he had told her he wouldn't last night. But that *was* last night. She lifted her chin. ''My grave will be a lonely one. I long to find some pieces of wood to fashion a cross to place at my head. 'Tis a simple thing.''

His lips twitched. ''Everything is a simple request with you, and yet, you have complicated my life.

Very well, come, but mind the bridge. Some of the wood is rotten.''

Tonia lifted her skirts and tripped down the hillside toward the stream. ''You are afraid that I will drown, and so cheat you out of the King's shilling? Methinks not, good executioner, for the water does not look very deep.''

He gave her a sidelong glance. '''Tis cold as iron, my... 'Twould chill you.''

She laughed lightly to herself at the absurdity of the situation. Then she asked, ''What about your horse? Will he follow us?'' Crossing her fingers under her cape for good luck, she prayed that the animal would.

The tall man shook his head. ''Baxtalo will stay in the field where he has the most hope of finding some good fodder to eat. He knows not to wander away.''

Tonia lifted one eyebrow. ''Truly? He must be well trained.''

The headsman chuckled. ''Aye, by myself,'' he said with a note of pride.

The air grew cooler when they stepped among the trees. Dry leaves from the previous autumn carpeted the ground, while twigs and small branches snapped underfoot with sharp cracks that echoed off the surrounding hillsides. Tonia's escort took the opportunity to gather some windfall kindling. Every so often he held out a stick to her with a silent question in his eyes. Each time, she shook her head. She was in no hurry to find the materials for her cross.

Her foot slipped on a damp, moss-covered rock. The headsman caught her hand before she fell. The shock of that physical encounter ran through her like wildfire. His skin was warm and, though hard calluses had roughed the pads of his fingers and palms, his touch was oddly soft—almost caressing. Startled, she looked up at him. His steady gaze bore into her as he tightened his hold on her. A tremor shook her and she was glad of his support. A strange aching took hold of her limbs.

I must be coming down with a fever or am faint from lack of food.

"Methinks breaking your leg is not in the warrant, Tonia," he murmured. A sudden twinkle lit his eyes before he looked away. He squeezed her hand briefly before he released it. Tonia's breath caught in her throat. Her name on his lips gave her an unexpected rush of warm pleasure. She coughed to cover her momentary confusion.

"I agree," she replied. He started to turn back toward the meadow. "Sir!" she called to stop him. She didn't want him to return to his gruesome chore. When he looked over his shoulder, she continued in a more controlled voice. "Sir, since we will be together a little longer, will you not please tell me your name? Surely you must be weary of hearing yourself called Master Death."

Sandor heartily agreed. He enjoyed saying Tonia's name. It had a pleasing roll on his tongue. But the inherent caution that marked all the Roms' interaction with outsiders held him back from sharing his identity with her, though he had a strong desire to hear her say his name. He pulled his gaze away from her pleading eyes. He found it harder and harder to resist the lady when he looked into those bewitching blue orbs.

"I could give you one name today, another tomorrow and a third the day after that," he replied.

Tonia drew closer to his side. Her cape brushed the back of his hand, sending a shiver of awareness rippling through him. The temptation to slip his arm around her waist and pull her against him grew harder to resist. *She is a dead woman who merely breathes for a time. She is nothing to me but a cold corpse.* Even as he thought it, he did not believe a word of it.

She touched his arm. "But none of those fine names would be your own true one, would it?"

His body burned. "The Rom consider a person's name to be the most intimate thing we possess. Knowing your name gives someone power over you."

She smiled up at him. He could barely breathe. "You know my name. Does that give you power over me?"

How I wish it were true! He cleared his throat. "The Rom never reveal their private lives to *gadje.* 'Tis our way to protect ourselves."

She furrowed her brow. "What is a *gadje?*"

A smile trembled on his lips. "You, your family, the king who desires your death, his ministers and churchmen, everyone in England who is not a Rom."

While Tonia considered this piece of information, he admired the beauty of her face. She reminded him of the saints that were painted on the stained glass windows of the Christian churches he had visited in France.

She laughed, a sound like dainty silver bells on the wristlets of dancers. "You say the word *gadje* as if it were coated in mud."

You cannot guess how close to the mark you have hit. How could he tell this beautiful, pure, holy lady that his family would consider her worse than the dung in the streets? That her mere touch, her nearby presence defiled him? Yet Sandor craved her smiles, the brush of her fingertips—and more. *'Tis nothing but wanton lust that tortures my loins.* Yet he had known lust with others—even *gadji*. With Tonia his feelings were much different, even different from those he had experienced with his dead wife. Nothing in his twenty-five years of living helped him to understand why the power of Tonia's attraction shook him to his core.

Sandor shifted the weight of his armload of wood. "'Tis for protection that the Rom do not mix with the *gadje* except to do business. Did you know that in England there is a harsh law against the Gypsies? In truth, I am a felon."

Tonia's eyes widened, though she did not draw away from him. "What is this law?"

"Twenty years ago, when the English saw so many Rom come into their land, they grew sore afraid. We were called lewd people and outlanders. King Henry VIII decreed that we were to be banished forever from his kingdom. Just three years ago, King Edward signed a law that said any Rom found in England would be branded and made a slave for two years."

Halting, Tonia stared at him. "Are you so marked?"

Should he show her his livid scar or should he lie? Why did her opinion matter to him anyway? She was to die by his hand in the very near future. Sandor put down his load of sticks, untied his jerkin's laces, then the laces of his shirt. He pulled back the cloth so that she could see the wine-colored "V" seared on his chest.

Her body stiffened; she could not smother her gasp of shock at the sight. "'Tis a cruel mark," she whispered, her eyes wide. "It must have hurt you beyond imagining."

"Aye," he replied, closing up his shirt and retying his jerkin. "Fortunately I fainted afore they were done."

"What does the 'V' mean?"

Sandor curled his lips with disgust. "Vagrants. Yet we have always worked for our bread."

Worked to dupe the dull-witted *gadje*, but Sandor decided against revealing the details of his clan's many shady professions. He, at least, had always been fair in his horse trading with the English, even though Uncle Gheorghe had often called him *prosto*, a fool, for doing so.

"Why did you stay in England after…that?"

Sandor picked up the firewood. "One trip across the Channel was enough for me. Life is good in England. The weather is kinder than in Flanders or the German kingdoms. The land is fat, full of fruit that falls from the trees and chickens that wander far from home." He gave her a sidelong grin.

Tonia pursed her lips. "You mean you steal chickens from honest farmers."

Sandor shrugged. "'Tis not so bad. A Gypsy may convey a hen or two to feed his family, but we would never steal the whole henhouse. That would deprive the farmer of his livelihood."

"But 'tis wrong to steal. 'Tis a sin."

He shook his head at her innocence. "Methinks that God looks at your sins and mine with a different eye, Tonia. The Lord Jesus knew hunger when he was a man upon the earth. Tell me, noble lady, have you ever been hungry?''

"Not until I came to this place," she answered with distaste.

Sandor decided to change the subject. This talk of laws and sins with such a holy woman as Tonia made him very uncomfortable. "Well, I am hungry now. What say you to a fine dinner of fresh fish?''

She quirked a half smile. "I would say you were a wonder-worker. Can you truly conjure up a fish?''

He laughed, pleased by her amazement. "Not conjure them, but entice them, if luck is with me and yon stream is well supplied. Come.''

Together they went back to the place where the bridge crossed the clear running water. Sandor set down his bundle of sticks, then searched along the bank for a spot in deep shade so that the wily fish could not see his shadow. Finding a place that satisfied him, he hunkered down beside the water. Gathering her cape under her, Tonia seated herself beside him.

Sandor put his finger to his lips signaling her to remain still. She nodded. Whispering a charm for luck, his slipped his hand into the icy water and rested it on the shallow bottom. Within a few minutes the cold had numbed his fingers, but Sandor did not move. He had promised Tonia a fish; his pride demanded that he procure one. After a long while, a large, fat trout swam upstream with lazy undulations. Sandor waved his fingers in the stream's current as if they were an underwater plant. He wet his lips with anticipation but otherwise did not move. The trout edged nearer, as if drawn by the swaying fingers. Tonia craned her neck to see better.

The trout swam closer until it hovered over Sandor's fingers. When the trout nosed him, looking for something to eat, Sandor gently brushed against the fish's silvery flank. It shivered but did not dart away. Sandor smiled to himself. This fat one liked to be tickled. He brushed it again. The fish sank a little lower, closer to Sandor's open palm. He touched its other flank. He could almost imagine the fish sighing with pleasure. After another drawn-out minute of tickling his quarry, Sandor's hand closed around it. Before the lulled trout could react, it was flopping on the bank, practically in Tonia's lap.

Sandor sat back on his heels and grinned at her. Giving up its useless struggle, the trout lay on the brown grass, gasping for breath. Sandor rubbed some warmth back into his hand and flexed his stiff fingers.

"'Tis a goodly fish but methinks two would be better. I pray your patience a little longer, Tonia. In the meantime do not let this fine fellow slither back into the water or he will swim away and warn his friends."

Her gaze fixed on the fish, Tonia bobbed her head. With another charm on his tongue, Sandor again put his hand in the water. The wait seemed longer, only because his fingers were so cold. Soon enough a second trout, not as large as the first but rounder in the middle, swam up the stream. Sandor's fingers waved in the current. Unlike the first fish, this one was more cautious, touching several of Sandor's fingers with its mouth as if trying to taste him. His shoulders ached from holding his uncomfortable posture, but he could not pull back now—not with Tonia watching him so intently. He willed the fish to swim over his hand just as the first one had.

Instead, the perverse creature swam upstream. Sandor didn't move. Years of tickling fish had taught him the necessary patience required. Sure enough, the trout's curiosity overcame its prudence. It turned round and drifted back toward Sandor's hand. This time it swam closer to his fingers. Sandor lightly brushed it. The fish wiggled away. Sandor didn't flinch but continued to wave his fingers. Once again the fish edged closer and brushed itself against him. Sandor almost chuckled aloud. The trout drifted over his palm, He touched its underside with his thumb. The fish rubbed against his other fingers. Sandor decided to seize his chance now before his skittish quarry grew tired of the game. He flipped his quivering prey out of the water and tossed it on the ground on the far side of the first catch.

Tonia clapped her approval. "Well done! 'Tis the most wondrous sight that I have ever seen. My cousin Kitt would be very envious of your skill, Master Fisherman."

Sandor dried his hand on his thigh while he basked in her praise. His heart swelled as she continued to smile at him and compliment his prowess. He much preferred that Tonia call him a fisherman rather than an executioner. He hooked his fingers through the gills of his two prizes, then helped her rise with his free hand.

"We will cross the bridge," he told her as he scooped up most of their gathered sticks. "Then we will eat. Do you know how to clean a fish?" he asked, suspecting that such a fine lady would not.

She stared at the trout, bit her lip and then shook her head. "I must plead ignorance. My lady mother taught me how to distill medicines from plants and how to make wine and beer, but not how to cook.''

Sandor shook his head with a rueful smile. ''Among my people, even little girls know how to bake bread.''

She gave him an injured look, though her eyes sparkled with a glint of mischief. ''I suppose they also know how to roast stolen chickens.''

Sandor chuckled. ''Wandering hens are the most toothsome.''

They picked their way over the bridge's treacherous planking and walked up the hillside to the spot Tonia had chosen for her gravesite. The sun now stood at its zenith in the azure sky. Sandor dropped the firewood onto the bare earth of the grave. Building a fire here would warm the dirt, making it easier to dig, though his heart grew heavy at the thought. Delighting in the pleasure of their stroll, he had almost forgotten his primary duty. Cousin Demeo had already been in the Tower for nearly a week. Sandor must complete his grim task by this evening so that he could leave by the morrow's first light. He glanced at Tonia. She had seemed so happy while they were in the woods, but the sight of her grave had banished her laughter. When she caught him looking at her, she gave him a little smile then pointed to the bundle of windfall sticks.

''Methinks you will never get a fire started with that lot. The wood is damp,'' she remarked. ''There are dry logs inside the fortress at the guards' hearth. We should go there to cook our dinner.'' She averted her eyes from the scored earth.

Sandor didn't blame her, but he needed to make quick work of the digging. Assuming a levity that he did not feel, he replied, "A true Gypsy can start a fire in a rainstorm."

He busied himself with breaking up the sticks and arranging them in an orderly pile in the middle of the turned earth. Then he drew out his tinderbox from the ditty bag that hung on his belt. The spark from his flint ignited the kindling. He blew on it to encourage the fire's life. As he predicted to Tonia, the flames responded. Soon a cheerful fire crackled in the depression, chasing the remnants of the morning's chill.

While the wood burned down to hot coals, Sandor gutted and cleaned the fish on one of the nearby stones. Tonia watched him with a studied interest.

"Your hands are quick and sure with your knife," she remarked with a light bitterness. "I am relieved that the warrant forbids you to shed my blood."

Sandor didn't look at her. He could never reveal the macabre duty he was instructed to perform after she was dead. He skewered the larger fish on a green wood twig and set it over the bed of coals. May the dogs eat the heart of the *gadjo* who had desired such a final indignity against so beautiful and gentle a woman.

One day, I vow I will avenge your death, sweet Tonia.

Chapter Five

The afternoon passed pleasantly enough for Tonia, as long as she didn't think too much about the hole that her companion was digging. In the warmth generated by the sun and the man's exertions, he had shed his jerkin and forearm dagger, and rolled his long, loose sleeves to his elbow. Sitting on her rock, Tonia couldn't help but admire the play of his muscles that strained the unbleached muslin of his shirt and bulged against the leather breeches that molded around his legs like a second skin.

When he paused in his work, which was often, he sent her smiles that made her heart beat faster. What a difference between this man and the lordlings that had come a-wooing her—and her father's fortune—at Snape Castle! Not one of her suitors had exuded half as much virility as this intriguing Gypsy—a man sent to kill her in the name of the King. Tonia had to keep reminding herself of that sobering fact, lest she fall completely under his spell.

Standing up, she shook out her skirts. It was a little late in the game for her to admire the comeliness of any man when she was within hours of meeting her

Maker. Her thoughts should be centered on the promised delights of heaven, not the pleasures of the flesh on earth. Years ago, Tonia had forsworn men and marriage in search of the greater good—and because she had never found anyone in Northumberland with whom she could imagine making love. Her cheeks warmed at that candid admission. She shot a quick glance at the Gypsy, but he was bent over, prying yet another rock out of the hole. His position only served to emphasize the force of his thighs and the slimness of his hips. Her flush deepened and she quickly turned away lest he notice her change in color.

Tonia prayed that he would uncover a boulder too large to dislodge. Then he would have to start on another hole—and buy her more time.

A scant twenty yards away, his beautiful silver-gray horse nosed among the brown grasses, searching for a tender shoot or two. Tonia forced her mind from its wanton musings as she sauntered over to the magnificent animal, so like his owner. Baxtalo lifted his head as she drew closer. His nostrils widened as he inhaled her scent.

"You are a pretty one," Tonia crooned, keeping eye contact with the horse as she moved toward him. "So fine with such a broad chest and strong legs." So like his owner.

The horse pricked his ears forward but did not shy away when Tonia touched his forehead. She wished she had an apple or a carrot to sweeten her introduction. Still murmuring endearments, she ran her hand along his neck. He sidestepped a little but did not pull away.

"My father would pay your master a wealth of golden angels for you, I am sure," she said as she noted the firmness of his muscles under his well-groomed coat. She glanced over her shoulder at the man, but he worked with his back to her. "Methinks your master will not part willingly from you."

If Tonia was ever going to dash for freedom, now was the moment. She moved around to the horse's near side and laid her arm over his back to see if he would accept her. Baxtalo stood very still. One ear twitched. Tonia looked over the horse's withers for one last glimpse of her would-be executioner. Oddly, she regretted leaving him in the lurch like this. In his own quiet way, the Gypsy was very charming. And quite handsome as well.

She sighed. "I am sorry that I never saw his face," she murmured to the horse as she took a firm grip on his mane. "'Tis a pity that I must steal you from him, for I know he loves you dearly. I will try to return you when I am safely home."

With one last look at the Gypsy's back, Tonia hiked up her skirts to her knee, then vaulted onto the horse's back—a feat she had learned as a child from her French godfather, Gaston. Baxtalo snorted and tossed his head. Tonia hung on with her knees clamped against his sides, and both hands entwined in his mane.

"Go!" she commanded the horse, kicking his flanks.

With another snort, Baxtalo bolted across the meadow toward the stream. Tonia lay low over his neck as the two of them crossed the water in two quick, wet strides. Behind her, she heard the headsman shout.

"Be sure to tell your master how sorry I am," she

said to the horse as they dashed into the woods. "Truly, I am not a thief at heart."

Tonia pointed him downhill, where she suspected there was a village or town. She knew that her former guards had gone somewhere to replenish their food supplies while they had waited for the King's executioner. She did not think beyond reaching that village. Surely there would be a church where she could claim sanctuary and send for her father. For now it took all her strength to hang on to her prize as Baxtalo raced under low-hanging tree branches. Her blood sang, intoxicated with her freedom.

Suddenly the horse wheeled and came to an abrupt halt. Had Tonia not been an experienced rider, she would have been thrown from his back. Renewing her grip on his mane, she again kicked his sides.

"Please, I pray you, sweet Baxtalo, let us be gone!"

A sharp whistle pierced the silence of the woods. It hung on the air then rose in its pitch. Tonia realized it must be the Gypsy calling. Lying over the horse's neck, she implored the animal to go. "'Twill be the death of me if we linger here!"

Snorting, Baxtalo stamped the leaf-covered ground. Once more, the same signal whistled through the trees. This time the horse responded. To Tonia's horror, he turned again then dashed back up the slope toward Hawksnest.

"Nay, Baxtalo! Please!" Tonia pulled his mane to the left and dug her knee in his side. The horse paid her no more attention than if she were a fly.

Her stomach clenched into a knot; panic as she had never before experienced welled up in her throat. She looked down at the uneven ground that raced under the horse's hooves. She should let go of his mane and jump, but the fear of possibly breaking an arm or her neck kept her clinging to Baxtalo's back. They crossed the stream with a splash. Once again in the meadow, the horse increased his speed.

Looking over his head, Tonia saw the Gypsy standing on the edge of her grave, his hands planted on his hips and his feet wide apart as he waited. With a final burst of speed Baxtalo thundered toward him. The horse leaped over the hole in the ground, circled around it and came to a stop beside his master.

Hiding her face in Baxtalo's mane, Tonia wept silent tears of frustration. She didn't dare to look at the headsman. She knew that he must be furious at her. Whatever charitable feelings he may have had for her earlier would be shattered after this escapade.

Patting the horse, the Gypsy spoke soothingly to him in a strange language. Then he touched her foot. "Tonia?" he asked. "Are you well?"

She shut her eyes. "Nay, Master of Death. The sun has grown cold for me." Filled with despair, she felt chilled and nauseous.

To her bewilderment, he chuckled. "So you thought you could steal my horse?" he asked.

Tonia peeked at him through her lashes. A half smile hung on his full lips and a twinkle lurked in the depths of his flashing blue eyes. She moistened her dry lips.

"Not steal, merely borrow for a time," she whispered.

His smile widened. "*My* horse?" Then he stroked her cheek where a tear hung. "*Na rov,* little *gadji.* Do not cry. 'Tis not your fault that you failed. You did not know that 'tis impossible to steal a horse from a Rom. We are the horse masters of the world,'' he added in a tone that did not boast.

Tonia pulled herself upright on Baxtalo's back and held up her head. ''Your eyes deceive you, Gypsy. I am not crying. 'Tis the wind from the ride that makes my eyes tear.'' She wiped away the offending evidence. At all costs she must maintain what shreds of her dignity remained.

The headsman gave her a long look. Tonia wished she dared to rip off his mask so that she could read his expression better, but having already offended him, she would not risk his further anger. She wondered how long she had to live now.

The Gypsy said something to the horse, then turned and started up the hillside toward the fortress. Baxtalo followed close behind him. Tonia groaned to herself. *Not now! Not yet!* She didn't want to die today. Her sudden fierce desire for life surprised her. When she had lived among her friends in their little convent, she had often meditated upon the lives of the holy martyrs and had secretly wished she had been able to show the depth of her faith by dying in Rome's Colosseum during the ancient days of the cruel emperors. Now, faced with the prospect of her own all-too-real execution, she quailed. Tonia hung her head at her cowardice. God must be very disappointed with her.

Sandor led them through Hawksnest's crumbling archway. The remaining walls of her prison looked even more foreboding than earlier this morning when she had so happily skipped out of them. She gave her shoulders a shake. Above all else, she must not betray her terror to this man. She would not give him that power over her.

Tonia swallowed the knot in her throat before she

asked, "What do you mean to do with me, my Lord Executioner?"

He looked back over his shoulder. "I crave your pardon, my lady, but I must return you to your cell." He halted Baxtalo before the yawning doorway, then held out his hands to help her down. "I cannot trust you not to bolt again."

Tonia looked down her nose at him. She tried to gauge the expression in his eyes, but she could not discern his true feelings. Best not to irritate him. She offered him her hand.

The Gypsy stepped closer and put both his hands around her waist. He swung her off the horse's back as if she had been a feather bolster. Staring deep into her eyes, he lowered her slowly to the ground, allowing her body to slide down his. She inhaled sharply at the contact. Never taking his gaze from her face, his broad shoulders heaved as he breathed. Tonia's hands skimmed along his muscular chest covered only by his muslin shirt. He tensed under her fingers. Her heartbeat drummed against her temples.

He wet his lips. For a split second, Tonia wondered if he would dare to kiss her. She half hoped that he would. Quickly, before he could read the wanton desire in her eyes, she looked down at the cracked cobblestones of the courtyard, unnerved by her physical reaction. The shock of his physical presence made her body tingle in the most secret places. She could not ignore the attraction that drew her to him. She wondered if he felt it, too.

The Gypsy did not release her when she stood on her feet within his embrace. Not looking up at him, she asked again, "What do you mean to do with me?"

* * *

Sandor swallowed. This pretty *gadji* filled his senses with a fierce desire that refused to concede to common sense. He wanted Tonia, both her body and her spirit. Hot blood coursed through his veins like a raging torrent. *'Tis lust only. I have been too long without a woman.* Though Tonia did not look at him, she quivered in his hands. His experience told him that she desired him as much as he wanted her. Uncle Gheorghe had said it was Sandor's right to have her. Yet, the lady was a virgin and did not realize what a whirlwind their lovemaking would unleash.

Sandor drew in a deep breath. Tonia was marked for death and by his hand. He would not send her to the Lord God broken and stained by him. In any case, the death warrant expressly forbade him to shed the lady's blood and that included the scarlet tears of her maidenhead. He dropped his hands to his sides and stepped away from her.

She regarded him for a heartbeat. ''Are you going to kill me now?''

Sandor clenched his hands behind his back. ''Nay, Tonia.'' He tried to introduce some levity into this dark and dangerous moment. ''You are not ready, I am not ready and your grave is not ready to receive you. Also, I must give Baxtalo a good rubdown after his…ah…exercise. Please.'' He pointed toward the doorway. The sooner he locked her out of his sight the better it would be for all of them.

She gave him a searching look, then turned on her heel and went inside the ruined keep. Sandor followed close behind her. His fingers itched to reach out and touch the wild tangle of her hair that cascaded down her back. He gritted his teeth and fought against the demons of his desires.

Tonia stumbled at the entrance to her cell. Sandor reached out to steady her, but she held up her hand to stop him. Then she lifted her chin and walked with a firm stately grace into the tiny, dank chamber. She stood with her arrow-straight back to him while he swung shut the heavy timber door and turned the key in the lock. He all but fled back to the guardroom.

Sandor sank down on the bench, pulled off the irritating mask and mopped the cold sweat from his face. What was he to do? The beautiful *gadji* had bewitched him, just as his mother and his aunt had always warned him. He should kill Tonia and be done with it. Demeo needed his freedom. What if the boy had already caught some pestilence? The *gadje* Tower guards would not lift a finger to help a mere Gypsy; they would let him die among the vermin. Sandor's return was already overdue. He should have been on the road today. His obligations to his family pressed against the back of his neck. Rubbing his eyes, he noticed that his hands trembled.

"Black Sara, help me," he prayed to the Rom's most beloved saint, Sara-la-Kali, the Egyptian handmaiden of the Blessed Virgin Mary. "Tell me what I should do." He closed his eyes.

The image of his grandmother surfaced in his memory. She was reading the tarot—his fortune. He saw the Death card in her thin fingers and heard again her laughter. "Afraid of change, are you, Sandor? Remember what I say. You will have a friend who was your enemy. You will find life holding hands with death."

Opening his eyes, Sandor stared at his hands as if

he had never seen them before. Wide palms with long fingers—good for working with horses—and for loving a woman. These were not killing hands. Curling his fingers into a ball, he cursed the misfortune that had sent him into the northern mountains on this ill-favored mission.

He fumbled in his ditty bag, then pulled out the garrote. He fingered the hard knots in the leather thong that would stop up a victim's windpipe and bring a quick death. He thought of the angry red marks the cord would leave on Tonia's smooth white skin.

"I am no murderer," he assured Black Sara, as if the saint hovered in the air over his head. "How can I do this cruel thing?"

In his mind's eye he saw his uncle, ill in his bed, jeering Sandor's lack of courage. He could almost hear Uncle Gheorghe tell him that he had the heart of a chicken. He saw Aunt Mindra squatting by the fire, keening for her son, the boy whose life depended upon Sandor. From the cradle, Sandor had been taught the importance of loyalty to his clan. The wide world was a harsh place for the Rom; his family must cleave together for protection and survival. To disregard the *kris,* the fundamental code of all Rom, would condemn him to a fate worse than the one decreed for Tonia. Sandor would be exiled from his people, cast out alone into a world that despised him.

Sandor gripped the garrote. Just down the corridor was the beginning and the end of this worst trial of his life. *Do it now. Make it quick. Do not look into her eyes. Just take her life and do not look back.*

Sandor pushed himself up from the bench. On silent feet, he moved down the stone corridor. He reached her door in too short a time. Pausing, he took a deep breath to calm his nerves. The knots in the thong bit deep into his palm, just as they would bite into her neck—in just a few moments' time.

Make it quick. Do not look into her eyes. *May God forgive me for what I am about to do*. He turned the key in the lock.

Chapter Six

The lady knelt beside her stool, head bowed and hands clasped in prayer. A single ray of sunlight shone through the high arrow loop bathing her in its golden light—as if the heavens reached out to bless her. Sandor stopped in his tracks, his breath taken away by Tonia's unworldly beauty. He had come to kill an angel.

Do it now. Take her from behind and dispatch her quickly. Holding the garrote between his hands, he started toward her.

Just then she looked up and saw him. The dark lashes that shadowed her cheeks flew up. A soft gasp escaped her. Gathering her skirts, she rose, then immediately dropped a deep curtsy to Sandor as she had done at their first meeting.

He felt hot under his neckerchief. Tonia was a gentle-born lady, he a Gypsy outcast from the mainstream of common folk. She shouldn't render him such an honor, especially not now. The silence between them stretched more taut than the cord he gripped in his hands.

Finally Tonia cleared her throat. "I was praying to God just now."

"So was I."

"And I was asking Him why I had to die," she continued in a whisper.

Sandor looked down at his hands. They shook. "I asked Him the same question."

She stepped a little closer, her gaze fastened on his face. "Did God give you an answer?"

He shook his head. "Nay."

She crept even closer. "Nor I. It seems that we are left to muddle out this problem on our own." Her lips fluttered. Reaching up, Tonia touched his cheek—his bare cheek. "You have misplaced your mask," she murmured.

Cursing himself for his stupidity, especially at this dire moment, Sandor turned away from her. "My mind was...was on other matters."

"I am glad to see your face, at last," she replied, circling around him so that she could look at him again. "By my troth, Gypsy, you are very easy on the eyes. Methinks I have seen you often in my dreams."

Sandor groaned inwardly. His mask had helped to distance himself from her; now all his defenses were down. Her admiring expression melted his murderous resolve. "Then you have dreamed of *Beng,* the devil."

Tonia shook her head. "In faith, you are no devil—nor do you look much like an executioner."

"I am not an executioner, Tonia. That is my uncle's calling. He was ill, so he sent me in his stead."

Her finger tapped her chin. "I am right glad that he did."

Sandor twisted his mouth in a rueful grimace. "Aye, my lady, for if my uncle had come yester eve, you would be dead and buried."

She swallowed, then looked down at the garrote that he had wadded up in his hand. "Did you mean to kill me—now?"

Sandor stared over her head so that he did not have to see her expression. "My time grows late. While I dally here with you, the King's soldiers keep my young cousin in the Tower of London. Demeo is my pledge that I will fulfill my duty and return quickly."

She released a choked, desperate laugh that grated on his already taut nerves. "Ha! I had no idea how much the King lusted for my death."

"Methinks 'tis the King's minions, and not Edward himself. He is but a boy who knows only what is whispered in his ear."

"Their hate for me and my religion runs deeper than I thought."

Sandor had no answer to this. From the first moment he had set eyes on Tonia, he had been aghast at the disparity between her alleged crime of treason and the beautiful innocent who stood condemned. He turned to go, but Tonia stopped him.

She touched the end of the cord that dangled from his fist. "Is this a garrote?"

"Aye," he snapped, wishing he were a hundred miles away.

She tugged it from his fingers. "I have never seen one," she said in a low tone.

"'Tis no sight for a lady."

Breathing in shallow, quick gasps, she held up the thong to the light. She paled as she touched the hard knots. "What are these for?"

He gritted his teeth. "'Tis best that you do not know. 'Twill be easier for you when…when the time comes."

Clutching the garrote, Tonia began to sway. "Sweet Jesu," she murmured. Her eyes rolled back in her head.

Sandor caught her before she fell against the sharp hearthstone. Holding her tightly to his chest, he lowered her gently to the cold floor. She lay still in his arms like a waxen figure, her black lashes fanned over her white cheeks. Without thinking, Sandor leaned down and brushed his lips against her cool forehead. His senses reeled. Cradling her in his arms, he rocked on his knees.

What was he to do? If he squeezed the life out of her now, she would go to heaven with her heart still beating like that of a frightened hen instead of the courageous woman that she had proved herself to be. He could not kill her now, he reasoned—her grave was only half-dug. She was safe from him for one more night. Sandor gazed down at Tonia. He wished he could keep her safe from danger forever.

Spirits crowded his imagination. His uncle admonished him to do the wretched deed; his aunt berated him for leaving poor Demeo in prison. Chuckling, his ancient grandmother reminded him of her words. Demeo's pinched face looked out through rusty bars, imploring Sandor to come home soon.

"I am truly Prosto, the Fool," he whispered to Tonia before he kissed her again.

Tonia slowly opened her eyes, then gasped. High flames leapt before her, heating her face. *I have died and gone down to hell. How did that happen?* Pulling herself upright, she realized that she was on the floor of her cell, staring at the roaring fire that danced in her hearth. She stretched her hands out to the warmth while she tried to remember what had happened. The Gypsy had come to her with death on his mind. Yet he had *not* killed her.

She smiled to herself as she recalled his face. What a handsome rogue he was! Tonia had never met anyone quite as intriguing as this man. His hair was thicker than she had presumed, dark and full of unruly waves. When he had looked down at her, one curl had fallen across his wide forehead, making him seem almost boyish. The touch of humor that she had detected around his mouth also hovered in the corners of his impossibly blue eyes, yet his expression cloaked a certain air of hidden mystery. Tonia liked the strong planes of his cheekbones and jawline, and his even, white teeth that contrasted most pleasingly with his bronze-colored skin. The Gypsy possessed a ruggedness and vital power that drew her like a lodestar.

Tonia realized that she was not sitting on the cold, uneven stones but instead she lay on a thick lamb's fleece. Then she spied a covered bowl and cup on the hearthstone. Lifting the scrap of muslin, she saw that the Gypsy had left her a wedge of cheese, a part of his bread and a handful of dry raisins. The cup held clean water.

Tonia quickly ate the food, blessing her jailer even as she wondered what he would do next. She considered calling to him to thank him for her supper—and to see his face once more—but she rejected the idea as soon as it was born. Best not to attract any attention to herself, in case he should change his mind and return with his wicked garrote. She shuddered at the memory of that cruel cord with its hideous knots. She should have listened when he told her not to look at it.

Fortified by the food, and thankful that she still breathed in the land of the living, Tonia lay down again, snuggling in her cape and rejoicing in the warmth of the sheepskin. Her eyelids hung heavy as she gazed at the flames playing in the hearth. Soon sleep overcame her, wrapping Tonia in its blissful embrace.

Venus, the evening star, sparkled in the twilight as Sir Guy Cavendish rode through York's old city gate. Attended by his son, Francis, and his nephew, Kitt, Guy went straight to the town hall before he sought a decent inn for the night's lodging. Since the hour was late, the municipal building was closed for the night. Guy vented his anger and frustration on the two soldiers who stood at the portal. In turn, the men were only too happy to direct the irate blond giant and his kin to the home of Sir Tobias Whalley, the city's magistrate. Upon arriving at the Whalley residence, Guy, usually the courtliest of men, wasted no time or breath apologizing for interrupting Sir Tobias and his family at supper.

Dispensing with the usual courtesies, Lord Cavendish came straight to the point. "Where the hell have they taken my daughter?" he thundered at the quaking Sir Tobias.

Mopping his florid face, the heavyset official replied, "What daughter is that, my lord? What is her name?"

Kitt Cavendish felt sorry for the rattled man. He

had never before seen his uncle so furious. He gave Lady Whalley and their children a little smile and bow to calm their fright.

"Lady Gastonia Cavendish, you dolt!" Guy bellowed, shaking the magistrate by his shoulders.

"You are a Cavendish?" Sir Tobias gasped out between shakings. "The Earl of Thornbury, perchance?"

"He is my brother!" Guy snapped, looking all the more like the snarling wolf that graced the Cavendish coat of arms. "I trust you have heard of our family?"

The magistrate looked exceedingly ill. "Aye, my Lord Cavendish! Who does not know your illustrious name?"

"Good," Guy continued. "Then where is Gastonia? I received word yesterday that she had been arrested and brought here to trial within this past fortnight. Where is she now?"

The magistrate's eyes bulged. "God in heaven! I didn't think…that is…I did not know that Mistress Cavendish was related to *you,* my lord. Neither her title nor her family were mentioned."

"Dogs," muttered Francis under his breath.

Kitt said nothing, but his anger rose steadily. From earliest childhood, he had always idolized Tonia, who had led him in their games and sport. Of all his cousins, she was Kitt's favorite. If his uncle didn't throttle the magistrate to death, Kitt might very well do the job in payment for Tonia's ignominious treatment.

Francis put his hand on his father's arm. "Do not choke him, Father, or he will not be able to tell us what we most desire to know."

Before his marriage three years ago, Francis had been both a diplomat and a spy in King Edward's service. Now he used his skills to defuse the situation. One of the younger Whalley children began to weep into her napkin. Francis bowed to the mistress of the house.

"I see that we have distressed your family, my lady. Pray take the children and withdraw to another chamber. I promise that no harm shall come to your good husband."

Lady Whalley opened her mouth to say something, thought better of it and rose from the table. Like a mother hen, she gathered her chicks around her and shepherded them out a side door. The two serving men scampered after her, leaving the quaking magistrate to deal with the legendary Cavendishes on his own. Kitt lounged against the mantel, his fingers lightly drumming the hilt of his dagger. Giving the young man a sidelong glance, Sir Tobias whimpered. Backing away from Guy, he stumbled and collapsed in the settle.

Guy leaned over him. "Tell me what I want to know, malt worm. My fingers itch to flay you."

"Softly, Father," Francis suggested. "You will make him swallow his tongue."

Whalley looked from one tall, blond man to the next. His lower lip wobbled. Kitt wondered if he was going to bawl.

"Gastonia Cavendish was brought before a special session of the court. Three judges had traveled up from London to try her. I merely observed the proceedings, my lord. Truly I had no hand in her fate."

"And?" Guy prompted. His blue eyes narrowed into slits.

Sir Tobias ran his fat tongue across his lips. "Your daughter was charged with treason for daring to open a Catholic nunnery within England's borders. The King, God save him, has outlawed all such popish practices. The justices were most precise on this point.'' Sweat beaded on the magistrate's brow. ''They condemned her to death for her obstinacy.''

Guy lifted the man out of the chair and shook him as if he were a rag poppet. ''Tell me something that I do not already know. Where is my daughter *now?*''

Whalley groaned. ''The soldiers took her away, my lord. I know not where except that 'tis out of this city. The justices sent a message posthaste to London for the services of the Tower's executioner.''

With a sound between a growl and a cry, Guy dropped the magistrate onto the floor.

'''Twas over a week ago, my lord,'' Whalley groveled. ''Methinks that your daughter would be dead by now unless the headsman has been delayed. You have my deepest sympathies,'' he added in a rush.

Guy's expression turned to fury. ''And you did *nothing* in Tonia's defense? She is but three-and-twenty years old, and as innocent as the angels.''

The magistrate curled himself into a ball on the floor. ''What could I do, Lord Cavendish? They were the *King's* justices and not my own. I must consider the consequences to my own family. In truth, methinks the King's men had already condemned her before they ever saw her,'' he muttered into the furred collar of his gown.

Guy pulled him up to his feet. ''Why do you say that?'' he asked in a voice that was low and therefore very dangerous.

Straightening his clothing, the magistrate attempted to regain some of his composure. ''They hardly gave the lady a chance to defend herself. They seemed to know all the particulars of her so-called convent. And I heard one of the judges say that her death will 'clip the wings of her overweening family and teach them to mend their ways'—his very words, my lord.''

The fire went out of Guy's eyes. He sat down hard on the magistrate's chair. Kitt shot an inquiring glance at Francis, who lifted an eyebrow in return. His kinsman was as much mystified by the justice's words as Kitt was. The youngest Cavendish pushed himself away from the mantelpiece.

''Let us quit this place, Uncle, and find some inn for the night.''

''Aye, 'tis true.'' Francis touched his father's sleeve. ''In the morning, we will ferret out Tonia's prison. 'Tis too late to seek her now.''

With a muttered oath under his breath, Guy pulled himself out of the chair. Without a backward glance at the ashen magistrate or the half-eaten supper cooling on the table, he stalked out the door. Francis followed on his heels. As Kitt turned to go, he gave Sir Tobias a shadow of a bow.

''A pleasant evening to you, my lord magistrate, and sweet dreams attend you—if you can sleep with my cousin's blood on your conscience. Trust me when I say that Tonia is the most virtuous lady in the land. If she is dead, then you and I will meet again to discuss your...cowardice.''

Satisfied that he had given Whalley an uncomfortable bone to gnaw with his supper, Kitt hurried after the other two.

The Cavendishes easily found good lodging near the Minster, York's great cathedral. As the season was Lent, no fairs or feast days filled the city. Guy spoke little during their light supper. Afterward he went immediately to bed. At the foot of the stairs to the inn's upper gallery, Kitt pulled Francis aside.

"Stay close to your father this night for his heart is sore wounded and methinks he might do some damage, either to his bedding or to himself."

Francis gave his cousin a searching look. "And where do you roam at this hour?"

Kitt chuckled without mirth. "Among the gutters and riffraff of the city." He slipped off the three heavy gold rings that he always wore and gave them to Francis. "Keep these for me until I return."

Francis studied Kitt's face for a long moment before he said, "I wonder how you can think of pleasuring yourself when we are on such a doleful errand."

Kitt clapped Francis on the shoulder. "'Tis not pleasure I seek, but information. I may be gone awhile," he added, as he turned toward the door. "Do not wait up for me and on no account tell Uncle Guy where I have gone."

Francis gave his young cousin a two-fingered archer's salute. "How can I tell him where you are when I do not know myself? May Saint Michael ride on your shoulder this night," he added, invoking the family's patron saint.

Kitt grinned. "Mayhap he will bring me luck with the dice as well as some useful news."

Wrapping his plain cloak around him against the evening's chill air, Kitt stepped into the street. The bells of Saint Michael-le-Belfrey chimed half-past nine o'clock as the young man hurried toward the less savory part of York. Only a few people were abroad at this hour. From a passing rat catcher, Kitt got directions to an inn near the Stonegate where the city's men-at-arms usually took their ease. Ye Olde Starr proved to be a noisy, smoky den, filled with soldiers on a carouse. Kitt ordered a pint of the local brew, then chose a table shared by a foursome who were already well into their cups.

After winning Kitt's small change in several dice games, the soldiers were more than happy to share the city's latest gossip. Kitt nursed his ale while he listened to several tales of drunken wool merchants from Flanders and the latest escapades of a toothsome whore named Jenny, then the young man steered the conversation toward trials and executions.

''Oh, aye,'' burped one heavyset man. ''There was a story I heard some days ago about a woman condemned for being a Roman nun.''

Kitt gripped his jack mug though he kept his facial expression carefree. ''A woman, eh? Did they burn her at the stake? Haint never seen the like of that.''

With a hiccup, the soldier shook his head. Then he signaled the tap boy to refresh his mug while he continued his tale. ''Nay, more's the pity, for I hear the wench was a looker.''

Kitt leaned forward. ''So what did they do with this piece of sweetmeat? Mayhap she would like someone to…ah…comfort her.'' Elbowing the nearest soldier, he gave him a wink.

The first man shrugged. ''No chance o' that. The King's soldiers popped her into a coach and drove her away. 'Twas a week or ten days past. Lucky bastards!'' he added to his companions. ''Most likely they had their way with her afore the executioner got her. I know I would!''

Kitt's fury at their slurs almost choked him. He drank down half his ale before he felt sufficiently calm enough to continue his questioning. "And so they cheated the good citizens of York out of a fine burning." He shook his head, pretending to be sorry to have missed such a grisly spectacle. "Any idea where they took her? Where was the lucky village to have a pretty wench to burn?"

One of the other guards spoke up. "I heard tell they took her into the mountains."

A third man nodded in agreement. "Aye, now I remember! The coach came back two days later. I was on duty at the Monkgate and waved him through."

Kitt could barely contain his excitement. "Did the driver say where he had been?"

"Aye, I asked him that selfsame question for I had seen the woman and was interested. The driver said that he drove them as far as Harewold. 'Tis a wee village at the end of a cleft in the mountains. The driver told me that they had no more need of the coach for the rest of the way was too steep. They put the wench on the back of one of their horses. The driver heard them say they were going higher to somewhere called Eaglesnest or Hawksnest. Some such bird." He scratched his greasy hair. "The King's men ne'er came back here again."

Kitt couldn't understand why Tonia had been taken to such a remote place to await execution. He prayed that the soldier's memory was not too addled by his drink. "So she still lives?"

"Nay," snorted the first speaker. "'Tis been a week and more. That headsman from London surely has come and gone, and there's an end to it. Pity, for she were a sweet piece."

Kitt refused to believe that his cousin was already

dead. They had been as close as brother and sister in their youth. He would have felt the void in the very marrow of his bones if she were truly gone.

Hold fast, Tonia! We are coming for you!

Chapter Seven

When Tonia opened her eyes on the following morning, she found that the sun dawned as clear and as bright as the day before. Though the wind still blew through her arrow slit, the cool air carried a hint of the coming spring. Closing her eyes and inhaling deeply, Tonia could almost smell the earth being plowed for the planting and the scent of delicate blossoms decking the trees in the warmer valleys below her eyrie.

When the Gypsy opened her door, he caught her singing for the pure joy of the new day. Her song died in her throat when she saw him.

"Good morrow." Tonia gave him a shy smile. "'Tis a good day to be alive, is it not?" Though the man did not return her smile, at least he did not have that gruesome mask over his face.

He averted his gaze and looked instead at the cooling embers in the fireplace when she mentioned being alive. A muscle twitched along his jawline. "You have a good voice," he finally said.

Tonia released the breath she had been holding. "My thanks for your compliment. Both my parents are very musical.'' A small lump rose in her throat when she thought of her mother and father. Tonia swallowed with difficulty. She must maintain her cheerful demeanor if she hoped to persuade him to let her live yet another night. She knew that a weeping woman could drive a man's patience over the brink.

''I have brought you some water…to bathe… ah…your face and other things.''

Before Tonia could express her surprised gratitude, he spun on his heel, stepped into the corridor and returned with a mossy oaken bucket slopping at the brim with water. He set it before the hearth. '''Tis cold but clean,'' he told her, though he still did not meet her gaze. ''When you are finished, please join me at the table by my fire. There is some cheese left. No bread.'' He ran his hand through his thick brown-black hair.

Tonia stared at the bucket, hardly daring to believe her good fortune. ''Does this mean that you do not plan to kill me today?'' she whispered.

He glanced at her briefly before looking down to the floor. ''Your grave is not deep enough,'' he mumbled. Then he turned away and headed toward the door. ''I will leave you to wash.'' He practically fled from her presence.

Tonia knelt down beside the bucket and rolled up the sleeves of her gown. Though the water was icy, it felt wonderful to bathe her face for the first time in over a week. Her other guards had been miserly in their care of her while they waited for the executioner. As she washed her ears, neck and hands, Tonia day-dreamed of a tub full of hot water and a cake of her mother's rose-scented soap from Paris. She would have loved to wash her hair, though she knew that if she gave into the temptation at this chilly time of year, she might die from fever and a cough before the Gypsy ever got around to strangling her.

The memory of the garrote made her shudder. At least that dreadful cord had not been hanging from the man's belt. After rinsing out her mouth and combing her hair as best she could with her fingers, Tonia poured the dirty water down the privy hole that was sunk in the wall at the far corner of her cell. Then, carrying the bucket by its stout rope handle, she ventured down the corridor to the guardroom. She considered it a good omen that her executioner had given her this much freedom of movement. When she turned the corner, the Gypsy rose from the bench.

He studied her face with an inscrutable look for an extra heartbeat, then his gaze softened a fraction. "I see that the water pleased you."

Tonia put the bucket down on the hearth and warmed her still damp hands at his fire. "Aye, Master of the Morn, 'twas as sweet as swimming in damask roses."

He cocked an eyebrow. "You can swim?"

She laughed at his surprise. "Aye, my cousin Kitt taught me—after he had pitched me into the cow pond and discovered that I could not."

A shadow of annoyance crossed the man's face. "Your cousin sounds much ill-mannered."

With a smile, Tonia shook her head. "Nay, Kitt is only full of high spirits," she replied with fondness.

"You like this cousin?" he asked with a certain coolness. "Were you betrothed to him?"

His question startled her. "Me marry Kitt?" She laughed at the very notion. "Nay, we are too close in blood. He was my playfellow and best friend for many years—but marry Kitt? Hoy day! I pity the poor woman who will wed him. He will lead her a merry chase. What made you think I would marry my cousin?'' She sat down near him.

He pushed the cheese closer to her. '''Tis the custom among the Rom to marry within the extended family. I married my father's cousin's daughter when she was thirteen.''

Tonia stared at him for a moment. She had not given a thought that he might be married. It seemed unlikely for an executioner to be a family man. Now that she had learned he was, she felt a twinge of disappointment—and a hot spurt of jealousy. She gave herself a shake. Why should his wife matter to her?

''Thirteen is young to be married,'' Tonia remarked. She bit into the hard cheese.

He gave her a wry grin. ''I was sixteen and considered myself fully a man. I have since learned that there is a great deal more to marriage than bedding a bride.''

Tonia felt a blush creep up her neck and into her face. She hoped that he did not notice her change of color. She tried not to think of him in bed…naked with those wonderful broad shoulders…and those slim hips…and those long legs…kissing his bride…holding her close to his bare chest…. Tonia choked on her cheese.

He thumped her on the back several times. ''Tonia?''

Swallowing, she held up her hand. ''Hold! I am recovered.'' She flashed him a quick sidelong glance. ''You could have let the cheese do your work for you, you know.''

Pursing his lips, he stared up at the low-vaulted ceiling. "You must think me a true villain."

Tonia admired his profile for a moment, musing how noble he would look if he were dressed in a fine shirt of cambric and a doublet of velvet. As he was, his gold earring gave him a certain raffish appearance that she found very attractive. She stifled a sigh of desire. He's a married man, she reminded herself.

"Do you have many children?" Tonia asked in an offhand manner.

He puffed out his cheeks. "Nay. My wife died in childbirth. She left none for me to remember her."

Tonia's sudden elation shocked her. She should never rejoice at the news of someone's death. "I am sorry for that and for your loss," she murmured. "What is her name that I may pray for her?"

He gave her a long, cool look before he replied, "'Tis not the custom of my people to speak the names of the dead. 'Tis bad luck."

"Oh." Tonia chewed another bit of her cheese while she gathered her courage to broach the real subject that burned in her mind. "Very well. Since we two are still among the living, you can tell me *your* name."

For once, her question seemed to amuse him. "'Tis important to you?"

"Aye, methinks we have kept company long enough and I am tired of making up titles for you. Surely you can trust me with your name by now. You have already told me your *horse's* name and I know how precious he is to you."

The Gypsy considered her request in silence before he finally nodded. "Very well." Lacing his hands behind his head, he leaned back against the wall. "I was baptized Sandor after Saint Alexander.'' The *r* sounds rolled off his tongue.

Intense astonishment made Tonia forget the last morsel of the cheese she held in her hand. ''You were baptized? In a church?''

He nodded and a smug grin crossed his face.

Tonia knotted her brows. ''But you are a Gypsy!''

A wide smile replaced his grin, transforming his features into those of an angel. ''Even so I was well and truly baptized in a holy church—in seven of them if the truth be told. 'Twas my father's little bit of *bujo*.''

Tonia gave him an arched look. ''Methinks I spy a rat in the larder. What is this *bujo?*''

His lips curled with merriment. ''It means...'' He rolled his dancing eyes as he searched for the word. ''Gypsy work—not hard labor. To coney—catch the *gadje*.''

Tonia gasped at this bold admission. ''You hood-winked some elderly priest while you stole from the poor box?''

Sandor held up his hands. ''Nay, 'twas not I! I was but a babe at the time—an innocent party. And my father did not *steal* anything.'' He chuckled to himself.

Despite her shock, Tonia found herself smiling back at him. ''So how *did* your father trick the priest?''

Sandor swirled the watered wine in his cup. '''Twas the custom in the bishopric of Paris that every new-baptized child should receive a gold ecu from the parish treasury. 'Twas a most generous gift.'' His eyes sparkled with mischief. ''So first I was baptized in Sainte Marguerite's church, then in Sainte

Marie's church, then at Sacre Coeur, and so forth. Each time the parish priest gave my mother an ecu. At the end of the day, my family had seven ecus in our bag, and I was named seven times over.''

Tonia glared at him. "'Tis a sacrilege to steal from the church!''

Sandor merely laughed. ''How could it be called stealing if the money was freely *given* to us? We did not even have to ask for it. My grandmother always said that you can get more with cunning than with power. That is *bujo*.''

Tonia considered this skewered logic for a moment. ''Were you really baptized seven times, or is your story just another tale like the donkey eating the cabbage leaves?''

Sandor raised one hand toward heaven. ''Let me die if I lie!''

The talk of dying cast a pall over Tonia's good spirits. ''Methinks I am much closer to death than you are at this moment.''

His expression clouded. Then he pushed himself up from the table. ''We burn daylight, my lady.'' He picked up the shovel that had been leaning against the wall. ''Come. We must give Baxtalo an airing. Methinks he will be glad of your company.''

Tonia popped the last piece of cheese in her mouth then, wrapping her cloak around her, she followed him out into the courtyard. She berated herself for bringing up the distasteful subject and so spoiling his cheerful humor, yet her ultimate fate preyed on her mind. How could such a charming man laugh with her even as he contemplated her murder?

Sandor attacked the cold ground with his shovel, venting his anger on the thick clods of earth that he tossed by the side of the grave. While he dug, he tried to decide what he was going to do about the increasingly desirable Lady Gastonia Cavendish. The time had come for him to be honest with himself. He knew in his heart that he was not going to kill her. He should have admitted that truth from the first moment when he saw her. Even as she curtsied to him, he had been thunderstruck by her beauty and her radiance. Had the lady been a gnarled crone ready for death, perhaps he could have done the deed, but he knew that God would be angry if Sandor snuffed out the life of such a beautiful example of his handiwork.

Pausing to sip some watered wine from his *bota,* he watched Tonia stroke and pet Baxtalo. Lucky horse! Sandor wished that she would run her fingers through his hair as she did with Baxtalo's mane. His skin prickled. Sandor mopped his brow with his neckerchief then squinted up at the sun. Time moved forward, one more day that Demeo lay in the Tower.

By his calculation, Sandor realized that he was expected to arrive in London on the morrow or the day after. He was supposed to deliver the small box containing Tonia's heart to the Constable of the Tower as soon as he reached the city. Only then would Demeo be freed. If Sandor did not appear within the week, he knew that the King's officials would send soldiers to Hawksnest to investigate. He must be long gone by then. And the lady?

Across the meadow, Tonia sang a lighthearted ballad. Its pleasing notes floated back to Sandor. When she turned to look at him, he grinned and waved to her. Then he returned his attention to the hole that he now stood in. He guessed its depth was three feet and a bit. Not that he intended to use it for its original purpose. Digging it bought him time and occupied his body. Otherwise he might be tempted to seduce the enchanting woman who played with his horse.

Sandor gripped the handle of the shovel. The devil would punish him for thinking such lustful thoughts. Tonia was dedicated to God, not to be a man's plaything. Yet what a waste! He glanced again at her. Even dressed in her plain gray gown with no ornamentation save for her wooden cross, she was as beautiful as a May morn. He recalled another one of old Towla's sayings, "Beauty cannot be eaten with a spoon." But then again, his grandmother had never laid eyes on Tonia. She was a feast.

She is a *gadji,* Sandor reminded himself. His shovel struck a good-sized rock. He worked the spade around it while his mind examined this problem. All *gadje,* most especially their women, polluted the Rom, or so Sandor had been taught ever since he was old enough to understand the differences between his people and everyone else in the world. Yet Sandor did not feel soiled by his contact with Tonia. On the contrary, she lifted his soul more than he had ever felt with any other. Was there evil in this magic?

He glanced toward the edge of the meadow where he had laid several snares in hopes of catching a wayward rabbit or two. His food store was very low. He had not intended to remain for so long at Hawksnest, nor had he planned to feed the woman who was supposed to be dead by now. This holiday from his responsibilities would come to a jarring end within another day or two. Then what?

Sandor looked over his shoulder at Tonia, but he did not see her. Baxtalo grazed near the stream, but the dark-haired beauty had vanished. Cursing himself under his breath, Sandor dropped the shovel and vaulted out of the hole. He should have guessed that she would make another bid for her freedom. After all, she did not know the truth inside his heart. He ran toward the last spot where he had seen her. The bent and broken grass, dry from the previous summer, showed plainly the direction she had taken. Sandor shaded his eyes as he scanned the edge of the forest. Tonia was clever in many ways, but he didn't think she realized the dangers that lurked within the tangled undergrowth.

Sandor crossed the field in her wake. On a rock in the stream, he saw the wet print of her shoe. Tonia would soon rue her cold feet. He cleared the water in two strides, then moved into the woods where he paused to listen. No point in calling to her. She would never answer. It did not matter, for she had left a trail that was easy to follow. He only hoped that in her rush, she had not disturbed any of the wild animals. Many predators were lean and hungry at the end of a long winter and they would not hesitate to attack a lone human.

Not too far down the hill, Sandor spotted Tonia ahead of him. It appeared that a thick bramble held fast to her skirts. Relieved to find her unharmed, though frustrated, he quietly descended behind her. When Sandor was close enough to hear her muttering under her breath, he stopped and leaned against the nearest tree.

"'Tis not the best place for a stroll, is it, Tonia?" he remarked.

She glanced over her shoulder, formed a round "o" with her lips then regarded her entangled skirts with disgust. "You seem to have an annoying habit of following me," she replied.

Sandor picked his way around the bush, then hunkered down to inspect the situation. "By the command of our sovereign lord, you are my responsibility," he reminded her. He broke off a branch, pulled it free from the bush, then pried the cloth loose from several long thorns.

"I am well able to fend for myself," she fumed, watching him free her clothing.

He flashed her a look that was gentle but carried a warning. "Can you kill a boar?" he asked, unwinding her ragged petticoat from another thorn.

Tonia gasped. "What boar?" With a shiver, she looked quickly around. "I see nothing. Methinks 'tis a trick of yours to make me afraid."

Sandor broke off another branch that held her fast in its thorny clutches. "I speak the truth to you, Tonia. There is a boar hereabouts and a large one judging from the size of his droppings. He is the king of this mountain, and he will not take kindly to your invasion of his realm."

Tonia continued to search the area, now a little less sure of herself. "A boar, you say?"

Sandor nodded. "A very large one, fit for the table of the lord mayor of York."

"Perchance 'tis not hungry." She chewed her lower lip.

"Boars need no excuse to attack," he said, pulling the last of her skirt free. "They are hag-ridden brutes spawned by the devil himself."

"So my father has said. He often goes a-hunting the boar in the winter."

Sandor offered her his hand. "Then let us quit this place."

Tonia regarded him with a speculative gaze. "You could leave me to my own defenses. Mayhap the boar would do to me what King Edward most desires. 'Twould relieve you of your duty."

He narrowed his eyes. "You may think me a monster, my lady, but I would not wish that bloody, painful fate on an enemy much less on you."

"Am I not your enemy?" she asked in a low voice. "I am a *gadji*."

He smiled at her use of his language. "You were never an enemy of mine, Tonia," he replied. The depth of his feeling made his voice husky. "Take my hand," he whispered.

Tonia hesitated a moment, trying to fathom his intentions but, as always, he shuttered his true thoughts behind a charming facade. There was no denying his charm now that he had discarded his headsman's mask. With a sigh of resignation, Tonia gathered up her skirts in one hand then placed her other within his.

Sandor's long fingers closed over hers in a warm, gentle clasp. A pleasurable shiver rippled through her. Her heartbeat increased. A wave of giddiness washed over her. Gripping his hand more firmly, she glanced up at him. His steady gaze bored into her as if he sought to read the very secrets of her soul. Then his lips parted in a wide smile that set her blood racing through her veins. Her breath came in small gasps.

Sandor helped her up the steep incline. When they were back in the meadow, he turned to her. Cupping her chin between his thumb and forefinger, he stared deeply into her eyes.

"I know that I frighten you, Tonia," he said in his deep-timbre voice. "And that fact is my misfortune more than yours. Please believe me when I tell you that there is nothing to fear. All I ask is that you trust me."

Chapter Eight

Tonia rolled over on her sheepskin pallet and stared at the low fire. Though she had been outside in the fresh air for most of the day, sleep refused to come. Her stomach growled, but it wasn't her hunger that kept her awake so late in the night. Up until now, she had been able to suppress the panic that hovered on the edge of her every waking minute. From the first horrifying moment of her arrest and abduction, she had fought against the tide of black fright that threatened to engulf her. During the carriage journey to York when her younger companions had wept and bewailed their fates, Tonia had been an island of calm, soothing the others' terror while she masked her own.

Even after the white-whiskered judges had pronounced her doom and dispatched her to this forgotten fortress, Tonia maintained her facade of optimism. Her self-control had served Tonia well when the executioner finally arrived, but the constant dread of death grew during the days that followed, eroding her courage. Her clever wits dulled until she could think of nothing else except surviving one more day, one more night.

Since her second escape attempt, Sandor had grown more distant. Every so often during the long afternoon, she caught him staring at her with a very grim expression on his face. By the time the twilight crept over the mountain's crest, her grave yawned wide and deep enough to fulfill its purpose. Yet Sandor said nothing of his plans, not even when she had asked him outright what time he planned to kill her. Instead, he asked her again to trust him.

No rabbits, fat or otherwise, had wandered into his snares. Tonight, Sandor gave her the last piece of his cheese while he himself drank only water. Her intellect advised her to take a measure of comfort because he had fed her instead of himself, but her nerves had been rubbed raw over the past fortnight. Despite the warmth of the fire, she could not control her shivering.

Tonia sat up, drawing her cloak around her. On the table, a fat candle end glowed inside the lantern. Sandor always left it with her to keep the evil spirits at bay, but tonight, she could not find solace in its light.

She slipped on her shoes, tied their laces and then stood. Grasping the lantern's handle, she tiptoed to the door that Sandor had not bothered to lock and pressed her ear against the wood. She heard nothing from the guardroom where she surmised the Gypsy slept. She cracked open the door wide enough to allow her to peer out. Light from his fire danced on the far wall at the turn of the passage, though she could not see Sandor.

She slipped out, then picked her way down the corridor toward the stairway that led to the wall walk.

When she stepped out onto the narrow parapet, the night's cold wind slapped her cheeks and sent her unbound hair flying about her face. A half-moon hung over the opposite mountaintop. She lifted her face to its cold silver light.

When Tonia had been a child and was restless in the night, she had often communed with the moon, dreaming of the faraway places and strange people that the silver orb smiled down upon. She would wonder if there were any other children living in a distant land who were also awake, looking at the same moon and dreaming of meeting someone like her.

Behind her, Sandor cleared his throat. Tonia almost dropped the lantern over the crumbling wall.

"Do you make a wish?" he asked, drawing beside her.

Tonia cast a sidelong glance at him, but his face was shadowed. "I have always wished on the moon, but she rarely pays any attention to me."

"Like many mortal women, the Lady Gana of the moon is fickle," he remarked as he slipped his arm around Tonia, drawing her close against him. "You shiver with the cold," he murmured in her ear. He draped his cloak over her so that it enveloped both of them.

The warmth of his body seeped into Tonia. She leaned against him, seeking what comfort she could. He wound his arms around her, locking her in his embrace. Tonia relaxed a little, basking in his strength.

"'Tis a wet moon that looks down upon us," Sandor continued. His uneven breath warmed her cheek.

"Why do you call it that?" Tonia asked, her gaze on the gleaming orb.

"'Tis when a cloud cuts across it. See, it comes again. There will be rain tomorrow. Or snow perchance."

Tonia said nothing, but she imagined her grave filling with icy water. She huddled deeper within their cloaks.

"'Tis too cold for you out here," he chided.

"'Tis warmer than lying in my tomb," she replied. "Therefore I do not complain."

With a deep sigh, he tightened his grasp around her as if he feared she might sprout wings and fly away. Tonia felt his thigh muscles tense against the backs of her legs. The power that he controlled within himself made her dizzy both with apprehension—and with appreciation. She wondered what would have happened if she had met him in another time and another place. Perhaps her life would have taken a different turning.

Sandor again cleared his throat. "Tell me, sweet lady, why did you never marry?"

Tonia stiffened. Did this Gypsy possess the skill to read her mind? She searched for an answer she could tell him. She didn't want to confess to him that she had never found anyone that had interested her enough to consider matrimony. For a reason that she didn't understand, Tonia did not want Sandor to think that handsome, intelligent men might find her unappealing. "I preferred to devote my life to God," she finally replied.

He snorted under his breath. "Your pardon, Tonia, but that is not what your body tells me."

Glad that the darkness hid the hot blush that rose in her cheeks, she pulled herself a little away from him but not so far that his cloak would not cover her.

"Methinks you have a wealth of nerve to presume the workings of my...er...mind."

"Ha!" Sandor rumbled. "I may not be able to decipher words on a parchment, but I can read the heart of a horse—and that of a woman. You should have married years ago."

Tonia laughed to cover her annoyance at his candor. "You make me sound as if I am a dried-up spinster. I am only three-and-twenty."

"A Gypsy woman would have had five children by that age," he observed, unruffled by her cool tone.

Stung by his remark, she snapped, "I am not a Gypsy."

He tucked a lock of her hair behind her ear. "But you *are* a woman—one who possesses fire and the spirit of passion."

His shocking words and gentle touch sent a pleasurable quiver through her veins. Tonia's breath stuck in her throat as Sandor smoothed another one of her windblown tresses beside the first. Though his fingers barely grazed her skin, gooseflesh rose on the back of her neck. She burrowed deeper into her cloak.

"You are right—it has grown much colder," she muttered, not daring to look into his eyes. "Let us go inside."

He slid his hand under her elbow and turned her toward the archway that led to the spiral stairs. "You still have not answered my question," he remarked as he guided her back to her cell.

He is as stubborn as a terrier chasing a rat. Aloud, Tonia replied, "Nor have you answered mine." She sat down on the stool.

"What question is that?"

"What do you intend to do with me?"

Turning away from her, Sandor tossed several more logs on her fire. The greedy flames licked the wood. Staring at his handiwork, Sandor said in a low voice, "I must leave this place at dawn tomorrow."

Tonia stifled a cry in the back of her throat. Of course she had known this moment would come, but now that it had, she discovered how unprepared she was—and how angry she was at this handsome rogue for beguiling her into a false sense of security.

"Will you kill me now or then? I need to know so that I may ready myself." She gripped the folds of her cloak to keep her hands from trembling, though the ploy was pointless. She shook all over. "You did promise me some time of preparation."

Sandor rotated on the balls of his feet so that he looked fully upon her. "I must go down the mountain to seek food. There is a good-sized village a half-day's ride from the fork in the road that leads here. Even Baxtalo needs a good meal."

Tonia drew in a breath. "And what of me?"

His clear eyes gave her a tortured look. "Aye, there's the rub of it. I do not know *what* to do with you—and that is God's own truth."

The fire's golden light made Tonia appear far younger than her years. Her lower lip quivered before she caught it with her small, white teeth. Sandor didn't blame the maid for being afraid of him. He wished there was something he could say or do that would banish all her fears.

Tonia lifted her chin. "Let me come with you on the morrow. Like your horse, I too could use a good dinner."

Sandor grinned at her. What courage she possessed! She would breed brave sons—if she were allowed to live long enough. Sandor longed to give her those sons. With a jerk, he turned away from her before her allure drove him over the brink.

He jabbed the burning logs with a rusted poker. "Tell me true, Tonia, would you be content merely to ride behind me or would you flee at your first opportunity?"

She said nothing in reply.

He nodded. "As I thought. 'Tis why I must leave you here."

She swallowed. "Alive or dead?"

He couldn't tell her of his decision not to harm her—not yet. She would be clever enough to use that knowledge against him. First Sandor had to cobble together a plan that would satisfy both his conscience and the hard-hearted *gadje* in London. "You will sleep in peace tonight."

"Ha!" she snapped. "You speak in a ghastly riddle, Gypsy. Is it your pleasure to taunt me into madness? Kill me now and be done with it."

Sandor recognized the knife edge of hysteria in her voice. She shivered so much that both their heavy cloaks shook around her shoulders. The tension between them increased with a stifling intensity. Pity overcame Sandor's logic. He reached for her.

With a cry, Tonia threw up her arms as if to shield her face. Crooning endearments in his own language, Sandor gathered her into his arms. Cradling her against his chest, he laid her head on his shoulder. He stroked his fingers down her stiff spine, wishing he could sweep away her terror.

"Hush, *sukar luludi,* my sweet flower, I am not a demon. *Jaj!* You are colder than iron." He hugged her tighter.

Though frightened, Tonia softened in his embrace, allowing her body to mold itself to his contours. She buried her face in the hollow between his neck and collarbone. Her ragged breath warmed his skin—and his desire. He swallowed before he spoke again.

"May God strike me dead if I harm you tonight or tomorrow, sweet Tonia Cavendish. I am not your killer but your protector. You must trust me."

"'Tis easy for you to say," she whispered into his shirt. "You are the one with the warrant and the weapons."

Nay, your fire has already slain me.

A sudden blast of wind howled through the arrow slit, slamming the cell's door shut and extinguishing the candle, despite the lantern's housing. Sandor muttered a quick prayer against evil ghosts. Hawksnest was filled with ill fortune. He had sensed it from the moment Baxtalo had walked under the main archway. The sooner they left this place, the better things would be.

"What did you say?" she asked.

He brushed his lips across the top of her head. "'Tis a message for God, not for you," he replied in a husky voice. "I asked him to lend me some of His wisdom."

Tonia looked up at him. "I didn't know that Gypsies really prayed."

Her beauty wrung his heart. "This one does."

"Did God answer you?" Her sugar-sweet lips hovered too near his.

"He suggests sleep for both of us while he ponders our problem." Sandor tucked the ends of the cloaks under them to keep out the draft.

Tonia touched the deep cleft in his chin with the

tip of her finger. "And you promise that I will awake in *this* world come the morning?"

He gave her a squeeze. "Upon my life, I swear it."

Sandor laid her down on the sheepskin beside him. Tonia curled herself against his side, pillowing her head on his shoulder. He said nothing but reveled in her nearness. At length, her shivers abated. Soon he could tell by the evenness of her breathing that Tonia was finally asleep.

Sandor leaned over her. He pressed his lips against hers, then covered her mouth. Her breath mingled with his. Sandor felt giddy, as if he had been drinking strong summer wine. He pulled himself away before his carnal desires took hold of his reason. Willing his throbbing body to ignore Tonia's proximity, he stared up at the low ceiling and began to count the stones. *Yek…dui…trin….* He drifted into sleep sometime after he passed one hundred.

Though the grave-digging, as well as the day's physical tension, had fatigued Sandor, he slept lightly as was his habit born of a childhood filled with sudden escapes from *gadje* sheriffs who often came calling at midnight. Now a stealthy movement woke him, though he did not open his eyes. He realized that he still lay on the sheepskin, but that his bed partner no longer slept in his arms. Tonia knelt beside him, looking down at him. He could feel the heat of her gaze even with his lids closed.

Sandor maintained the pose of sleep, though he was ready to give chase if Tonia decided to bolt for her freedom. Why couldn't she realize that the forest surrounding Hawksnest held more danger for her than the man who lay beside her? Sandor breathed steadily while Tonia decided what she was going to do.

Then he felt her fumbling at his belt. Sandor willed his body to ignore her feather-light touch and remain still. Did she search for the garrote? Would she throw it into the fire? Her fingers skimmed over his *putsi* wherein lay the lethal cords. Then she touched the hilt of his razor-edged *chiv*. Sandor slitted his eyelids. Tonia bent closer over him, chewing on her lower lip. The low firelight illuminated the grim determination on her face.

She closed her hand around the dagger's leather handle and gave it a little tug. The blade moved in its sheath. Tonia paused, watching Sandor with the concentration of a cat at a mouse hole. The short hairs on the back of Sandor's neck prickled. *She means to kill me!*

That possibility had never crossed his mind. Just because he couldn't kill her didn't mean that she felt the same way about him. Sandor had forgotten that Tonia was the daughter of a famous warrior. Sir Guy Cavendish's fighting blood ran deep in her veins, as her great courage had already demonstrated. Of course she would kill Sandor to gain her liberty!

He remained still even as he felt his dagger slowly leaving its sheath. In an odd way, he was disappointed in Tonia. He had thought that she liked him, at least a little bit. Obviously he had been mistaken. His nerve endings tingled as he waited for her to begin the final downward stroke. He would not move until the last possible second in the hope that the same compassion he had felt for her would stay her hand. He had asked her to trust him, and now he must test his trust in her. But it was going to be very close.

Tonia drew the dagger free. Still biting her lips, she held the blade shoulder high. Again she paused.

Sandor breathed lightly between his parted lips. Mentally he coiled himself to roll away before springing at her.

Tonia did not move. She clutched the dagger a foot or so above his chest. Then, with her free hand, she reached down and brushed a lock of his hair from his forehead. Her fingers grazed his skin like a butterfly's wing on a summer's day. A warm tremor ran through Sandor's veins. He watched her through the curtain of his thick lashes. Tonia hovered closer. He saw the shimmer of confusion in the depths of her eyes. His heart raced with sudden hope. So cold-blooded murder was not her pleasure either.

Tonia ran the backs of her fingers down his dark-stubbled cheek. Her touch was exquisite torture. If Sandor was fated to die by her hand, at least the moment would be pleasurable before the pain. She touched the cleft in his chin. The dagger's blade wavered above him.

Sandor tensed. A small gasp escaped her lips. A lone tear spilled from her eye and rolled down her cheek. Its watery path glistened in the firelight. A second followed the first. The sight of her tears encouraged him. Tonia's womanly heart fought with her natural desire for self-preservation. Mayhap she did like Sandor—at least a little bit.

She touched his neck, then loosened the knot of his neckerchief. Her fingernail scraped the sensitive skin at the base of his throat. Sandor clenched his teeth so that he would not swallow and betray himself. Cold sweat dampened the hair on his forehead.

Tonia widened the neck of his shirt. A cold lump formed inside Sandor's gut. Again she touched his neck. Did she seek the vein that carried his life's blood? More tears ran down her cheeks. Tonia bit down on her lower lip. Anguish etched every line of her body. She raised the dagger higher in preparation to strike. Sandor's instincts screamed inside his brain. Still he lay as if in blissful repose. He wanted to give Tonia every opportunity to back away from this terrible deed.

Dashing the tears from her face, she drew in a deep breath and raised the knife high above her head.

Chapter Nine

With a low moan, Tonia dropped the dagger and buried her face in her hands. Sandor bolted upright and kicked the blade across the chamber. Then he took Tonia into his arms and gently rocked her. Through the tight bodice of her gown, he felt the pounding of her heartbeat.

"You knew?" She wept against his shoulder. "I...I couldn't do it."

"Aye, murder is a tricky thing. It kills the murderer far worse than the victim." He rubbed her back.

She collapsed against him. "I am no mur...murderer."

Sandor pulled her into his lap. "'Tis not in your soul to kill," he said, with relief in his voice. He never wanted to lie that close to death again. His own heart drummed against his chest.

"I only wanted my freedom," she whispered. "I am innocent of the King's trumped-up charges."

I know that you are, sukar luludi. But he could not tell her his conviction, not until he had devised an escape from their dilemma. Burying his face in the dark cloud of her hair, he allowed his silent tears to flow. *Jaj!* How he wished an angel would fly down from heaven and whisk them both away to France!

Tonia curled against him like a kitten. Spent by her emotions, she slipped into a deep sleep. Sandor held her in his arms for the remainder of the night.

When Tonia opened her eyes, she saw a pewter-gray light outside her window. Sandor came through the door carrying a large load of dry firewood from the pile her former guards had left in an antechamber. He was dressed in a fresh shirt and a sheepskin jacket. His face shone clean of his dark bristles. When he saw her, he grinned.

"As I promised, you have awakened in this world and not the next, though 'tis a chilly morn to greet you." He stacked the split logs and kindling on the hearth. "And there is nothing to break your fast but icy water from the well."

She gave him a wry look. "In short, you offer me cold comfort." It was a weak jest, but he laughed, releasing the tension between them.

"Aye," he replied, "but your wit will keep you warm." He grew more serious. "In truth, Tonia, the weather has turned as the moon foretold. Snow hovers in the sky."

Taking his work-stained shirt from the sack he carried over his shoulder, he stuffed the cloth in the arrow loop window to block out the wind. "Methinks 'twill be better to trade daylight for warmth."

Tonia stretched out her cold fingers to the renewed fire. "'Tis no matter." *As long as I still live and breathe upon this earth.*

While she warmed herself and shook the last wisps of sleep from her body, Sandor bustled out of the chamber. He soon returned, carrying a jug of the promised well water and a bucket of the same for washing. A thick wool blanket, woven with wide colorful stripes unlike any Tonia had ever seen, hung over his arm. He placed the jug on the table next to her chipped cup as if he served her the finest French wine. Then he draped the blanket over her shoulders. Smelling faintly of horse, its weight and its warmth took her by surprise. With a gasp of pleasure, she snuggled within its depths.

"'Tis old and travel-worn," Sandor apologized, "but it has served me well for years. My grandmother wove it and knitted spells of protection within the stripes. 'Twill keep you safe as well as warm while I am gone."

His words acted like a knifepoint, puncturing her fragile sense of well-being. "You are going away? Now?"

He looked away. "Aye, for food, my lady."

She stood, clasping the blanket around her like a shield. "Let me come with you. I am weary of this place."

He made a dismissive gesture with his hand though he still did not look at her. "Nay, upon my bond and oath, I cannot do that."

Anger flared in Tonia's breast. By his oath and bond he was her executioner, but by the gentleness of his look and touch, she had thought him otherwise. "How now? Has the Master of Death returned?" Was this to be their final moments together—and her last day on earth?

He winced at her rebuke. "By the *tarocchi* cards, Death means a change. 'Tis a new beginning as well as an end—or so my grandmother told me."

Tonia sniffed. "I do not read a pack of pasteboards to tell me what I should believe. My Book of Hours holds all the truth I need for this world and the next. I wish that I had it with me now! 'Twould give me more solace than your slippery words."

Sandor buttoned up his jacket, adjusted his neckerchief and pulled his pointed-brim felt cap down over his ears. A clutch of black cockerel's feathers bobbed jauntily from the hatband. His expression turned grim. "Tell me one truth, my lady. If I took you with me, wouldn't you escape from me at your first opportunity, no matter what vow you had given me that you would not?"

"I...I..." Tonia bit her lower lip. Of course she would grasp for her freedom if given the chance. "I just want to go home," she finally replied. Her anguish colored the simple words.

Sandor finally met her eyes with his. "You will anon," he told her. "You may rely upon my word, though only God knows when or how." He pulled on his gloves. His right forefinger poked through a hole in the old leather. He touched his hat brim by way of a salute to her. "Baxtalo is saddled in the forecourt and awaits me. Be of good cheer, Lady Gastonia, and think of the feast I will bring you." The wind moaned down the corridor behind him. "And say a prayer or two for my safe return. I fear that your life depends upon it."

With that, he went through the doorway, slammed the heavy portal and turned the key in the lock. The grating sound terrified Tonia. Shaking off the blanket, she raced to the grilled window and shook the bars. "Perfidious knave with honey words!" she shouted at him. "You have sealed me in my tomb. Why?"

He slung his black cloak around his shoulders. "If I did not lock you in, would you still be here upon my return?" He snapped shut the cloak's brass clasp under his chin. "Here you are safe. Outside in the forest? You would surely meet the death that you fear so much. Trust me on this point."

Sandor turned away from her. "You had best bundle up in yon blanket, Tonia. 'Twill be a long cold day and—" he gave her a meaningful look over his shoulder "—I have left you my eating knife by your jug. 'Tis not much more than a thorn, but 'twill serve you if…if someone else comes."

Tonia's mouth went dry. "Who? No one comes here except the damned!"

Sandor paused at the bend of the corridor. "Aye, you speak the truth. Should a devil seek shelter from yon storm and discover you here, do not hesitate but skewer him under the ribs near the heart. But if you hear the whistle of a meadowlark, then sheath your *chiv* and put on a smile for 'twill be me—and our supper." He touched his cap brim again. "Fare thee well, Tonia. *Jel sa Duvvel.*" He rounded the corner.

Standing on her toes, Tonia shook the cold bars. "What did you say?" she shouted after him.

"Go with God." His blessing echoed off the stone walls.

Tonia leaned her cheek against the door's rough wood. "And with you, you double-dealing, two-faced churl!" she whispered.

Never had a day stretched so long. Every minute was an hour; each hour lasted a year. Tonia spent the creeping time maintaining the fire, listening to the wind that grew in strength and saying her rosary on her fingers since her judges had stripped her of her holy beads. As the day waned toward twilight, she prayed for strength and courage, for safe deliverance and, most of all, for Sandor's promised return.

He wouldn't leave her to starve a slow death in this dank prison, she told herself, but as the hours dragged by, she became less sure. For the first time since her arrest, Tonia found herself completely alone. The solitude crept around her, chilling her more than the cold stones of her cell. She moved as close to the hearth as she dared, but the fire's heat did little to stop the shivers in her soul.

Sandor had duped her! Treating her like a gullible coney rabbit, he had left her in this cage and so fulfilled his commission. She would certainly die—of starvation, of thirst or of the cold, but not by the shedding of her blood as the warrant had decreed, nor by his hand, as he had promised her.

She pulled the little knife from its plain leather sheath and touched its chill blade with a fingertip. If any blood was spilled, it would be by her hand. Was that why he had left her this final escape? Shuddering, she resheathed the weapon. Suicide was the worst sin on the church's list of offenses against God's laws. 'Twas a crime against oneself as well as against God who alone had the right to give or take a life. How could that man think that Tonia would kill herself, even in the depths of her abandonment? But of course, Sandor was only a Gypsy and not schooled in good Christian morals, in spite of his seven baptisms.

Thinking of him made her body ache, not for lack of food nor cold, but for him—his touch, his warmth, the sound of his melodic voice telling her the most outrageous stories as if they were gospel-true. To her surprise, she realized that she missed him, not just for the company of another human being, but for himself. Wrapped in his thick blanket, Tonia lay down on Sandor's sheepskin rug and inhaled the comforting scent of horse and a fainter musk that was his own. Despite her intentions to the contrary, she dozed.

When she awoke, the chamber was much darker. Her fire burned low in the grate. Chiding herself for her lapse, Tonia tossed on several more logs and blew the red embers to encourage a renewed flame. She eyed the woodpile. It had shrunk to half the size it had been this morning. She realized that she must husband her fuel, no matter how cold it got. Once the wood was reduced to ash, she would freeze to death within a day.

When the logs caught fire, Tonia set the stool under the narrow window, stood on tiptoe and pulled a little bit of the shirt away from the frame. A thick veil of snow fell outside her walls. At least Sandor had spoken the truth in one respect—the weather had indeed turned wet as his moon goddess had prophesied to him. Tonia replaced the cloth and hurried back to the fire.

The silence beyond her locked door seemed louder than a thunderstorm in summer—and more ominous. Night was nearly here and Sandor had not returned. For the first time, Tonia ceased to worry about her own fate as she considered that of the man and his horse who were out somewhere in this white tempest. Tonia had heard stories of people getting lost in a snowstorm and freezing to death only yards from their doors. What if Sandor was riding around in circles, unable to find the way back to Hawksnest?

A wave of apprehension swept through her. He

could not be lost! That thought had barely crossed her mind when a second, even more shocking one followed: she could not bear it if she never saw him again. With trembling fingers, Tonia lighted a small twig, then touched it to the wick of her candle end in the lantern Sandor always left beside her pallet "to keep away the troublesome spirits." If she put the lantern in her window, its light would give him a beacon to guide his way back to her. She paused. Or it might beckon other, more sinister men—the very ones that Sandor had warned her about.

Tonia stared into the candle's light. That was a risk she would have to take. Sandor must return to her, not only with food to feed the hunger of her body but also to satisfy the cravings of her heart. She shut the little glass door tightly so that the wind would not threaten it, then she went to the window. After pulling away the protective cloth, she hooked the lantern's handle over a protruding bit of the upper frame. Then she made a hasty retreat to the fire. Her lantern swayed in the wind that now blew through the cell, but the candlelight did not waver. Picking up the dagger, Tonia held it between her hands and stared at its hilt, imagining the holy cross. Kneeling before the fire, she prayed to God to send back the intriguing man whose image filled her mind.

The wind howled louder around the ruined battlements and snowflakes fluttered through the window's bars. And blind darkness enveloped the fortress—except for one lone spark of light.

Sandor thought that he would feel free once he and Baxtalo left the fortress behind them. At least, his horse had perked up as soon as they had crossed over the drawbridge. Now Baxtalo deftly picked his way down the narrow, overgrown path toward the valley. Sandor gave his mount a slack rein while he retreated into the dark corner of his mind that he had ignored for the past week and more.

He should have been in London by now, even with the unexpected delays that wet or icy roads presented. By allowing his heart to rule his head, Sandor had put not only cousin Demeo in greater jeopardy of the King's rough vengeance but also the rest of his family. And for what? A *gadji* with eyes like sapphires, though Sandor had only seen a real sapphire once in his life. Lady Gastonia should mean nothing to him. She was not a member of his family or clan, not even a Rom. Yet, he had only to conjure up her face in his mind's eye to know that he could not do what he had been sent north to do.

There was no murder in his heart, only love. He gasped aloud, causing Baxtalo to prick his ears. Love? Where did that word come from? How did Sandor know he was in love? Lust, yes. Tonia's lush body, though hidden within her prim gown, enticed and seduced him past all common sense. But love? What did he know of that elusive emotion?

His parents had died when Sandor was too young to remember his mother's kisses or his father's laughter, though old Towla had often soothed him in the dark nights with stories of his mother's beauty and his father's cleverness. His grandmother told Sandor that his parents had loved him, but he could not remember it. He couldn't even remember their faces.

Had Sandor ever really loved his little wife? They had been children when they were married. He had liked his bride well enough and his body took pleasure from hers when he had tried to get a child on her. When he had finally succeeded, she had died giving birth to their stillborn babe. Remembering her, he felt no love, only shame to have killed so young a flower.

Sandor recalled the *tarocchi* his grandmother had cast for him just before he had set out on this impossible journey. The Lovers—a happy couple embracing under a striped umbrella while Cupid flew over their heads. 'Twill be a soul mate for you, his grandmother had predicted. Was Tonia his soul mate? Aye, from the first moment of their meeting, even before she had greeted him, Sandor had known that she was like no other woman he had ever met. But Tonia was also a *gadji,* a member of a society that hated Gypsies and who were, in turn, despised by the Rom for their unclean ways. Where did his loyalties lie?

Use this time away to examine your heart, his grandmother had advised him when she turned over the Hermit card. Sandor shifted in the saddle and patted Baxtalo on the neck while he summoned up the courage he needed to look where wise old Towla had directed him. The Hermit signified a search for self-knowledge. Sandor pulled his hat lower over his face in an effort to keep the stinging of the wind out of his eyes.

He was a Rom, born in a tent in a French field and cradled in a horse collar like all true Rom were. The open road was his life. Home was where he stood during the day and where he laid down his head at night. There was no past for him—and no future—only the eternal present.

Once, when Sandor was a boy, he had peered through the window of a *gadje* cottage and seen the family within sitting around the fire. Though they were poor and their floor was only hard-packed earth, they had a dry roof over their heads and food in their bellies. Sandor had smelled the savory soup that the woman simmered in her kettle. The hungry child could almost taste its rich broth. Soaked and barefoot on a rainy April evening, Sandor turned away from the domestic scene, knowing that his supper would be a piece of two-day-old bread. The boy had envied the *gadje* and he yearned for the security of their world.

When Uncle Gheorghe learned the reason for Sandor's sad face and mumbled answers, he had cuffed the boy on both ears. One must accept how he is born, his uncle had shouted at him. *If you do not, your life will be very long and miserable.* Sandor never brought up the subject of a secure home again. But at night, his dreams were filled with it.

Sandor saw himself the master of a prosperous farm in a fat land that was well watered and lush with thick clover. He would breed his own horses, sons and daughters of Baxtalo. He was tired of working horses for the *gadje* men. If Sandor had to confess his innermost desire, it would be a permanent home for him and his family. It was a dirty *gadje* dream, one that Sandor should be ashamed to contemplate.

Still he yearned for it—and for a *gadji* wife to warm his wide four-poster bed at night. She would be slim as a willow, her long hair black as a raven and silky as fine ribbons. And her blue eyes would shine with love when Sandor smiled at her. Tonia!

Yet she was a nun, dedicated to God. He kept forgetting that fact.

Sandor gave himself a shake. "I am woolgathering,

Baxtalo," he explained to his patient horse. "I ask you true, how would you like a warm dry stable to call your own instead of a muddy field? Do you dream of a paddock full of mares for you to cover?" He patted Baxtalo again. "Aye, you would hate that life as much as I. It gladdens my heart to know that we two think alike.

"In truth, I am the very Prosto that the cards said I was," he continued, taking some comfort in voicing his disturbing thoughts aloud. "Like the Fool, I have one foot over the cliff already." He glanced over the side of the path at the steep drop toward the stream at the bottom of the ravine. "'Twould not be too difficult to take that second step, would it?"

Old Towla had warned him that there would be a choice and a risk—the Death card had pointed to a great change. Sandor hunched inside his cloak. He did not fear physical danger, for he had faced that all too often while growing up on the fringes of the *gadje* world. Beatings and branding at the hands of *gadje* sheriffs had been the stuff of his childhood. It was the danger to the core of his very existence that gave him pause.

"My family depends upon us, Baxtalo," Sandor said aloud. His breath took the form of small clouds in the freezing air. "I owe them my fealty. Uncle Gheorghe is sick and has not the strength to defend the women should the King's *musgre* come with their pikes and staves. And they will, you know, if I do not bring them Tonia's dripping heart in their fine little box."

Sandor leaned out of the saddle and spat on the frozen ground. "Let destruction gnaw at the King's entrails,'' he cursed under his breath. ''I care not a fig for his law or his justice.''

At the bottom of the incline, the path met with a wider roadway and more level ground. Glad for the excuse to take his mind off his perplexing questions, Sandor gathered up Baxtalo's reins and urged him into a trot. The sooner they arrived at the village and found food, the sooner they could return to Tonia.

As he rode farther into the valley, a grim thought crossed Sandor's mind. His problem would be solved if he did not go back to Hawksnest. Locked inside a cold cell with no food, little water and dwindling fuel, Tonia would freeze to death within a day or two at most. Sandor had heard that freezing was not a painful death. In fact, the old people said it was very pleasant toward the end, like falling to sleep. Tonia would not suffer, nor would her blood be spilled. Sandor's hands would be clean of her death.

''But not my soul,'' he said aloud. By abandoning Tonia to the Fates on that lonely mountaintop, he would have murdered her as sure as if he had tightened the garrote around her neck. And what about the macabre business of her heart in a box? What fiendish mind had conceived so vile a request? Sandor gripped the reins too hard, causing Baxtalo to toss his head. He patted his horse's neck.

''I agree, my friend, to desecrate her body would be a greater sacrilege.''

Though he had butchered his share of pigs and chickens, the thought of slicing through Tonia's breast, even if she had been dead a week, sickened him. He clamped his jaws together. Let the *musgre* whip him, tear at his flesh with flails and cut out his own heart while he still lived. Sandor would gladly give over his life if they would set Tonia and his family free from their wicked coils. He would think of some device to cheat the King and his bloody-minded ministers. The *gadje* themselves had proclaimed in their edict against "the many outlandish people calling themselves Egyptians" that the Rom practiced "subtle and crafty" skills to "deceive the people." Very well, Sandor would engage in some of this infamous trickery to protect the woman he loved.

Love Tonia? Sandor puffed out his cheeks. Aye, with all his soul he did. Like the painted Prosto on the gilded card dancing over a yawning abyss, Sandor felt giddy with his decision—and very happy.

Chapter Ten

Though it was nearly midday by the time Sandor reached the village of Harewold, the lowering sky made it look more like early evening. He approached the hamlet slowly, taking care not to draw unwarranted attention to himself. From long experience he knew that a stranger in any village, particularly one as remote as this, would attract open curiosity. Once the inhabitants saw his darker skin and southern Continental features, that curiosity could turn less friendly.

He dismounted and led Baxtalo through the cobbled streets that radiated from the ancient gray stone church that dominated the village center. Sandor paused at the public water trough where he broke the skin of ice and allowed his horse to drink. Meanwhile, he surveyed the unfamiliar surroundings.

As luck would have it, the day was the weekly open market in the square, though the customers did not linger and socialize. The frigid temperature and the smell of snow in the air hurried them through their business. Sandor noted that the village boasted several public houses. He chose the one sporting a sign of a large orange cat, which appeared to enjoy the most patronage. It was easier for a man to lose himself amid a crowd, especially if that man wore a golden hoop in his ear.

Before giving Baxtalo over to the care of the well-bundled ostler, Sandor eyed the stables that enclosed the inn's courtyard. Shabby but the straw smelled fresh.

"Give him a good rubdown," he told the boy, handing him a groat. "There will be another of these if you do a good job."

The boy only nodded, conferring more of his attention on the horse than its owner. Sandor watched with satisfaction as the ostler led Baxtalo toward the dark shelter of the stable. He knew intuitively that his best friend was in good hands. As he mounted the stone steps to the inn's side door, Sandor hoped that his welcome inside would be as cordial.

The Fat Cat's small public room was crowded with farmers, tradesmen and a few of the market's vendors, all seeking respite from the cold. A large fire roared in the wide hearth and savory cooking aromas mingled with the less pleasant odors of the clientele. Sandor found a vacant stool to one side next to the wall. In a *gadje* establishment such as this one, he always felt more secure with thick plaster at his back, less chance for some rapscallion to accost him from behind.

Only after he had given the tap boy his order for a mug of the house ale, a bowl of stew and a loaf of bread did Sandor undo his cloak and jacket. Though he took care not to reveal the location of his money pouch, he allowed the serving boy to see the sixpence that he held between his fingers. Experience had taught Sandor that his obvious foreign appearance might deny him service, but the silver sheen of ready money went a long way toward hospitality, especially in a coin-poor village such as this one.

When the stew arrived, Sandor fell upon it like a wolf in the dead of winter. It had been nearly a fortnight since he had last eaten a good meal, when his Aunt Mindra had cooked a feast of *hotchiwitchi* made from a fat hedgehog that had taken a fatal stroll across Hampstead Heath. Sandor sopped the thick gravy of the mutton broth with a heel of the rye bread. Then, twirling his sixpence between his fingers, he ordered another bowl.

"And two more loaves of your good bread for my journey," Sandor added, acutely aware that the sound of his accent had caused his nearest neighbors to stop their conversations and stare at him. "Have you any cheese?"

"Aye, 'tis hard but not stale," the boy replied, mesmerized by the sixpence.

Sandor knew that the value of his coin could buy a wealth of food for himself and Tonia, provided the innkeeper was an honest man, though Sandor doubted that honesty would be extended to him. Prices suddenly doubled for Gypsies and other outlanders.

"A pound of your not-stale cheese then." Sandor smiled at the lad. "And have you any meat pies?"

The server furrowed his brow. "Aye, 'tis made of hare—" he lowered his voice "—though there's more turnip and carrot in it than hare," he confided.

With a conspiratorial wink, Sandor nodded. "I will have two of these pies if they are not large. Tie them up in a cloth for I have far to go."

''Where away, stranger?'' asked one of the listeners.

Sandor gave the man an easy smile. ''All the way to Londontown and a cold ride 'twill be.''

The man narrowed his eyes. ''Harewold is middling far off the London post road. Might I ask what ye be a-doing in these parts?''

Sandor allowed his hand to drop under the table where he could reach his long dagger if necessary. ''You speak true, friend. I have been in the mountains on business, the King's business.'' Though Sandor kept his voice low, more of the inn's customers turned his way at the mention of the young monarch. The innkeeper stepped out from behind his counter.

He cocked his head at Sandor. ''Ye nae have the look of a King's man about ye.''

Sandor gave him a wolf's smile. ''Executioners are a breed apart, though a law-abiding man such as yourself need have no fear of the King's justice.'' For further effect, he pulled out his black hood from his pouch and dropped it on the rough-hewn table. ''Here is the badge of my office.''

There was a collective intake of breath among the nearby patrons, then everyone seemed to have something very important to say to his neighbor. The innkeeper scurried back to his counter leaving Sandor alone with his food and his thoughts. He had not intended to reveal so much information, but now that he had, perhaps he could use it to his advantage in case anyone came searching for him at a later date. The hazy outlines of a plan for Tonia's deliverance began to form in his mind. With an open smile, he turned to the man who had first spoken to him.

"I am sure that you saw some of the King's soldiers ride through here some days past, did you not?"

The man looked into the depths of his jack mug as if he were afraid that the executioner might curse him with the evil eye. "I nae have been to Harewold for a fortnight till now. With the weather fine, I had me fields to plow."

The tap boy laid a sack filled with the extra food on the table. "Aye, there were some four or five soldiers that came through some days ago." He wrinkled his nose.

Sandor played with the sixpence. "I pray that they did not dally too long with their refreshment. The King's captain of the guard does not approve of sluggards."

The lad shrugged his shoulders. "They came, took a short ease and then rode down toward the post road and were gone." He sounded relieved.

This bodes well for my purpose. Aloud, Sandor said, "And I too shall be on my way. There is much I need to do in London."

The innkeeper cleared his throat, then dared to ask Sandor, "What be the name of the one ye turned off? Ahem…so that we may remember the poor sot in our prayers come next Sunday."

Sandor shuddered inwardly. Why did the *gadje* continue to speak the names of the dead with love and reverence long after they were cold in the ground when people should pay more attention to those who still lived? "'Tis the King's pleasure and not mine to tell names. I only do my duty as I am commanded."

A strange glimmer stole into the man's watery eyes. "Mind if'n I ask how ye did it? Did ye hang him or cut off his head?"

Sandor gave him another wolfish grin. "Neither, my friend. I am the master of the garrote." He clenched his hands and made a pulling motion. "'Tis quick and very, very quiet."

The innkeeper and his customers stared at Sandor's hands. Enjoying his role, the Gypsy splayed out his fingers on the table for their ghoulish admiration. Then he rose, tossed the sixpence to the tap boy and gathered up his cloak and the sack of food. To his table companion, he smiled and touched his hat brim. "Good day and God save," he said.

He worked his way through the crowd out to the stable yard, where he retrieved a well-groomed Baxtalo. He tipped the ostler two groats for his horse's good care and for a bag of oats. Snow had begun to fall while Sandor had dined inside the Fat Cat. Though the streets had only a thin covering over the cobblestones, he knew that the way back to Hawksnest would be a good deal more difficult than the morning's ride to Harewold. He chided himself for having stayed so long.

Before he left the village, Sandor sought out the butcher's stall. The vendor was in the act of closing down his business when Sandor located him. He purchased a string of sausages that the butcher claimed were fresh made, several tallow candles and a pig's heart. Remnants of its life's blood were frozen on the organ. Sandor added the sausages to his other provisions, but he wrapped the heart in a rag and stuffed it in his saddlebag. The cold air would keep it from deteriorating too much.

Then Sandor turned Baxtalo toward the eastern road so if anyone watched his departure, as he expected the patrons of the Fat Cat would do, they would later say that they saw him take the route to the post road. Once past the prying eyes of Harewold, Sandor circled around the village. The snowfall covered his tracks within minutes.

The grating sound of the key in the door lock roused Tonia from her torpor. Hunger and the chill of her prison had made her groggy, but the new sound snapped her into full wakefulness. The person on the other side of her door had not called out her name nor said any soothing greeting. Her heart thudded into the pit of her stomach. What if it wasn't Sandor who was having so much trouble turning the lock? She grabbed the little knife that he had left her, then she scurried into the darkest corner of the tiny cell. Gulping down her fear, she raised her puny weapon as the lock clicked open in the keyhole.

A man's booted foot kicked back the door. Tonia tensed. Then a familiar form stepped into her cell. A load of dry firewood filled the crooks of his arms while he balanced a full jug of water in his hands. A heavy sack dangled from his teeth, making coherent speech impossible.

"Sandor," Tonia breathed. Relief flooded her body. He had not abandoned her to starvation and a lonely death! Lowering her knife, she sagged against the wall.

His azure eyes widened when he saw her and the naked blade that she held. He deposited the water and sack on the table, then turned to her. "Missed me?" he asked with a half smile on his lips. His gaze searched hers for the answer.

Her knife clattered to the floor, and its blade rang against the stones. With a cry of "Sandor!" Tonia threw herself against him. The bulk of his body and the warmth that emanated from him soothed her fears.

Sandor dropped the wood, then straddled the pile to take her in his arms. Trembling with joy, she clung to him, soaking up the comfort of his presence. Without thinking of the possible consequences, she rose on tiptoe to kiss him. She had meant to brush against his cheek, but he turned at the last split second so that their lips met.

Time stood still.

Sandor drew in his breath as her mouth closed over his. Then he pressed his lips to hers, caressing her more than kissing her. His velvet warmth touched Tonia like a whispered prayer, making her senses spin as he deepened his kiss. A quiver of pure delight surged through her veins. Her skin tingled and her lips burned. Though her eyes were closed, she felt as if the air surrounding them crackled with the golden sparks of a Twelfth Night fireworks display.

Sandor slowly pulled away. Tonia looked up at him. The smoldering flames that she saw in the depths of his bright eyes sent a tremor through her. She felt his heart beating rapidly against her own. Clearing her throat, she pretended that the pounding in her ears was nothing.

He did not speak but his hand slid down her spine, exploring each hollow of her back. His touch was oddly soft and caressing. A delicious shudder heated her body. Tonia knew that she should fight against her growing desire to move closer to him. A lifetime of prudence counseled her to resist. It was not too late to turn away and put him back in his place. She was a chaste virgin dedicated to God; he was a wild, unpredictable Gypsy.

But her body, and the passion that she had long denied herself, resisted all common sense. Tonia ached for more of his touch. She burned for another one of his kisses.

Still Sandor remained silent, though his eyes spoke volumes, making no attempt to conceal his desire for her. His gaze dropped from her face to her shoulders and finally to the swell of her breasts where he lingered for a long moment. Fettered within her bodice, her nipples tingled as they hardened against the rough linen of her chemise. She gasped under her breath as an urgent tingling sensation spread out and down, heating her loins.

When he looked back to her face, Tonia moistened her lips in mute invitation. She held her breath. The prolonged anticipation was almost unbearable, and her limbs felt suddenly very heavy.

Sandor swallowed. "Forgive my rashness, my lady. I forgot that you are a nun."

She blinked, then shook her head. "Nay, I never took formal vows. The King disbanded convents and forbade nunneries. My house of prayer was my own devising."

He cocked his head. "But you said that you had dedicated yourself to God, not to man. I would not dare to steal from God."

She tightened her arms around his neck. "You have stolen nothing from God—or me." *Except my heart.*

A slow smiled curled the corners of his mouth as he lowered his head to her.

"Do you truly want to do this?" Sandor murmured, his hot breath laving her cheek.

Her emotions, exploding from the hidden recesses

of her heart, melted away the last of her resistance. Tonia arched herself against him like a harlot, though she felt no shame. His hand tightened against the small of her back, supporting her weight. Her pulses raced.

"Please," she whispered, offering her lips again to him. "Or I will die."

"Then live, *sukar,*" he replied before he reclaimed her mouth.

Sandor's fiery possession seared Tonia, and her mouth burned with his desire. His tongue traced the fullness of her lips, inflaming her to greater heights. His hunger shattered her common sense. Rational thinking whirled away like dry leaves in a wind. Parting her lips, Tonia welcomed him with abandon. He devoured her. She drank in his nectar.

Were all kisses like these? She had never before tasted such heady wine as his lips now offered her. How barren her past had been before this Gypsy had come into her life and taught her the magic of a kiss.

Joy bubbled up inside of Tonia, and she seemed to float. She gripped Sandor harder lest she swoon. He crushed her against him as his lips demanded more. She gave him freely all that he asked. His kisses sang in her veins and took root in the marrow of her bones.

God save me, but I love this man!

With ragged breathing, Sandor released her lips. He took her face gently between his hands. His thumbs brushed across her cheekbones. "Sweet, so sweet," he murmured as he caressed her. "My *sukar.*"

Then he sighed and dropped his arms to his sides. "But I am not the one for you."

Tonia gripped the edge of the table for support as she tried to reel in her thoughts. "What do you mean?'' she asked. Her lips still burned with his passion. "Did I do something wrong? I realize that I have no experience in these matters. Please tell me my mistake and I will amend it.''

A sad smile tipped the corners of his mouth. "You are perfection,'' he replied. "A gift from heaven for a very fortunate man, but not me.''

Her skin turned to ice; the whole room became frigid. "You don't like me,'' she said flatly. What a cruel jest! For the first time in her life, Tonia allowed herself to love a man only to learn that he did not love her.

Sandor bent down and retrieved the wood he had dropped. "I am a Gypsy.''

Tonia frowned. "So you have told me on several occasions during our brief acquaintance.''

He hunkered on the balls of his feet before the fire. "You are a lady from a noble family." While he spoke, he added several split logs to the feeble flames. "I am too rough for you, too…foreign.''

A tiny curl of hope rose within her. Perhaps she had been a bit hasty in her judgment. "Am I too foreign for you?''

"You have hit the nut and core of it,'' he whispered.

Sandor didn't have to look at Tonia to know that his words had hurt her. How could he possibly explain the Rom's concept of *marime* to her? How could he tell this angel that his people believed she was defiled and that now he was defiled for kissing her? Worse than that, in the eyes of his family, Sandor was almost beyond redemption because he had *enjoyed* kissing Tonia. In fact, he desperately wanted to kiss her again this minute. He wanted to lay her down on his grandmother's sheepskin and make long passionate love to Lady Gastonia Cavendish, a *gadji*.

Grabbing his shoulder, Tonia swung him around to face her. Her sudden action upset his balance and he sat down hard on the cold floor.

Anger painted bright red spots on her cheeks. "Are you saying that *I* am not good enough for *you?* Pray explain this wonder to me, Gypsy, for my brains must have become addled by your...that is...recently." She seated herself on the stool, folded her arms over her enticing breasts and glared at him. Her indignation made her even more beautiful in his eyes.

Sandor crossed his legs while he pondered his answer. "Tell me true, my fine lady, would your father approve of me? Would he have minded me kissing your lips if he had spied us just now?"

Pursing her lips, she stared down to her lap. "Nay, he would not, but then..." She looked at him. "Methinks he would not approve of any man I kissed except for one of his own choice. My father has three daughters and he has always been very protective of us. My sister Gillian's husband had to practically wade through fire before my father allowed her to marry him."

Sandor whistled through his teeth. "There are two more as beautiful as you?" Lord Cavendish must have an army of guards stationed around his manor.

Tonia turned pink again, though not from displeasure. "My twin sisters are eighteen months younger than I. We share the same coloring and general looks. All three of us are too tall for current fashion."

He smiled at her modest description. "You are not

too tall for me,'' he murmured, hoping to make her smile in return.

Instead, she frowned. ''Not too tall, only not good enough.''

He clicked his tongue against his teeth. Tonia did not distract easily. ''I did not say that—exactly.''

She lifted one of her lovely dark brows. ''Then what do you mean—exactly? Tell me true.''

Sandor threw up his hands in the air as if he implored the angels for help. ''*Jaj!* You are worse than a shire reeve with your questions. Very well, but I warn you, you will not like my answers.''

Tonia cocked her head and waited.

He sighed. He would skirt the problem of *marime* if he could. ''If my uncle had seen us kissing, he too would not have approved.''

Tonia considered this for a moment. ''Then your uncle would have shown good sense. A noblewoman stains her family's honor if she is seen kissing a man in public.''

He shook his head. '''Tis not that, Tonia. Uncle Gheorghe would not approve of you because you are a *gadji*. A Rom man should kiss only Rom women.'' He twiddled his thumbs while he waited for her next ticklish question.

She was silent for a very long time. The renewed fire snapped and crackled in the grate. ''Methinks I understand,'' she finally said, then she sighed.

''We are from very different worlds,'' he added, relieved that he didn't have to explain things in any more detail.

''We are together now.''

He gazed at her, trying to conceal the longing that consumed his heart. ''But for how long, *sukar luludi?*

The snow will stop, but time does not. Have you so soon forgotten why I came here?''

A small rueful smile touched her lips, lips that were still swollen with his kisses. ''Nay, but I hoped that you had.''

He returned her smile with a broad one of his own. ''As to the problem of your execution, methinks I have hit upon a plan that will save both our necks.''

She sat up straighter on her stool. ''Hoy day! It has taken you *this* long to tell me? Out with it!''

He chuckled. ''Your pardon, my lady, but me-thought you did not mind my kisses. In fact, 'twas you, not I, that began it before I even got both feet in the door. You gave me no chance to speak a word.''

Tonia colored very prettily.

With another chuckle, Sandor rose, wiped his hands on his sleeves, then went to the table. ''Nor did you give me the opportunity to show you what I have brought.'' He untied the sack. ''Are you hungry?'' He lifted out one of the rabbit pies.

She lunged for it. ''Sweet Jesu!''

He laughed as he gave it to her. Then he poured two cups of water from the jug. ''Let us eat first. Serious matters sit better on a satisfied stomach.''

With her mouth full of the cold pastry, Tonia merely nodded. They ate in silence, enjoying the simple repast, the cheer of the fire and each other's company. Sandor savored the reprieve. All too soon, he must tell her his plan—and about the pig's heart that lay wrapped in his saddlebag. He watched as she licked the pie's brown gravy from her hands. Her little pink tongue curling around her long, slim fingers stirred hot desire in his loins.

He had fallen in love with Tonia. From the first moment of their meeting, he had been lost to her. Her sweet kisses only served to taunt him. How could she possibly love him in return? His was a fool's dream, like Prosto of his grandmother's cards. Aye, Sandor was exactly that man—except *both* his feet hung over the abyss. He had lost his heart to a lady of noble birth—and a *gadji*. Sandor was sure that she would leave him without a backward glance the minute he turned her loose. Wasn't that the real reason why he had locked her in her cell when he journeyed to Harewold?

After they had shared a wedge of the cheese, Sandor cleared his throat. "The hour grows later, *sukar*, and we must speak of many things. As soon as the snow stops, we will quit this place."

Tonia stared at him; her eyes shone a deep blue. "Leave Hawksnest? *Both* of us?" she whispered.

He could have wept for her distrust of him. "Aye, did I not tell you to believe in me?"

"You did," she acknowledged. "But I feel as if I have lived these past few weeks poised on the edge of a sharp knife. Do you promise me freedom?"

Sandor swallowed. Once, when he was a child, he had caught a particularly tuneful lark. Day after day, he had delighted to hear its song, but a week later, he noticed that the little bird sang less and less. Old Towla told him to release the creature. She said that if the lark truly loved him, it would stay of its own free will. Opening that cage door was the hardest thing Sandor had ever done in his young life. The bird had soared to the skies while he watched its joy with an ache in his heart. But his grandmother had been right, as always. The lark returned every day to eat Sandor's breadcrumbs and to sing for him. They remained friends until the bird had flown south for the winter.

Tonia was like the beautiful lark. She longed for her freedom. Had she only kissed him and pretended to like him so that he would allow her to flee the King's doleful sentence? Sandor gritted his teeth. He didn't like to think of her as a scheming woman. And yet, he knew that he would have done the same thing himself if he had been the one standing in the shadow of death. The *tarocchi* cards had prophesied that he must take a risk. Was this it?

"Will you truly set me free?" she asked again, breaking his reverie.

Sandor could not look at her. Her yearning for escape broke his heart. Instead, he watched the flames leap in the blackened hearth. "What is free? Are we not all bound to something?" A strange question for a Gypsy to ask, he thought as the words tumbled out of his mouth.

Her eyes narrowed into slits. "Then you *lied* to me. I see it now. Your freedom is to kill me, isn't it? Why have you kept me alive for so long? Did you mean to seduce me so you could take your pleasure of my body before you wrung the life out of me? What traitorous kisses you have! I almost believed you."

Her words ripped him apart like a dozen daggers thrown by a vengeful former friend. He winced inwardly. "My tongue did not lie to you. Neither my words nor my kisses were meant to lead you astray. I swear this upon my soul."

She twisted her lips. "Your *Gypsy* soul—and everyone knows how honest that is." She slid off the stool to the cold floor and knelt before him. "Kill me now, Master of Death. I have grown weary of your game and cannot abide to spend another night in your perfidious company.''

She scooped up her hair in her hands and held it away from her slender white neck. ''Do it now— quickly. I am as ready as I will ever be. I have run out of prayers.''

Sandor wanted to lift her into his arms and kiss away her fears and anger, but he did not dare to touch her. Instead, he pulled out the garrote from his pouch and flexed the braided leather cord before her wide eyes. He must be cruel before he could be kind. ''So you want to die?''

Tonia gulped.

Sandor stood up before her; the firelight cast his dark shadow over her. He dangled the garrote between his fingers. ''Do you really prefer death to me?''

Chapter Eleven

Tonia could not control the spasms of fear that shook her.

"Tell me what is truly in your heart, my lady," Sandor said in a much softer tone.

Despite her fright, she looked up into his eyes that gazed upon her with sad tenderness, searching her face, probing deep within her soul. Tonia clasped her hands together. What was the point of showing a brave face at this juncture? Why lie to him or to herself? There was nothing left to lose now.

"I want to live, Sandor. With you," she confessed. Tensing, she waited for him to laugh at her folly before he whipped the leather thong around her neck.

Instead, he knelt opposite her and cupped her chin between his thumb and forefinger. "This is the truth of your heart?" he asked, his eyes wide with wonderment.

She blinked. "May I die if I lie," she said, repeating his phrase though the words held a deeper meaning for her.

"You will not die, *sukar luludi*," he assured her in his deep-timbre voice. "At least, not by my hands."

With that, Sandor tossed the garrote into the fire. The leather curled in the flames until there was nothing left but a long, black ash.

Tonia's relief made her limbs weak as jellied eels. With a sob of joy, she fell into his arms. Her tears, dammed inside for so long, overflowed her eyes and ran down her cheeks. Sandor held her against his chest while she poured out the fears that she had locked in her heart ever since the arrest. Never had life seemed so sweet. She savored the salt taste of her tears. Sandor's soothing words of nonsense sang like poetry. Her dank cell was now a nest feathered with swans' down. The fire's crackle spoke of liberation.

While she wept, Sandor's hands rubbed tender circles over the taut muscles of her shoulders. He kissed the tips of her ears and whispered endearments in her hair. Wrapping her arms around his neck, Tonia locked her fingers together and held him tight as if she would never be parted from him. Tonight, no shadows would cloud her heart. The world was filled with brightness and good cheer. Her soul danced an exuberant galliard.

"My best beloved," he murmured.

"And you are mine," she replied. A knot of happiness swelled in her throat.

Sandor lowered them both onto the sheepskin before the fire. Tonia sighed as she snuggled against him. In the fire's light, she studied Sandor's lean, dark-skinned face and she liked what she found there. It seemed as if she had been waiting all her life for this special man, this special moment.

Sandor lay on his side facing her and propped himself up on his elbow. His eyes softened as he gazed at her with a heart-stopping tenderness that made

Tonia feel infinitely cherished. Her pulse leaped with excitement. With the tip of his finger, he traced the outline of her lips. A pleasure that she had never before experienced rippled through her.

He smiled, then lifted her hand to his lips and kissed it with almost a holy reverence. *"Av, pawdel dur chumbas,"* he sang softly in his rich voice. *"Av kitane mansa?"*

Tonia swallowed. "The words sound beautiful, but what do they mean?"

He took a tendril of her hair and curled it around his finger, all the while smiling at her. "'Tis an old love song. It says 'Come over the far hills. Will you come with me?' The singer is asking his love to run away with him. Would you come to the far hills with me, Tonia?"

Her heartbeat skittered. She took his hand in hers. "Methinks we are already *in* the far hills."

He slipped his arm under her and drew her closer to him. "I long to be your lover, sweet flower. Do you understand what I ask of you?"

Her breath stopped for a moment. Her blood burned within her veins. The echo of his invitation sang in her brain. Sandor struck her as a man who did not offer his love lightly as most men did. Tonia knew that if she accepted him, there would be no turning back for her.

A giggle born of her nervousness escaped her. "Aye, you wish to disobey the King's most direct order." When he looked perplexed, she continued in a whisper. "You wish to shed the blood of my maidenhead."

He caressed her cheek with the back of his knuckle. "I have already disobeyed His Majesty's first order.

You still live.'' He lowered his head to her. ''I would do more, much more, than take the gift of your virginity. I wish to love you now—and forever. Will you have me? I promise I will be gentle,'' he added. He sealed his vow with a kiss.

Tonia's blood throbbed for Sandor's touch, for his kisses, for joining him in the most intimate way she knew of, though had never experienced. Her mouth went suddenly dry. ''Be my love,'' she murmured, reaching up to stroke the cleft in his chin, ''and my teacher.'' She dispatched the vision of her shocked family to the smallest corner of her mind.

Sandor and Tonia looked into each other's eyes and their gazes locked in a moment of silent understanding. They breathed as one. Then his lips feather-touched hers with a tantalizing persuasion that she was unable to resist. Shivers of pure delight raced through her. She moistened her lips then offered them to him.

Once more Sandor claimed her, this time as a hunter claimed his prize at the end of a good chase. His mouth imprinted his passion on her skin. She burned where he touched her and yearned for more of his fire. When the tip of his tongue touched her lips, she opened to receive him. He took his time exploring the recesses of her mouth. Passion exploded within her.

Sandor raised his mouth from hers, then smiled into her eyes. He lowered his head again. The caress of his lips on her neck set her aflame. ''Oh, Sandor,'' she breathed as she gripped his shoulders.

He pulled them both upright so that they sat facing each other. He lifted the slim chain that supported her cross over her head. Laying the necklace on the table behind him, he said, "Methinks the Lord God would be more comfortable there for the time being."

"Aye," Tonia replied, not taking her gaze from his face.

With infinite care he untied the knot that held together the top of her bodice. She trembled, but she did not pull away. No man had ever dared to cross this line of propriety. Sandor pulled the silken laces through the first pair of eyelets while he hummed his Gypsy love song. When he loosened the second pair, he brushed against her breast, modestly covered by her chemise. Her skin tingled. He continued to undress her slowly and with great ceremony, as if she were a golden vessel to be offered upon an altar.

Once her bodice was gone, Sandor slid her shift from her shoulders. Tonia clasped her hands together in her lap, resisting the natural urge to cover herself. She held her breath as the cloth fell away, exposing her breasts to him. He touched her tentatively, almost shyly, murmuring his love for her in his strange yet melodic language.

Closing her eyes, Tonia threw back her head and gave herself up to the thrilling sensations of Sandor's lovemaking. Though his fingers were icy, his palm was hot as the fire before them as he fondled the swell of her breasts. Splaying his other hand across her back for her support, he traced a path with his tongue across the soft skin that no man had ever touched.

Tonia gasped as her breasts rose to his intimate caress. The first tremor of arousal caught her. Then Sandor's tongue teased one of her nipples into pebblelike hardness. Tonia clung to his shoulders. She felt as if she were floating in a pond perfumed with intoxicating flowers. His lips and tongue continued their sweet assault of her breasts and shoulders. The cool air kissing her wet skin only made the pleasure more exquisite. She moaned deep in her throat.

Whispering her name, Sandor eased her back down onto the fleece. The soft lambs' wool cushioned her bare skin. She opened her eyes. Sandor had already doffed his jacket. He pulled apart the lacing of his shirt, revealing his muscular chest. The sight of his strong body glowing bronze in the firelight made her heartbeat skitter.

"Forgive my badge of shame," he apologized, pointing to the wicked V-shaped scar on his chest.

"'Tis no matter," she crooned, reaching up and touching the ragged mark.

Sandor sucked in his breath. "By your blessing, you have healed the scar on my soul," he told her.

His words tore at her heart. Tonia wiped away a small tear that had formed in the corner of her eye. Sandor did not notice her silent weeping for him. Instead he fumbled with the thick knot that held her kirtle around her waist. His fingers, now warm, brushed against her flat stomach as he worked the stubborn lacing. Tonia admired the flex and roll of the corded muscles in his arms. She anticipated the moment when those arms would hold her close to him, with no cloth to separate their bodies.

With a chuckle of satisfaction he finally freed the knot. Slipping his fingers between her skirts and her waist, he loosened the material from the ribbons that had held them in their modest place. Then he slid off her gown and petticoat with infinite care as if they were fashioned from cobwebs. With deliberate motions, he rolled down her worsted stockings and pulled them from her feet. Each time his fingers grazed her skin, she quivered. Finally he removed the shift that had gathered around her hips and laid it on top of her other clothing.

Looking down at her, he drew in a deep breath. "*Jaj, sukar,* you are not just a feast for my eyes but a royal banquet."

Stretched out naked on his sheepskin, Tonia shamelessly basked in his open admiration. Then she gasped when Sandor lowered his body over hers. His chest lightly brushed her jutting nipples. With her blood humming and her skin burning as if on fire, she arched toward him. He molded her body against his contours, two halves coming together as a whole.

Supporting his weight with one elbow, he began a sensuous exploration with his free hand over her stomach, then her waist and around her hips. His stroking of her unexpected pleasure points sent jolts of sensual excitement radiating through her. Tonia had expected rough handling from this unpredictable, half-wild Gypsy, but his lovemaking proved the truth of his promise. He was both tender and restrained, taking his time while he explored, aroused and pleasured her beyond her most secret wanton dreams.

Sandor's expert lovemaking sent Tonia soaring to a high plateau of ecstasy. Panting, she whispered his name over and over like a prayer. When he found her inner core, she shivered at the first contact, then melted as he continued his stroking. Her thighs fell apart. Arching, writhing, moaning, Tonia begged Sandor for the release that she was sure must come. She couldn't breathe.

"You torture me," she panted as she bucked under his hand. "Have mercy!"

"Come to the far hills with me," he sang under his breath.

Gripping the fleece in her fingers, Tonia cried out

her sweet agony. Then, without warning, her body shuddered in a crescendo of pleasure. She felt as if she had shattered into a hundred shards of a Venetian looking glass, each piece reflecting her love for Sandor.

Opening her eyes, she asked, "Did I bleed much?"

Sandor chuckled. "'Tis not yet happened, best beloved, but the time is now. I will unsheathe my sword." He untied the waistband of his breeches and pulled them down over his slim hips.

Tonia gulped when she saw his manhood standing proudly erect between his legs. "'Tis a goodly size," she whispered. A coil of fright replaced her earlier passion. *'Twill rip me asunder!*

He knelt between her legs. "'Twill be a little pain, I confess. I cannot help that, *sukar,* but then I will take you up to the sun and you will forgive me."

Before Tonia could frame a reply, he began to stroke her again. Her quickened response took her by surprise. Her body warmed then flamed with his caresses. Closing her eyes, she writhed under him as he lowered himself over her. Taking her hand in his, Sandor guided her to touch his shaft, hot steel cloaked in satin and pulsating. He groaned as she closed her fingers around him.

"Take care, beloved," he gasped. "'Tis been a long time since I have made love. I could explode at any moment."

He took her wrists together in one hand and held them over her head. Then he crushed her mouth in a kiss that seared into her soul as if he sought to imprint his image there forever. Between her legs, he stroked against her.

Her growing passion made Tonia's blood pound against her temples. Sandor's heat coursed through her body. She rose to meet him, eager for more. Her heart burst with her love for him and her exquisite anguish. She abandoned all her fears. Opening to him, Tonia surrendered herself completely to the wildfire of Sandor's lovemaking. He returned his love for her in the fullest measure.

With a slow thrust, Sandor breached her maiden's wall. Tonia gasped with a momentary pain, but it was soon forgotten in the ascending passion that shook her. Sandor groaned under his breath as his love flowed into her like warm honey. Tonia quivered as his liquid fire filled her.

She released a long, surrendering moan as the tide of their ardor swept her to the height of a great wave. She felt as if she paused on the crest, then she plummeted down into the vortex of indescribable pleasure. As she floated back to reality once more, a deep peace seeped through her body. Tonia felt more complete and more alive than ever before in her life.

"I have found paradise," she murmured, sinking into the cushion of Sandor's embrace.

He pressed a gentle kiss on her lips before he replied, "Methinks paradise was not this cold."

Rolling away from her for a moment, he grabbed his striped horse blanket. After tucking it around them both, he gathered her in his arms once more. Tonia pillowed her head on his shoulder and gave herself up to the sleep that claimed her limbs. "I am home," she sighed.

Sandor brushed stray wisps of her hair from her face. *"Si kovvel ajaw,"* he whispered in her ear. "This thing is true. You *are* home with me."

Chapter Twelve

Tonia awoke with a start. Daylight illuminated the hallway beyond the open door. Sandor, fully dressed in his clothes, shook the snow from his hair and shoulders before he knelt to kiss her.

"I find you with God," he said with a beaming smile.

A little embarrassed to be discovered still naked in the morning's weak light, Tonia sat up on the fleece, drew her knees up to her chest and wrapped her cloak more tightly around her. "Good morrow," she replied with a little catch in her throat, remembering how shameless she had been in her lovemaking last night. What did Sandor think of her now?

Chuckling, he stroked the tips of her bare toes that protruded from under the heavy wool blanket. "I have just been to Baxtalo and told him of our new happiness." Sandor threw several logs on the sleeping fire. "He is very pleased for us." He rolled his *r*s in the way Tonia had grown to love. "He sends you his love. He would have come himself but he is too large to fit through the outer doorway."

She blinked at him. "Your *horse* understands what you say to him?"

Sandor added some brush to the firewood and prodded the pile with the old poker. "Baxtalo is a very intelligent animal. I trained him myself."

Tonia couldn't tell if he was jesting with her or if he was serious. Sandor's relationship with his horse was a very special one. "You make it sound as if you asked for his blessing," she remarked lightly.

Sandor looked at her. "I did. He is the closest thing to my family that I have at the moment. 'Tis a great regret that I cannot speak to your father as well." He tickled her foot. "Though methinks your father would not be in a listening mood if he saw us just now."

Tonia covered her toes. "I fear you speak the truth."

Sandor sat down beside her. "Is your father a patient man?"

Tonia thought of the great giant that was Guy Cavendish and smiled. She couldn't wait to see him and her mother again. "He is a thinking man," she replied. "He rarely acts in haste. That is what my Uncle Brandon does."

Sandor raised his brows. "You too have an uncle? *Jaj!* The world is filled with uncles, methinks. My Uncle Gheorghe—bah!" He waved away the disapproving image of his relative. "'Tis good for us that he too is not here."

Tonia dragged her fingers through her tangled hair and wished that she had been arrested with a comb in her hand. Until Sandor's arrival at Hawksnest, she had not bothered to worry over the state of her tresses. Now everything was different—everything.

"Why is my father's patience so important?"

Sandor gaped at her. "You do not know?" He puffed out his chest and thumped it. "I am an honorable man, my Lady Gastonia. I do not ravish virgins in the middle of the night then ride away." Pausing, he gave her a mischievous grin. "And you were well and truly a virgin."

Tonia's cheeks grew very warm. She did not dare to investigate the state of the sheepskin beneath her, at least not while Sandor was watching. She cleared her throat. "I am glad to hear that you are honorable. I would not have…ah…given myself to you if I had thought you were just a thief in the night."

His dark eyes sparkled. "Oh, I have been just such a thief in my past life, but that was for food. 'Tis unlucky to steal such a fortune as you, yet very lucky if one is given it as a gift."

Tonia cocked her head. "More of your grandmother's wisdom?"

He nodded. "I hope someday to introduce you to her. Methinks she, at least, would approve of what I have done." He shook his head a little then continued. "But you have not answered my question. Will your father listen to me before he tries to impale me on his sword?"

Tonia considered her answer. She did not have the slightest doubt that her father would probably try exactly that. Lord Cavendish would not consider a Gypsy fit company for his daughter, let alone her lover. Aloud, she asked, "What will you say to him?"

"We must discuss the bride-price, of course," he replied.

Tonia suddenly felt cold all over. What a fool she had been to allow herself to finally fall in love only to discover that Sandor was really a fortune hunter! She straightened her bare shoulders under the blanket. ''I should have known you to be a double-tongued snake from the very beginning!''

He reared back as if she had physically slapped his face. ''How now? What caused this sudden tempest? You did not think that I would offer your father a goodly price for you?''

Tonia paused in her anger. ''You want to *pay* my father for me? You are mistaken. 'Tis the woman's father who pays the man.''

Sandor shook his head. ''Not among the Rom. We have no such dishonorable custom as a dowry. 'Twould offend a girl to her very marrow if her family had to *sell* her in order to find her a husband. She would die of shame.''

Intrigued by this most novel idea, Tonia relaxed. With a gleam in her eyes, she asked, ''How much would you give my father for me?''

He whistled. ''*Jai!* My Lord Cavendish could ask a kingdom for you.''

Tonia couldn't help being flattered. ''In truth? Well, he owns a fair portion of land now. Methinks he would not require so much as that.''

Sandor appraised her with a serious look. ''Do not laugh at me, my best beloved. You do not know your worth. Your weight in gold or a long rope of pearls would not be too much.'' He sighed. ''I have none of these treasures to offer. But I am willing to work all my life in payment if we could strike such a bargain. 'Tis why I asked if your father was patient.''

Tonia could hardly believe what Sandor proposed. She tried to imagine how many bags of gold angels would equal her weight. Far more than the dowry that she knew Sir Guy had set aside for her. The thought made her feel vaguely uncomfortable. She rubbed the side of her nose. "'Tis no matter."

Sandor caught her hand and kissed it. "But it is, sweet Tonia. I wish to *marry* you. Didn't you understand that last night?" He gave her an anguished look.

Tonia's head swam. She gripped his hand tighter, afraid that she would swoon. Marriage—the one word that she had never expected to hear. "You want me to be your wife?"

He dropped to his knees before her. "Aye, 'tis what I had in mind from the first. Methought you did, too." A muscle in his jaw throbbed. "Is it the custom of bored noble ladies to toy with Gypsy hearts until they break? Or am I not good enough even to wash your foot with my bitter tears?"

Sorrow mixed with simmering anger in his expression was more than Tonia could bear. She took both his hands in hers, letting the blanket slip down to her lap. "I am truly honored to become your wife, Sandor Whatever-your-last-name. And I care not a fig for uncles, or dowries or bride-prices. I only wish there was a priest here and now to join us."

With a whoop, he swept her into his arms, and the blanket fell from her legs. Tonia did not notice the cold on her skin. Nor did she care that she was naked in this wonderful man's embrace. Sandor laughed, filling the tiny chamber with his joy.

"*Sukar luludi!* My heart is close to bursting!" He swung her around in a wide arc. "As for joining us, we have already done so! And will do so soon again. But we have no need of a priest to be married. God is already here with us. All we have to do is tell Him our vows." He saw that she was about to object.

"And when the snow stops falling and we are safe from the King's long arm, I will flush out a priest from his bolt-hole to marry us like the good Catholics we are. What say you?"

Tonia kissed him hard on his mouth. "I say aye, but can we eat something first? I am giddy with hunger—and with my love for you."

They kissed again, then while Tonia dressed and washed her face in the icy water that Sandor had brought from the courtyard well, he prepared their simple meal. They feasted on slices of bread slathered with butter and honey and drank loving toasts in two languages with chipped cupfuls of pure water. They seasoned their breakfast with more kisses.

When they had licked the last crumbs of honey-soaked bread from each other's lips, Sandor asked, "Are you now ready to tell the Lord God that you will be my wife and the mother of my sons?"

Tonia cocked her head. "And what if we have daughters?"

He returned her smile. "All the better, for they will be as pretty as their mother."

"Do you truly think I am pretty?"

He raised both eyebrows with surprise. "You jest with me! You are the most beautiful flower in the Lord God's garden. May I die if I lie."

Tonia ducked her head so that her grin was hidden behind the dark curtain of her hair. "Then I will be your wife, Sandor," she said.

Sandor watched Tonia as she washed the last trace of honey from her mouth and finger-combed her glorious hair. Her words drummed in his ears. This rare creature had just accepted his offer of marriage. He felt light-headed and flushed with pride. Yet, at the same time, he became fully aware of the harsh reality of his situation. The instant that he and Tonia were joined as man and wife, he would commit the most serious offense against the Rom's prohibition laws of *marime.* By marrying a *gadji,* he would become so defiled in the eyes of his people, he would be forever exiled from their company.

Banishment from his clan was the worst punishment that could befall a Gypsy. Abandoned by those who were sworn to protect him, Sandor would be a solitary man caught between two opposing cultures— despised and mistrusted by the smug Christians of Tonia's people, while shunned and hated by the Rom. In his mind's eye, he saw his uncle spit at his feet before turning away. He saw his aunt heave fistfuls of mud at him. He heard his cousins snarl insults at him and Tonia. And what would his grandmother do?

The mere idea of his family's alienation made Sandor's mouth go dry. Yet when he looked at Tonia, or only thought of her, his heart and soul told him that she was the one for him—his true soul mate. His first wife had been sweet, though he could barely recall the features of her young face. But he had never felt the same sense of completion with her as he did with Tonia.

The decision that old Towla had foretold to her grandson had now arrived. The Fool leaped from the cliff's edge, the Lovers entwined themselves against the world and the great risk of the Death card loomed before Sandor, appearing far more dangerous than a dozen knives in the hands of an enemy.

Tonia said something to him that broke through his thoughts.

When he looked at her, he knew she was worth every hazard. "Your pardon, sweet flower? I was woolgathering."

She slipped her hand in his. Her touch warmed him. "I asked where should we plight our troth?" She wrinkled her nose as she glanced around the cell. "I would rather stand outside in the snowstorm than be married inside a prison."

Sandor cupped her cheek with his free hand. "Would a chapel suit you?" he asked with a smile. How could he not smile when he looked at her?

Intense astonishment touched her face. "This hell-hole has a chapel?"

He shrugged. "'Tis in ruins on the far side of the courtyard. The roof is gone and so is the colored glass that its arched window once held. The altar table is mere rubble." Sandor saw the light leave her eyes. "But the baptismal font is still there in a small alcove to one side. Will that do?"

A smile of joy parted her lips. "Aye!" she breathed. She swung her cloak over her shoulders. "What should I bring? Alas, I have no flowers to deck my hair and a nun's habit makes a poor bridal gown."

Her perfection bathed his eyes. "*You* are the only flower needed." He inserted a fresh candle in the lantern, then lit it with a twig from the fire. "'Twill keep away the evil spirits while we speak with God. Come."

Taking her hand, he led her past the guardroom and up the stairs to the open courtyard. Tonia huddled deeper in her cloak and hood when the full force of the wind-driven snow hit them.

She surveyed the deep drifts that had piled up in the corners. "I had no idea how fierce the storm was," she said, raising her voice so that Sandor could hear her over the cry of the gale.

He bent down his head and said in her ear, "'Tis a godsend since it has given us the time we need and a respite from the King's long arm."

Sandor passed the lantern to Tonia, then he lifted her in his arms and carried her across the white expanse to a low archway on the far side. Shielding the flickering lantern's flame, she hid her face against his chest. He felt her warm breath even through his padded jerkin.

Once inside the old chapel, Sandor hugged the wall until he came to the baptismal alcove that he had described to Tonia. Fortunately the wind blew away from this direction so that the paving stones at the rear of the small vaulted chamber were relatively dry and free from the snowdrifts. After sweeping away dead leaves and other nameless refuse from the floor, he set Tonia on her feet. The chamber was chill as a gravestone and the lantern's brave light did little to encourage warmth.

When Sandor leaned down to apologize for the mean surroundings, Tonia stopped his speech with a fluttering kiss on his lips.

"'Tis a goodly place," she whispered. "I am content." She dropped her hood to her shoulders and shook the stray snowflakes from her midnight hair. "Now what do we do?"

He grinned at her. How exquisite she looked in the glow of their little candle! He knew deep within his soul that their marriage had been foreordained in heaven. He took her cold hands within his.

"I, Sandor Matskella, do promise from this moment on to love, to protect and to honor you, Gastonia, as your own true husband for as long as there is breath in my body. This I vow before God.''

Tonia kissed his fingertips then replied, ''I, Gastonia Alicia Cavendish, do promise to love, to obey and to be faithful to you, Sandor, as your own, true loving wife as long as there is breath in my body. This I vow before God.'' She sealed her pledge with another kiss on his hand.

Sandor gave her fingers a little squeeze. He knew she would hesitate over the next part. ''In a Rom ceremony, the bride and groom give each other gifts of bread and salt,'' he began.

She smiled at him. ''I pray that is not too important, since we lack salt and the bread is on the table in our room.''

''Aye, 'tis not necessary, but what follows is. I beg you to be brave and trust me.''

A shadow of fear darted into her deep blue eyes. Her lips trembled with a forced smile. ''I have just promised to obey you. What is it?''

Sandor swallowed before replying. ''We take a blood oath. I make a cut on your palm—only a very little cut, *sukar*,'' he hastened to assure her. ''And I do the same on my hand. Then we join our palms like this.'' He entwined their fingers so that their palms pressed against each other. ''I will tie our hands together then we recite the oath. 'Tis very quick. I have done it before and have lived to tell the tale.''

Tonia gulped. ''''Tis important?''

He nodded. ''Our blood will mingle together, then truly we will become one. 'Tis a very ancient custom among my people.''

Tonia drew in a deep breath. She stretched out her hand to him, palm up. ''I have come this far with you and I have sworn to follow your path always. What is a drop or two of blood?''

Sandor placed a grateful kiss on her lips. ''Bear me many sons, Tonia, for they will all have your fire in their veins.''

He untied his red silken neckerchief and placed it over the edge of the worn stone font. Then he drew out his small dagger. Its blade gleamed in the candle-light. ''Close your eyes,'' he whispered as he took her hand in his. ''I will be gentle.''

His own hand shook as he poised the knife above her soft, ivory skin. A decade ago at his first marriage, his bride's cousin had performed the incision. Sandor prayed that he would be as quick and painless for Tonia's sake. She flashed him a quick smile then scrunched her eyes closed. She bit her lower lip.

Holding his own breath, Sandor made a sudden slice across the pad of her hand. A spurt of crimson appeared.

''Oh!'' Tonia murmured.

Sandor cut his own hand then clasped hers quickly. '''Tis done, my beloved. Open your eyes and look into mine.'' With his free hand, he wound the scarf around their hands.

Tonia raised her lids, and when she saw what he was trying to do, she helped tie the knot. ''It didn't hurt much,'' she assured him. Relief replaced the fear in her face.

He kissed her again for encouragement—and because he enjoyed the taste of her lips. ''I will recite the oath in my own language, then you will repeat it in yours.''

She nodded and squeezed her fingers tighter around his. He felt the warm slickness between them.

"Mandi's ratti kate 'te amndi pirmni. Mendi dui si yek," he intoned. Then he smiled at her. "I give my life's blood to my lover. We two are now one."

Tonia repeated the oath slowly as she gazed into his eyes. With each word, Sandor felt himself grow stronger and more deeply in love with his beloved *gadji*. When she had finished, he released their hands, stepped out into the main chapel where he scooped up a handful of snow. He pressed some against her wound.

"'Twill aid the healing," he told her. Then he bandaged her hand with his scarf.

Tonia looked up at him, her eyes brimming with tears of joy. "Are we married now?" she asked.

Sandor chuckled, glad that the bloodletting had been accomplished. "Aye, except for the ring."

Tonia shook her head. "I need no ring to remind me of this moment."

"But you do," he insisted, opening the small leather bag that he wore on a leather lace around his neck. He pulled out a small dark ring. "'Tis a horseshoe nail," he told her. "One of Baxtalo's that I have carried for good luck. It worked, for I have found you." He slipped the ring over the third finger of her left hand. It proved to be a little large. "When we are free from care, I will give you a gold one that fits."

Tonia kissed the head of the nail. "But this is the only ring I want."

Sandor's heart swelled at her answer. "Do you remember that I told you I have two first names, one to use and one to hide from the devil?"

She nodded, looking a little perplexed.

"As the final bond between us, I will whisper my true name in your ear so that you will be able to call me in the afterlife." Bending down, he kissed her earlobe before he whispered, "I am Sandor *Mateo* Matskella."

"Mateo," she breathed.

"Aye," he replied, loving the way she pronounced his secret name. "But you must never say it aloud unless we are in a holy place, or when we make love, for that is a holy act. The devil must never learn it."

"I promise," she said. "I fear that I have no such secret to share with you. You have heard all the names I have."

"Then I will new-baptize you, Gastonia Alicia Cavendish, for you must have your own name that will keep you safe from evil spirits." Again he whispered in her ear. "From now on, you are named Gastonia *Caja* Alicia Cavendish Matskella." Straightening up, he smiled down at her. "'Twas my mother's name."

"Caja," she repeated, rolling the sound around her tongue.

"But it must remain your secret," he cautioned her. "The devil is always listening."

Tonia rose on tiptoe and twined her arms around her new husband's neck. "Methinks the devil is miles from here, frozen in some bog. I love you, Mateo," she whispered. "Your Caja loves you."

With a joy that he felt would burst through the seams of his jerkin, Sandor lifted her so that her feet swung free from the cold floor. "And I love you, my Caja," he whispered back. "Let us leave this cold place for a better one. Within this hour, I will warm you in our marriage bed, though 'tis only a cot in the guardroom."

Tonia grinned at her new husband. "At least, 'twill be off the floor."

With that, Sandor gathered her again in his arms. Tonia lifted the lantern from the font, then pulled her hood over her head. Sandor stepped into the snowy nave. Then he jumped in the air.

Startled, Tonia glanced up at him. Kissing her nose, he explained. "I pretended that a broomstick was lying across the threshold. 'Tis the last part of the wedding ceremony. We jump a broomstick to show that we are ready to start our new life together."

Tonia touched the cleft in his chin. "I am ready. As for the broomstick? We'll do that part when we find a priest. In the meantime, let us light up the world with our fire and banish all the evil spirits away."

With a laugh, he kissed her forehead. *"Jallin' a drom!"* he whooped as they raced through the snow back to their retreat.

"What does *that* mean?" Tonia shouted over the wind.

"Let us travel down the road!"

Chapter Thirteen

Greenwich Palace, London
Late April 1553

Sir John Dudley, Duke of Northumberland, loitered under the grand staircase, feeling uncomfortable and conspicuous while he waited for Sir Roderick Caitland to keep his appointment. Every so often, the wily duke glanced up and down the long gallery hoping to catch sight of his minion. He twirled his large emerald ring around his thumb and cursed Caitland's tardiness under his breath. As the clock in the ornate tower struck two in the afternoon, Northumberland spied his quarry and strode out to meet him. Before Caitland could finish his courtly greeting, the duke had propelled them both outside.

"Hold your tongue," Northumberland growled, hurrying them down one of the paths in the knot garden. The crushed cockleshells that covered the walkway crunched under their feet. "These walls have many ears."

Caitland said nothing but kept pace with his master.

The morning's rain had finally ceased, though the pruned rosebushes still dripped. Northumberland bunched his cloak in his hands to keep the damp from seeping into the hem. At the far end of the garden, they made a sharp turn to the left, which brought them into a small boxwood-lined bower large enough only for a stone bench. On warm spring and summer evenings, the retreat was the scene of many amorous assignations, but at this midday hour only a scolding jay kept company with itself. It flew away when the two men seated themselves on the cold marble.

Northumberland glanced down the path once more to make sure they had not been followed. Ever since King Edward's health had become more alarming, the simmer of intrigue about the palace had grown to a boil.

Satisfied that they were alone, the duke asked, "What news from the north?"

Caitland shook his head. "Little, your grace. The Cavendish wench was taken to Hawksnest to await execution. Her guard returned to the Tower two days ago with the report that the executioner had arrived at Hawksnest."

"Did they see her die?"

Caitland again shook his head. "Nay, your order said no witnesses and so the executioner dismissed them."

Northumberland twirled his ring. "Just so. And this executioner. Where is he? I must have my proof or this whole enterprise has been for naught."

The other man shrugged. "No one has seen or heard from him. I questioned his family myself this morning. A disgusting rabble, but methinks they spoke the truth when they said they knew nothing of him.''

Northumberland curled his thin lips. 'Twas a shocking state of affairs when good, stout Englishmen disdained the headsman's office, leaving it in the hands of heathen foreigners. ''Did you threaten these Gypsies?''

Caitland shifted on the hard seat. ''Aye, with the usual fines and torture. One of the women snarled something in their language but the man held firm.''

Northumberland twirled his ring in silence for the next few minutes while his thoughts raced. Great power had come into his hands within these past few years, and now he craved more of it like the elixir of poppy. This was possible only as long as the boy king or a young Protestant heir sat on England's throne. The duke needed someone innocent and pliable, one who was willing to listen to Northumberland's wise counsel. At all costs, the late King Henry's elder daughter, the Lady Mary, must be excluded from the succession forever. With her strong Catholic sympathies, especially in the north of England, and her equally headstrong Tudor will, she would grind Northumberland and his family into oblivion.

''I have worked too hard, too long for that,'' the duke muttered under his breath.

Caitland cleared his throat. ''There is one other piece of news from York, your grace.''

The duke gave him a sidelong glance.

''One of my men there sent a swift messenger who reports that the Cavendishes have been aroused. Sir Guy and two others from his family were seen in that city—asking questions.''

The duke closed his eyes and gritted his teeth. He

curbed the poisonous oath that scratched his tongue. It would not profit him to utter it. On the contrary, he must not let even Caitland know how much the Cavendish family's Catholic influence terrified him.

"What did they learn?" he snapped.

"Something, though my man did not know what. They rode out of York a day later, going on the westward road."

The duke tugged on his ring. "Away from their home. This bodes ill. I had wanted to keep that troublesome family in the dark until you arrived at Snape Castle with the proof of their daughter's demise."

Caitland flashed him a startled look. "You wish *me* to carry…ah…the box to them?"

Northumberland raised one eyebrow slowly. "Aye, whom else could I entrust with my most private mission? The honor is all yours. You will be amply compensated for your trouble in the new reign, I assure you."

The other lord took out his handkerchief from his sleeve and wiped his face with it. "You speak treason when you speak of the King's death," he whispered, looking over his shoulder as he spoke.

"I am no fool to bury my head in the sand, Caitland. The King grows weaker daily. Methinks only his religious zeal to root out all popish practices keeps him alive even now."

Caitland shifted his weight again. "And the heir?" he said through unmoving lips.

Northumberland permitted himself a small chuckle. "She already waits in the wings, though the Lady Jane Gray does not yet know of her good fortune to come."

"God shield her!" Caitland murmured.

The duke frowned at him. "Has your heart turned sheepish? Do you lack the fire that I need for this undertaking? Perchance you would like to retire to your country home now?"

Beads of sweat stood out on Caitland's brow. His skin turned a pasty color. "Nay, your grace, I am, as always, your liege m-man," he gabbled.

"See that you remain so." The duke gave him a wintry smile.

He couldn't completely trust anyone these restless days. Only when the Gray girl was firmly on the throne and just as firmly wedded to his youngest son would the duke feel free to draw an untroubled breath. Catholic Mary Tudor must be quelled, preferably locked away, and all those who supported her cause made to bend their knee to Protestant Queen Jane and King Guilford Dudley. Once the powerful Cavendish family was brought to heel, the other Catholics would follow suit. Influence in the north hinged on the Cavendishes.

The duke knotted his hand into a fist. His large ring bit into his flesh. "The chit must surely be dead and rotting in her grave by now."

"There was talk of a late spring snowstorm in the Pennines," Caitland suggested. "Mayhap the executioner has been delayed."

"Mayhap he is roistering in a sottish inn somewhere until my gold runs out of his pocket," the duke snarled. "Go back to his family. Tell them if you have not heard from him within these next two days, you will deliver that ragged boy of theirs from the Tower—piece by piece."

Caitland stared at his master. "How now, your grace?"

This man is too soft for my business. I will deal with him in good time. Aloud, the duke replied, "Use your imagination, slug! Send a finger one day, an ear the next, a foot thereafter. And so on. Hopefully, you will not run out of body parts before the rogue's return." He glowered at Caitland. "Well, see to it! Begone! I need to attend to my holy meditations."

The flustered lord made no reply. He executed a quick bow, and then scuttled down the cockleshell path like an overlarge beetle.

Once you have served my purpose, Caitland, I will squash you too.

Tonia hummed a sprightly country tune under her breath as she heated one of the hare pies on a makeshift hob. Today had been her wedding day—unorthodox, yet so perfect. Soon she would be reunited with her family where she and Sandor could settle down— Pausing, she frowned a little. What if Sandor didn't want to live the life of a country gentleman? He was a rover. Mayhap, he would want her to travel the highways and byways riding behind him on Baxtalo's broad back.

"A farthing for your thoughts, *sukar luludi*," said Sandor from the doorway of the guardroom. He stamped the snow from his boots before he came closer. "You had such a serious look on your face. I hope that you do not regret becoming my wife—at least not so soon." His lips smiled, but his eyes looked worried.

Tonia laughed to ease his concern. "I was thinking of the future." She cocked her head. "And I wondered if you wanted to live in a house instead of traveling hither and yon."

He set down the water bucket then removed his cloak before he said, "Is this very important to you?"

Tonia tried to read the real question in his eyes, but he did not look directly at her. "Our future together is very important to me."

He sat down on the bench beside her and slipped his arm around her waist. "'Tis important to me as well."

"Would you be unhappy to live in one place for the rest of your life?"

He puffed out his cheeks. "*Jaj!* If the truth be told, 'tis a question I have often asked myself. I have known no other way but on the road."

Tonia took his hand in hers. "Why do your people always travel? Why don't they become farmers or tradesmen? Surely, 'twould make a better life for them than sleeping in a ditch."

He chuckled. "A ditch does not make a bad bed, if it is dry." He pulled her closer to him so that his body heat warmed her. "The old people say that we Gypsies are doomed to roam the earth forever. 'Tis our destiny."

Tonia scanned his face. "What king or magistrate has decreed this?"

"The Lord God," he replied without bitterness. "Hundreds of years ago, a Rom blacksmith camped outside the walls of Jerusalem. One day, while he was shoeing a horse, two Roman soldiers came out of the city gate and stopped before the blacksmith's tent. They asked him to forge four nails, long and sharp, for a crucifixion."

"Oh," gasped Tonia, realizing for whom the nails were intended.

He nodded. "Aye, 'twas for the Son of God. The

soldiers had tried to buy nails throughout all of Jerusalem but no one would sell them any. The Rom blacksmith agreed, especially when he heard the price that the soldiers were willing to pay him. He told them to come back after the midday meal and the nails would be ready. Immediately he heated up his forge. He cast the first and the second and the third nail, but then he paused.''

''He was sorry for what he was doing?'' Tonia asked, swept up in the tale and not caring if it were true or not.

Again Sandor chuckled. ''Sorry? Nay, 'twas thrift that stayed his hand. The blacksmith knew the manner of a crucifixion and he thought to himself, 'The feet require only one nail, not two, for they can be crossed one on top of the other. I will give the soldiers these three, wrapped in a cloth, and they will think 'tis four. I will be twice paid—by the soldiers, who are nothing but *gadje*, and I will save the iron of the fourth nail for a future use.' As soon as the soldiers left with their nails inside the cloth, the blacksmith took down his tent, loaded his cart and drove down the road.''

Tonia bowed her head. ''And so they crucified Jesus with only three nails.''

''Aye.'' Sandor released a long sigh. ''That night 'twas very dark, for the clouds covered the moon when the blacksmith lay down to sleep. In the middle of the night, he was awakened by a strange hissing sound and when he looked outside his tent he saw a large nail, glowing red-hot, hanging in the air before him. The man was so frightened that he struck his tent immediately and hurried off into the desert. But the fiery nail followed him. Every night it hung over him, reminding him that he had made the Son of God suffer more for the lack of the fourth nail.''

"Sweet Jesu!" Tonia whispered.

"And so that is why the Rom can never stay in one place for very long. God is angry at our greed and the Christians revile us for forging the nails in the first place.'' Sandor shook his head. "At least that is what I was always told."

She touched his cheek. "Do you believe this story?"

He shrugged. "It could be true. The Rom have always worked in metal. I myself make the shoes and nails for my horses."

Tonia turned over his hand and caressed the hard calluses that were the hallmark of his work. "Will we too be pursued by God?"

He gave her a hug. "I know not, 'tis but no matter. You will be safe with me." They shared a moment of thoughtful silence before Sandor spoke again. "To tell you the truth, I must be a very bad Rom, for I have always wanted to live in a house."

Tonia relaxed and laid her head on his shoulder. "Methinks that you have repaid your own debt to God by sparing my life."

Sandor gave himself a shake, then tilted her face up to him. "Before we speak more of our future, we must consider the present."

"I am here with you."

He brushed her lips with a quick kiss. "Aye, but we cannot stay here. Even now, there are powerful men in London wondering why I have not returned."

"To report my death to them."

His expression grew very hard. "Aye, but there is more to it that was not written in the warrant. I warn you, 'twill curdle your blood with horror. It did mine when I first heard their command.''

His voice was completely emotionless and the sound chilled her. ''What more did they desire? The death of my family as well?''

Sandor closed his eyes. ''Your heart,'' he said in a strangled tone.

Tonia sagged against him. ''But…but there was to be no bloodletting. I read the warrant myself.''

Sandor hugged her tighter. ''I was ordered to take out your heart *after* your death and to put it in a small casket.'' He barked a sharp laugh. ''Ha! They even gave me the box, all bound with brass and a lock.''

Tonia clasped her cold hands together. Shudders racked her body. ''You would have done this? Plunged a knife into my…my breast?''

''Nay, my best beloved,'' he soothed. ''How could I do that? I could not even kill you, much less desecrate your beautiful body. I knew that I could not from the first moment that I beheld you.''

Tonia moaned under her breath while Sandor continued to hold her and kiss her hair. When the first shock receded, she considered the motivation behind such a barbaric request. ''Who are these bloodthirsty men?''

His eyes flashed. ''I know not. The Constable of the Tower gave the box and instructions to my uncle. When Gheorghe asked the same question, he was told 'twas the King's business and not his.''

Tonia furrowed her brow. ''Methinks King Edward knows nothing of this. 'Tis one or two of his ministers. But why?'' Suddenly the reason shone crystal clear in her mind. ''Sweet Saint Anne! 'Tis diabolical indeed!''

Sandor stared at her; a muscle along his jaw quivered. "Do you know the man?"

"Nay, but he has the devil's own mind. You take back that box with my heart in it—"

"Together with a lock of your hair and a piece of your gown," Sandor added.

"Exactly so!" Tonia grew angrier with each breath. "For true proof of my death. And this double-dyed villain will send it north again to my parents at Snape Castle. Oh, my poor mother! 'Twill kill her to see such a sight!"

Sandor whistled through his teeth. "To what purpose?"

"I was tried for treason because I wanted to practice my religion in the old-fashioned way. For the past few years, the laws of this land have grown very harsh toward any form of Catholic worship." Unable to contain the energy that her rage had unleashed, Tonia rose and began to pace up and down.

"In the churches, altars are smashed and replaced with common tables. Prayers are recited in English instead of Latin. Statues of the saints and holy candles have been outlawed. King Edward wishes to replace our beliefs with the so-called 'New Learning.' His half sister, the Princess Mary, has refused and she remains a steadfast Catholic. Should the King die, she is next in line for the throne, and Edward is very ill, I hear. His ministers must be quaking in their boots!"

"But what are kings and queens to you? Is your family royal?"

Tonia paused before the fire. The family's motto flashed across her mind: Neither Collar nor Crown. "Nay, but the Cavendishes are the most influential family in the north—and we are Catholic. Howsoever we lead, the good people of the fells and moors will follow. Aye, Sandor, we are cause for fear among those who crave power. By proving my death to my parents in such a gruesome way, these vile men demonstrate their might and so keep the Cavendishes at home should the common people rise up in revolt against the government.''

Sandor struck his thigh with his fist. ''And I was to be their black hand.''

''Aye.'' Tonia sighed. Her fury waned and was replaced by a heavy fatigue. ''I was to be executed in secret. No one to know of the deed till it was long past done. None of my blood spilled in the execution so that no one's tender conscience would be stained. My parents probably do not even realize that I was in such dire danger. By the time they should see my heart, I would be cold in the ground in an unknown grave. 'Tis too wicked to contemplate!''

Rising, Sandor took her in his arms. Hugging him, she wept fresh tears of relief. How close her family had come to perdition and sorrow!

''I will avenge your honor, for 'tis my honor now,'' he said, rubbing the nape of her neck.

Tonia gripped his arms. His muscles tensed under her fingers. ''Revenge, aye! But not yourself alone. We must go to my father and—''

Sandor shook his head. ''Nay! Remember, you are dead, and for both our sakes, as well as my family's, you must stay dead to the world's eyes. Even now my little cousin Demeo lies in the Tower's dungeons as surety for my swift return with the proof of the deed.''

Tonia gasped. ''In my happiness, I had forgotten him! You have tarried here too long.''

He sighed. "Aye, 'tis why I must be gone tomorrow. When I went to tend Baxtalo, I saw that the snow had stopped some hours ago. The wind has turned, bringing warm air from the south. Methinks, 'twill melt tomorrow if the sun shines. Tonight, we must devise our plans with care."

Tonia stiffened.

"How, now?" He looked around as if he expected someone to burst in upon them.

She gave him a wry look, then pointed to the hob. "Methinks our supper is burning."

Chapter Fourteen

Overshadowed by the separation that they knew lay ahead, Sandor and Tonia shared their supper of the salvaged hare pie in a silence filled with poignant tenderness. Tonia feasted her eyes on her new husband, trying to imprint his features in her heart. He, in turn, held her in his steady gaze while he ate. Afterward he took her in his arms and pillowed her against his chest while they spoke long into the night.

"You will be safe enough here, *sukar*," he reassured her. "I will leave you all the food, and the woodpile is still high. Your guards must have done nothing but chop dead trees to fill up their time while they were here."

She traced the furrows and ridges of his hands with her fingertip. "Indeed, they left me alone in my cell save for pushing food and scanty fuel through the hatch. At night, methinks they overimbibed their ale, for their voices were loud and raucous like a flock of ravens."

He raised her hand to his lips and kissed it. "'Tis fortunate for their future health that they did not harm you."

Tonia said nothing but snuggled deeper in his embrace. It would serve no purpose to tell Sandor that she had feared the rough men who had brought her to Hawksnest. Daily, she had expected ravishment, despite the fact that the soldiers had been ordered not to touch her. Who would have known what they had done? The victim was already condemned. One terrifying night she had even heard them debating the matter. Only the cooler head of the sergeant in charge had stopped the others. At least one man among them had been honorable.

"I was protected by my angels," she finally said. Tonia believed it was true.

"Then I pray that your angels have not abandoned you now," Sandor rumbled deep in his throat. "Tomorrow, I must make all speed to London. 'Twill be a hard journey for Baxtalo, but he has a great heart." His jaw tensed. "I wish to God that I did not have to leave you here alone."

She agreed, but for both their sakes, she assumed the veneer of courage that she had used when Sandor had first arrived. "We have already chewed that subject to shreds, my love," she soothed, though she trembled inside.

"If I took refuge at one of the inns in Harewold, the whole village would know of it within the hour. If anyone came looking for a young woman of my description, 'twould be child's play to find me there. And my home is too far to the north for you to take me there first." Regret tinged her sigh. "You would lose valuable time."

He sighed. "When I return, I will take you to your parents, though we will have to travel under the cover of night. No one must see us."

Tonia nodded. ''You will come back soon?'' she asked, although she had already asked this question twice before.

Sandor kissed her ear. ''As soon as I have delivered the box to the Constable and made sure of Demeo's release. 'Twill be a week if the roads are good. Ten days at the most. How could I stay away when you have my heart?''

She shuddered at the mention of hearts. She had almost gagged when Sandor had shown her the pig's that he had purchased from a butcher. Now it lay in the King's infernal box, along with a swatch of her gown and a curl of hair from the nape of her neck. She wrapped herself around him. ''Speak to me of love, not of hearts.''

''Aye, I will show you once again the depth of my love soon, but first there are a few more things you must know,'' he replied. He pulled out a dagger from his boot and laid it in her hand. The metal chilled her skin. ''Could you use this to defend yourself? Could you kill a man if needs be?''

Tonia gripped the leather-wrapped haft. In her soul, she knew that she possessed neither the physical strength nor the bloodlust to do such a vile deed, but she could not tell Sandor. His worries for his family already weighed him down. ''Am I not the daughter of the best swordsman in England?'' she sidestepped her answer.

He chuckled. ''Aye, so you have said, but this is a *chiv,* not a sword. *Jaj,* I wish I had the time to teach you how to throw it.''

''Is it very hard to learn?''

''It takes many hours of practice.''

Sandor gently untwined her from his side, then he

rose from their cot. He plucked a bit of charcoal from the edge of the fire and drew the outline of a man on the wooden door. He marked the spot where the human heart lodged, and set the lantern so that it cast its light on the target. Then he stepped back to the far end of the room. He drew out his hidden arsenal of knives: one from his belt, a second from his other boot and one from the sheath that Tonia knew was strapped to his forearm. He pulled the final blade from the casing that hung down his back.

She attempted a jest to soften the set expression in his face. "By my troth, Sandor, I never realized that I had married a hedgehog full of prickly bristles."

He flashed her a grin that showed a great deal of white teeth. "English law forbids Gypsies to carry arms, even a bow and arrow. 'Tis why I call these my eating knives. Now watch."

He had barely finished speaking before he threw the first one at the door. The others followed in a flashing blur. Tonia gasped. Three out of the four impaled the charcoal heart. The fourth lodged in the figure's left arm at the shoulder.

"'Tis a marvelous wonder!" Tonia breathed. "Not even my father could do such a feat as that," she added truthfully, staring at the four quivering daggers.

Sandor lifted his chin a notch as he worked to free his blades from the wood. "You think so? Pah! I missed one. 'Twas the poor light." But he looked pleased with himself despite his protestations.

After he returned his weapons to their hidden recesses, he sat down next to her again. "Practice," he reiterated. He opened his arms to her.

Tonia curled against him once more. "I will be watchful," she assured him. "Besides, no one has passed by save yourself since I was first brought here.''

Sandor furrowed his brow. ''Praise the Lord God for that. But if you are forced to leave Hawksnest before my return, I want you to lay a trail of *patrin* so that I can follow where you have gone.''

Tonia rubbed the side of her nose. *''Patrin?''* she repeated.

'''Tis a sign made of grasses bent a certain way, or a twig broken just so that will point your direction. 'Tis how the Rom find each other in unknown countryside.''

''Oh!''

Using her fingers and his, Sandor taught her the various *patrin* common to his people. Tonia sucked on her lower lip. She was not sure she could remember all the patterns. ''I will be here when you return,'' she promised him. ''Just hurry!''

He kissed her on the tip of her nose. ''Use these signs. But if you cannot, I will still find you, even if I must travel to the ends of the earth.''

Tonia returned his kiss. ''They say that the earth is round.'' He tasted of honey and hare pie.

''Ha! How do you know this? You have never traveled anywhere. 'Tis flat, and filled with a great many mud holes in the middle of poor roads.'' Sandor unlaced her bodice. ''Let us put away this dull talk of knives and pigs' hearts. 'Tis our wedding night and I wish to lie with my bride to make sure that she will remember me.''

His warm hands cupped her breasts. With a deep sigh of pleasure, Tonia lay down on the fleece. She would worry about tomorrow when tomorrow came. For tonight, she wanted only Sandor's love.

Jaj! Now I am starting to think like a Gypsy!

Guy paced the narrow confines of the inn's main bedchamber that he shared with his son and nephew. Though darkness still cloaked the moor beyond his dirt-speckled window, a thin sliver of pale gray light sliced the horizon, signaling the approach of a new day. Guy pressed his face against the bottle-thick glass of the panes and watched the rose-hued dawn arrive. Knotting his hands into fists, he dug his fingernails into his palms.

Tonia was dead. In his heart he knew it. By now, she had been imprisoned too long to have escaped the King's unjust sentence. All he could hope for was to locate her body and return it home for a proper burial under Snape's chapel floor. 'Twould give his wife cold comfort, but perhaps it would ease her grief a little to know that their eldest child lay within their walls. After that, Guy would ride to London and ferret out the villains responsible for this heinous crime against the most innocent maiden in England.

"How now, Father?" Francis sat up in the trundle bed he shared with Kitt. "What's amiss?"

Guy gave his only son a brief smile. "The morning comes apace."

Francis jabbed his elbow into the side of his sleeping cousin. "Up, Kitt!"

The youngest Cavendish rolled out of the low bed onto the floor. He rose to his knees bleary-eyed but alert. "What ho! Are we attacked?" He fumbled for his sword.

Guy shook his head. "'Tis time we were away. I am a-weary of this lice palace." He rapped on the windowpane with his knuckle. "It grows more light. Today will be fair."

Francis struggled into his tight-fitting doublet. "We shall find Tonia today, Father."

Guy did not meet his son's eyes. "I fear that you speak the truth," he replied in a low voice.

Sandor found his leave-taking to be more painful than he had anticipated. He fought the urge to pull Tonia up behind him and ride away with her to Scotland, instead of returning to London by himself. Holding Baxtalo's bridle while he saddled his steed, Tonia gave Sandor brave smiles but he saw the sheen of concern in her jewel eyes.

"One kiss more," he said in a husky tone, after he had tightened the girth. "Kiss me until I cannot breathe."

She flew into his arms and hugged him as an ivy vine clung to an ancient oak. "I love you, Sandor," she whispered between their kisses. "Hurry back soon."

"I will," he promised. With a final, bruising embrace that left him on fire and short of breath, he swung into the saddle. *"Jel 'sa Duvvel,"* he blessed her. "Go with God."

"And with you," she whispered. She swallowed back her tears. There would be time enough for them later.

Sandor wanted to kiss away her sorrow, but the sun had already sent his rays over the crest of the mountain. Not trusting himself to say anything else, he turned Baxtalo toward the front gate and kneed him into a trot. Once they were on the post road, he would push his faithful mount to eat the miles to London.

Sandor looked back over his shoulder just before Baxtalo crossed over the moat's bridge. Tonia waved and flashed him a brave smile. Gritting his teeth, Sandor turned away to face the journey at hand.

The track down to Harewold was slippery in many spots, but at least the snow had melted enough to make the going easy for Baxtalo. An hour later, Sandor skirted around the village where people were already up and about their daily business. In the sky above the trees that ringed Harewold, he saw plumes of smoke from many chimneys. The breeze carried the sounds of men and dogs and the scents of a hundred breakfasts. His stomach rumbled, reminding him that he must eat well at whatever public house he found near noontime. He would allow himself only one full meal a day while on the road. Tonight he expected to sleep under a hedgerow.

"Or a warm hayrack, if we are lucky," he said aloud to Baxtalo.

Harewold was less than a mile behind him when he spied a party of men coming toward him. As the riders drew closer, Sandor's heartbeat increased, though he kept his expression neutral. By the look of the fine horseflesh, by the rich cloth of the riders' apparel and by the long swords that hung from the belts of the three men in the lead, he deduced that he had blundered into a party of nobles.

The aristocracy had always made Sandor uneasy. Experience had taught him that gentlemen were usually hand-in-glove with officers of the law. Sandor's brand mark itched under his shirt. He hoped that the men were merely hunters out for a day's sport, though they carried no falcons on their wrists nor did a pack of hounds accompany them. Pulling his cap low to cover his earring, Sandor slowed Baxtalo to a walk and sat back easy in the saddle with his arms away from his sides to show that he carried no weapons. He prayed that the noblemen would not mistake him for a highwayman.

When the horsemen reined to a halt, Sandor marveled at the stature of the three who wore the swords. The eldest man in the middle sat particularly tall astride his warhorse and he held himself with an air of command. Sandor was tempted to stand in his stirrups to equal them.

The youngest gentleman lifted his hand in greeting. "Good day to you."

"And to ye, m'lords," Sandor replied, mimicking the accent of the local folk. He too raised his empty hand. "'Tis a fine day to be abroad a-hunting."

The second young man smiled at him, though he regarded Sandor with an unsettling intensity. "Aye, my friend, you have hit upon the nut and core of it. 'Tis a hunt we are on, though the lay of this land is strange to us. Do you know these parts?"

"Middling well," Sandor hedged. He eyed the four men-at-arms who rode behind the gentlemen.

"Is there a castle called Hawksnest nearby?" snapped the eldest man.

"Or Eaglesnest?" added the youngest. "We were told 'twas in this direction." He pointed down the road that led into Harewold and from there to the mountain where Tonia waited among the ruins.

Sandor's heart thudded as if a bolt from a crossbow had skewered it. *The devil take these* gadje! *They are King's men sent from London to see if I have killed my beloved.*

Thinking quickly, he nodded. "Aye, m'lord," he

answered. "'Tis an abandoned abbey ye seek, but ye have taken a wrong turning at the fork. 'Tis way on the other side of this mountain. To get there, ye must backtrack a wee bit, then take the trail to the left. 'Twill lead ye round to the pass. From there 'tis another few leagues. Ye canna miss it. 'Tis a great crumbing mass o' stone.''

The oldest man swore an oath that set Sandor's teeth on edge. Without a word of thanks for the false directions, he wheeled his horse around and started back down the road they had just come. The men-at-arms and the second gentleman followed after him.

The youngest noble again raised his hand, this time in farewell. "Our thanks to you." He pointed to Harewold's church tower that was just visible above the bare branches of the trees. "What village lies yonder?"

Sandor did not think twice about the second lie he knew he must tell. After all, this young lord was only a *gadjo* and it was no sin for a Rom to mislead one of them. Besides, Tonia's precious life was at stake, and Sandor would do anything to protect her from the wicked swords of these tall men.

"'Tis but a wee spot in the road, m'lord, called Tip o' the Wold by them that lives there. I know not what others call the place. 'Tis nothing there for yer lordship but a flock o'sheep.''

By now, the other horsemen had disappeared over the rise in the road. Sandor wet his lips. This unlucky meeting wasted daylight, but there was no help for it. "God speed ye on yer hunt, m'lord," he said, eager to put some distance between himself and these noblemen.

The young man turned his horse. "Do you come

this way?'' he suddenly asked. ''You are welcome to join us.''

'Tis a nightmare of the devil's devising! The hideous truth was that Sandor indeed had to travel to the east in order to reach the main post road. He touched his cap like a good commoner would and replied, ''Me thanks to ye, m'lord. I am on me way to York. I will ride with ye and point the turning for ye, so please ye.''

The young man nodded, then spurred his horse to catch up with the others. Sandor patted Baxtalo. ''We find ourselves in strange company, my friend. Let us hope that there is a turn in the road soon. Once free of them, we will fly with the wind.''

Baxtalo snorted in answer. Sandor lightly touched the horse's flanks and they trotted after the others. A few miles down the road, a fork branched away to the left—almost in answer to Sandor's unspoken prayer.

''Paika tut 'te, Sara-la-Kali.'' He whispered his thanks under his breath to his patron saint, Black Sara. Surely she had been watching from heaven and had helped him hoodwink these *gadje*. He vowed to light a candle before her statue the next time he visited her shrine in Saintes-Maries-de-la-Mer in the south of France. There he would introduce Tonia to his favorite protector.

Sandor pointed down the faint track. ''Aye, there it be, m'lords, and good hunting to ye.''

The oldest nobleman nodded. He dipped into the scrip at his belt then flipped a silver coin at Sandor. ''My thanks for your service,'' he said before he headed down the track.

`Sandor caught the sixpence as if it had been a fly

buzzing around his face. "Godspeed, m'lords," he replied, touching his cap brim again.

Pocketing his reward for his lies, he chuckled to himself at this little bit of *bujo,* Gypsy coney-catching. Then he kneed Baxtalo into an easy canter toward the post road. The sooner he put some distance between him and the gentry, the better he would feel. As for sweet Tonia, Sandor had to leave her fate between the hands of God.

"Jallin a drom!" he encouraged Baxtalo. "Let us go down the road!"

Kitt shielded his eyes against the morning's bright sun as he watched their guide ride away. Though the man had spoken civilly enough there was something about him that bothered Kitt, though he could not put his finger on the spot. Perhaps it was the stranger's skin that looked so tanned at this pale time of the year. Or maybe it was because he did not appear to be a farmer or craftsman, though he spoke like one. Kitt touched the hilt of his sword. If the stranger turned out to be a highwayman, he would pay dearly for it. Within a few minutes, the rider disappeared from view.

Kitt's stallion stamped his hoof with impatience while his master still watched the empty road. "Aye, boy," he calmed the horse. "I heed your concern. We are not lost in this wild country—at least, not yet."

Still mulling over the disturbing guide, Kitt urged his mount forward, following after his uncle and cousin.

Chapter Fifteen

Kitt kept his misgivings to himself until near the twilight hour, when his uncle reined to a halt. The track had run out after they had forded a cold stream. Now deep within the mountains, it was obvious that they were miles from any pretense to civilization.

"A pox upon that dog-hearted knave who sent us here!" Guy bellowed. The mountains echoed his frustration.

Giving Francis a meaningful glance, Kitt said out of the side of his mouth, "I had wondered about that man myself."

Guy overheard his nephew. His eyes narrowed into slits. "Tell me your mind." A silken thread of danger laced his tone.

Kitt drew up beside his uncle. "Methought our guide spoke false, though why I suspected this, I cannot say. But 'twas enough to make my neck itch."

Francis nodded. "I had the same feeling at the time. 'Twas his eyes. He did not look at us straight as any honest man would have."

"Why?" Guy asked, scanning the narrow valley around them.

Kitt also looked around, half-expecting to see a horde of bandits swarm out of the hills. "Mayhap he is in league with a pack of brigands. He has sent us into a trap and tonight they mean to rob us. 'Tis a goodly spot for a massacre."

Guy bared his teeth. "Let them come. My blood already boils over Tonia's fate. A bit of swordplay would do me a world of good."

Francis rolled his eyes, though he did not smile. "Celeste would disagree, methinks. I gave her my promise that I would bring you back home in one piece."

Guy snapped his fingers under his son's nose. "I care not for my well-being. 'Tis Tonia's sweet ghost that haunts my hours, day and night. The devil damn that detestable villain who sent us here! If ever I lay eyes on him again, I will tear him apart with my bare hands."

Jenkins, one of the men-at-arms, cleared his throat before he dared to break into his master's conversation. "My lord, we had best make a campsite here while there is still light to find wood and build a shelter."

Guy nodded. "See to it!"

Then he dismounted and led his horse away from the others. Kitt started to follow after him, but Francis leaned over his saddle and caught his cousin's arm. "Give Father some time alone. His heart is broken with the thought that Tonia is dead. We are poor company for a grieving man."

"Then it rests on our shoulders to maintain a sharp watch tonight lest we be taken unawares," Kitt replied. "Jenkins and I will stand guard for the first part of the night."

Francis agreed. "Brooks and I will spell you. Horton and Stiles will take the early morning watch." He glanced up at the evening sky. "At least, methinks 'twill not rain or snow."

For Tonia, the day crawled by like a year of Lent. Though the sun was warm, the breeze that blew her hair about her face was chill. She did not mind. At least she was not locked in that horrid cell, away from the light and fresh air. To while away the time, she walked down toward the stream where Sandor had tickled the trout. She wondered if she had the skill to do that trick.

The sight of her open grave, now half-filled with water and muddy slush stopped Tonia in her tracks. For a fleeting instant, she reexperienced the stab of fear that had ruled her body until Sandor's gentle love had banished the terror. Sickened by the image of herself lying white and cold in that dirty hole made her turn away. She almost bolted back to the ruined fortress before an interesting thought occurred to her.

In the world's eyes, I am dead—and if dead, then I must have a grave.

Her courage returning, she studied Sandor's handiwork more closely. Though it had rained and snowed since he had turned the earth, she didn't think the mound of dirt beside the hole was too hard packed as yet. Furthermore, he had left his shovel in the stable. Spurred by her restlessness and the need for some activity to engage the dragging hours, Tonia practically skipped down to the gurgling stream at the base of the incline. She plucked a fist-size stone from the creek bed and carried it back to the grave, where she tossed it into the bottom of the hole. It landed with a small splash.

"'Tis a start," she said under her breath. Then she returned for another rock.

After an hour of stone gathering, Tonia felt satisfied that she had filled the grave with enough rocks to approximate the size and shape of her body. She knew that if the grave was to look authentic, it should be rounded above the surrounding land, instead of sunk below the lip of the hole. By now, the sun had risen to its noon height. Tonia's stomach growled, reminding her that she had eaten little breakfast. She had had no appetite that morning. Her sorrow that Sandor was leaving had filled her instead. Now, after this short piece of hard work, she found that she was both hungry and exhausted.

I have grown into a weakling since a month ago. No wonder caged birds seem so listless. I swear I will never imprison another creature again.

Shaking the mud from her fingers, she returned to her small corner of comfort amid the ruins of Hawksnest. After washing her hands and face at the well, she toasted some of the bread and cheese over the low fire in the guardroom. The silence closed around her. She drew her knees to her chest and wrapped an arm around them. While she waited for the cheese to melt, she said a little prayer for Sandor's safety. She wondered how far he had traveled down the London post road by now.

After her simple meal, washed down with more well water, Tonia curled up on the fleece that Sandor had left for her. She covered herself with the blanket and closed her eyes.

I'll just take a little rest.

When she awoke, the sun was much lower in the sky. Scolding herself for her laziness, Tonia hurried out to the stable, located the shovel with no difficulty and then marched down to her sham grave. In the waning afternoon's light, she could not discern what exactly lay at the bottom of the hole. All to the better, she thought. She stuck the spade into the mound and lifted up a few clods of earth. With an unladylike grunt, she heaved the handful into the pit.

"Hoy day!" she muttered to herself as she scooped up another pitiful pile. "Sandor made this work look like child's play." She tossed it after the first.

Thinking of him and how handsome he was when bare chested, with the muscles rippling down his arms, she whimpered in the back of her throat. Sandor was truly a man among men. All the other men she had known, save for her family, were wet rags compared to him. The good Lord had indeed worked in a mysterious way when he had sent the fascinating Gypsy into her life. And how she thanked God for him!

"Ugh!" she exclaimed as her shovel sliced through a thick red worm that had made an unexpected appearance in the mound.

Tonia had seen men digging in her father's fields all her life, but until now she had always taken their labors for granted. After this experience, she knew that she never would underestimate farmers again. She had only dug a few shovelfuls and already her shoulders ached. The rough wooden handle chafed the tender skin of her palms.

Arching her back, Tonia squinted at the sun. Twilight already? She stared down at the hole. Her efforts had only covered the top of the stones. She groaned aloud. *What a hopeless milksop I am!* Gritting her teeth, she jabbed the shovel deep into the dirt. *Sandor would laugh if he could see me now.*

Only after the sun had completely set did Tonia trudge back up the hill to her room. Her head ached; her arms burned; blisters puffed up on her palms. Her neck, shoulders and back protested the harsh activity. The well's cold water felt like paradise. While she warmed another hare pie, her eyelids drooped with fatigue. The fresh air and the exercise had sharpened her appetite and she was tempted to eat a second pie. Only the knowledge that she had to conserve her food supplies stopped her. After banking the fire, she fell back into the hard cot. Sleep claimed her before she finished her nighttime prayers.

The following morning dawned cloudy and colder than the previous day, but Tonia could not smell any rain. Someday she would have to ask Sandor to teach her how to read the weather signs. Before attacking the still-high dirt mound, she ripped the hem of her bedraggled petticoat and wrapped her blistered hands with the strips. Even so, digging was agony. To take her mind off the pain, Tonia sang old familiar songs under her breath.

With her arms feeling as if they were clothed in leaden sleeves, she was forced to take more rest breaks. Tripping over her hems, she swore at her long skirts. In exasperation, she threw down the shovel, grabbed the bottom of her gown and pulled it up between her legs. Though her calves, clad in her torn stockings, were now immodestly exposed, she didn't care a fig. Whom would she shock with her wanton display? The birds had the more important tasks of mating and nest building to hold their attention, nor had she seen or heard any of the animals that she knew must dwell in the wood across the stream.

Thinking of the boar that Sandor had said lurked on the mountainside, Tonia paused and scanned the edge of the trees along the stream's bank. Then she glanced down at his dagger that lay on the grass nearby. She smiled grimly. *Let it try to attack me. I am starving for a nice platter of roast boar.* Recalling her family's succulent Christmastime treat with a polished apple stuck between its tusked jaws, Tonia's mouth watered. *Methinks I could eat the whole thing in one sitting—stiff tail and all!* She went back to work with vigor.

By sunset, Tonia patted the last shovelful of dirt onto the finished gravesite. She stepped back a few paces to admire the product of her aches, bruises and blisters. Pursing her lips, she nodded her satisfaction. *'Tis the very image of a fresh grave.* A shiver chilled her heart; she rubbed her arms. *I am a goose to be afraid. 'Tis only the evening wind and nothing more.* Nevertheless, Tonia decided to light the lantern in case Sandor's "troublesome spirits" wafted about Hawksnest.

She gathered up the shovel and dagger. Then she gave the site a final look. *Tomorrow I will make a cross for it.*

After another solitary meal with only the moan of the freshening wind to break the silence, Tonia huddled under her blanket and was asleep long before the moon rose.

The public room of the Fat Cat was filled with the cheerful inhabitants of Harewold. The innkeeper looked especially pleased to be serving men of such noble bearing as the three weary Cavendishes. He dashed back and forth between the counter and kitchen hatch, bearing trays full of cool ale and hot stew.

"'Tis a pleasure to wait upon ye, m'lord," the host gushed, nearly spilling a mug of ale down Kitt's back. "Indeed, indeed, 'tis so."

Kitt steadied the tray that the man balanced just over his head. "Tell me, good master, is there a place called Hawksnest hereabouts?"

The innkeeper wiggled his bushy eyebrows as he deposited his latest offering in the middle of the table. "'Tis passing strange that ye ask that very question, indeed, indeed, 'tis so."

Guy stared at the red-faced little man. "How now?" he asked softly.

The host bobbed his head several times. "Ye be the second, nay, the third that's been asking after that selfsame place. As to Hawksnest, 'tis nothing but a ruin."

"So we have been told," Kitt muttered, remembering their perfidious guide of several days ago.

Guy swirled the ale in his pewter mug. "Who else has been inquiring after Hawksnest?"

The innkeeper pushed his tongue against one cheek while he thought. He looked as if a large tumor grew from his jaw. "Now I remember! 'Twas first a soldier. Great brute of a fellow. He comes in, his chain mail a-rattling like me knees do when the chilblains come down, and he asks me that very question."

"Was he alone?" Francis asked.

The innkeeper thought some more while his tongue switched cheeks. "Not so, never. I recollect that there were more of them in the street. Couldn't rightly tell how many, fur there was a great covered coach in the way.''

Kitt gripped the haft of his eating knife and shot a knowing look to Francis. His cousin nodded in return.

Guy continued to swirl his ale. ''A coach? That must have been a sight to see.''

''Oh, indeed, indeed, 'tis so,'' agreed the innkeeper with a broad smile. ''I said to meself, 'There's money in this,' thinking that 'twas royalty lost and perchance hungry.'' He frowned as he continued his tale. ''But the man a-standing afore me would not let me by to speak to the travelers in the coach. 'Twas none o'me business, he told me, bold as ye please. And since he was the one that was armed and I was not, I agreed with him—ifin' ye understand me meaning, sir?''

Guy pushed his mug aside. ''Exactly so. Then what happened?''

The rotund host shrugged. ''Then they went on.''

''After you gave them directions to Hawksnest?'' prodded Francis.

''Indeed, indeed—''

Guy held up his hand to stop further affirmations. ''Who *else* sought this place?''

The man's eyebrows wiggled again. ''Why, no one, sir—for at least a week or mayhap 'twas ten days.'' He shrugged. ''I am not one fur much reckoning, me lord. I cannot read an almanac.''

Kitt could see that his uncle was fast running out of his already-fragile patience. ''Who came a week or so later?''

''Why, 'twas other men-at-arms. Said they'd been on the mountain and were sore in need of fresh ale. Well, I knew straightaway that they was at Hawksnest fur there's nothing else up there save that. 'Twas once a grand fortress built to protect us from the wicked Norsemen but that was time out o'mind ago.'' The innkeeper shook his head. ''They never came, ye know. The Norsemen.''

''But some soldiers did recently?'' urged Francis, jerking the man back to the present day.

''Oh, aye, as I tole ye. Three, four of them a-come one cold afternoon. Said they wanted some company to cheer them fur they were keeping cold company on the mountain.'' He gave the Cavendishes a leer followed by a wink. ''So I called Judy and Pol—good girls they are, me lords, if ye have a-yearning.''

Guy narrowed his eyes, always a dangerous sign. Kitt jumped into the conversational breach. ''Did the soldiers say what they were doing up on that lonely mountain?''

The man rocked back on his heels and rolled his tongue around his mouth while he considered the question. ''They sang a great deal. 'Twere a right merry lot. Said the usual frippery to the girls, I should think. But to me, they only said that they were a-waiting fur someone who was late.''

Guy sat up straighter on the bench. ''Who would that be?''

The innkeeper shrugged. ''I know not. The soldier said that I would recognize him by his London speech.'' He put his hands on his hips. ''Now I ask you plain and true, me lord. Since I hain't ne'er been to Londontown, how was I to know how a London man talks?''

Guy wrapped his long fingers around his mug. ''They are the men who speak with double meaning out of both sides of their mouths.''

''Oh,'' muttered the host. ''In that case, no London

man came this way. Only the soldiers again a few days later. They stopped by for another carouse and stayed all night.'' He rubbed his fingers together to indicate the expenditure of coin. ''There was the chinks in that frolic, indeed, indeed, 'tis so.'' He grinned, showing a few gaps in his teeth.

''And that was all?'' Kitt asked quickly before the man could catch his breath.

''Not so, neither! I said there was another. He came by one noontime a few days ago.'' He snapped his fingers. ''Now that I think of it, *he* said he was a-going *to* London, not coming from it! Or was it York that he be headed?'' He furrowed his brow with the effort to remember.

''And did this man speak with a different accent?'' asked Francis.

''Oh, aye, he did, didn't he! Foreigner, to be sure. Mayhap Scots. We get them here now and again, ye know. Strange fellow for all his smiles. Looked like the devil with his dark face.'' The man lowered his voice. ''Methought he was a lord in disguise at first, for he wore an earring of bright gold, but after he talked some, I thought not.''

Kitt caught his breath. Earring! That was what their mysterious guide had worn, though he had tried to conceal it under his cap. That was the niggling detail that had bothered Kitt for the past two days. Though the stranger had spoken with a rough North Country accent, the cut of his clothing looked too outlandish for a simple farmer. Most perplexing of all: what was a common landsman doing with a valuable earring? Kitt swallowed down his excitement lest he rouse the innkeeper's interest.

"So this man was the third who asked after Hawks-nest?"

The man cocked his head. "Now did I say that to ye? Nay, he was like yerself—asking if any strangers had *come* a-searching fur that ruin. He seemed not to care to find it himself. He bought a bag o'victuals fur his journey to York and off he went. Took the east road to the post road like he said."

Francis broke a piece of bread from their communal loaf and dipped it into the cooling stew. "Did you happen to notice the *horse* that this man rode? Do you think he might have stolen it?"

Kitt grinned to himself. He was fascinated to watch how Francis, the one-time spy, extracted information from their gregarious innkeeper.

The man snapped his fingers again. "Aye! Now that ye mention it, I did meself wonder that very thing, fur 'twas a fine piece of horseflesh he rode—seeing how he was not dressed to fit the horse, so to speak. 'Twas a pewter color, but with a mane and tale of charcoal. Well groomed. God save me, do ye think that man was a horse thief?"

"Do you have many in these parts?" Francis countered.

The host chuckled. "Horses or thieves, me lord?" He guffawed at his jest.

Guy winced. Then he said under his breath, "'Twas the same horse we saw."

"Aye," Kitt breathed. "But who was the *rider?*"

Chapter Sixteen

When Tonia awoke the following morning, she could barely move. All her muscles felt as if they were bound in iron shackles and stabbed with hot pokers. Groaning, she pulled herself into a sitting position. How did the farm girls do such heavy work day after day? She stared glumly at the low embers in the hearth. She had been so tired last night that she had forgotten to bank the fire. A stack of split wood awaited her in the other chamber, but even the simple job of picking it up was agony.

Once Tonia renewed the fire, she faced the task of fetching water from the well. How easy that chore had been yesterday! Grumbling to herself, she dragged the bucket up the stairs and out into the courtyard. Looking up toward the brilliant sun, she realized that the day was already well advanced. She rubbed her stomach. No wonder she felt so hungry!

Slowly she winched up the full bucket from the cold depths of the well. After pouring its contents into her own bucket, she eyed the brimming container with misgiving. It was heavy enough under normal circumstances, but today—

A covey of screeching birds soared overhead, obviously startled by something in the forest beyond the walls. Tonia tensed, her aches and pains forgotten. She stood rooted to the spot as she strained to catch the sound of something out of the ordinary. She clenched her empty fingers. Her dagger was back in the guardroom on the table.

A shout, not loud but clear on the morning breeze, echoed across the mountainside. A second cry answered the first—men on the trail and coming closer! Tonia began to shake as fearful images assailed her imagination. Were they the King's soldiers, returned to verify her death? Had they apprehended Sandor and tortured the truth from his lips?

The water bucket forgotten, Tonia spun round and dashed back to her chamber. She stuck the dagger in the waistband of her gown, then she piled her few belongings on the sheepskin. Gathering the corners together, she fashioned a clumsy bag. Clutching it to her breast, she raced down to the far end of the corridor to the stairway leading to the wall walk. She dragged her bundle up the steps to the narrow parapet, where she wedged it between the wall and the battlement. Then she retraced her route. Her bruised joints cried out for mercy, but she paid no heed to the pain.

At the top of the stairs to the courtyard, she paused, listening. Though no one had come inside the fortress, she plainly discerned the muffled voices of several men beyond the moat. Gripping the dagger's handle, she ran along the edge of the yard, pausing every few steps to listen. Near the stables, she encountered some stone steps that led to the top of the outer wall—or what was left of it. Biting her lip, she studied the chipped stone and wondered if its mortar would support her weight.

Every aching fiber of her body warned against the climb, but she ignored common sense. She would surely be killed if these men discovered her. Hunching low against the wall, she crept to the top and peered through the chinks in the wall at the greensward below.

Seven horsemen milled around her gravesite. Then one of them half fell out of his saddle in his haste to reach the ground. Tonia's heartbeat pounded in her inner ear. She withdrew her knife from its sheath.

Dear Lord, I beg that they do not open the hole! Please let them think that I am dead.

Suddenly, a great despairing wail split the stillness.

"Jesu!" the man cried as he fell to his knees beside the mound of dirt. He buried his face in his hand.

Confused by his actions, Tonia pressed her eye closer to her peephole. Who was this person and why had her grave so upset him? She wished that he would turn toward her so that she could see his face. Yet even then, the distance was still too great to discern his features.

The other six dismounted. Two of the taller men joined the first and knelt beside him. One of them pushed back the hood of his cloak and pulled off his hat. The sun caught the flash of his red-golden hair. Tonia's breath nearly stopped in her throat. Only one person she knew had that exact hair color—her half brother.

"Francis?" she whispered. "And Pappa?"

It had to be! No King's minion would lament so grievously at her gravesite. Steadying herself against the rough stone wall, she rose to her feet and peered over the ragged battlement. By now all the men had doffed their caps. The Cavendish golden hair blazed like three welcoming beacons.

A warm rush of incredible joy flooded through Tonia's veins. She stood on tiptoe. "Pappa!" she shouted down to them.

As one, the men looked up in her direction. Tonia called again and waved her hand, forgetting for the moment that her numb fingers still clutched the dagger.

The four men-at-arms backed toward their grazing horses, while the three Cavendishes gaped at her. Then one of them, Kitt, she thought, made a hasty sign of the cross.

They think I am a ghost! "'Tis I, Pappa! I am alive!"

At this, the tallest man scrambled to his feet and started running, stumbling, clawing his way up the hill toward the fortress. Tonia watched his rapid progress with tears freely flowing down her cheeks. "Oh, Pappa. Pappa! How glad I am to see you!" she whispered.

Then she scampered down the stairs. Pebbles and chunks of mortar scattered at her footfalls. "Pappa! Pappa!" she continued to call as she ran toward the drawbridge.

When they met under the arched gateway, Guy swept Tonia into his fierce embrace. He pressed his wet cheeks against hers and murmured her name over and over. Tonia hugged him and made soothing noises. Never before had she seen her strong, steady father cry and the sight moved her deeply.

Then her half brother and cousin joined them, enfolding the two with outflung arms and heaving bodies. Everyone talked at once and none of them made any sense.

"Pappa," Tonia murmured in his ear when he finally stopped babbling, "I fear I cannot breathe. I pray you, put me down, but don't let go of my hand or else I will think that you are all nothing but a happy dream."

Guy lowered his daughter to the cobblestones but held her close to his side. "I would to God that I never let go of you again," he said in a very hoarse voice.

"Whose grave is yonder?" Francis asked with a half smile. "Did you overpower the headsman?"

You have hit the bull's-eye. But Tonia decided that now was not the time to announce her marriage. Instead, she replied, "'Tis a counterfeit." She showed them her blistered hands. "And I have done duty as a digger."

Kitt whistled with surprise and appreciation. "I shall remember your new skill when I have need of a ditch or moat, coz."

Tonia laughed. It felt so good to laugh without care. Then she remembered her laughter with Sandor and wished that he stood by her side now to share in her kinsmen's joy. *He will return soon anon.* Bolstering herself with this thought, she invited her family down to the guardroom.

The Cavendish men filled the chamber. Kitt made quick work of building up the fire. When Tonia went up to the wall walk to retrieve her sheepskin bundle, she discovered several officious jackdaws trying to pull open the pack with their long, black beaks. She waved them away and returned with her few belongings.

Guy dropped down onto the bench. "'Tis a pla-guey rat hole that those malt worms have kept you in, sweetling," he grumbled.

Tonia only chuckled. "Nay, Pappa. This is a grand manor. My former rat hole is down the passageway—the one with the stout door and the thick bars."

Her father muttered one of his seldom-heard oaths under his breath. "We shall discover who the villains of this piece are, and when I do, their lives will become much more tenuous."

Her father's quiet anger made Tonia wonder if she ought to show him the warrant now or wait until his passion had cooled a bit. She had never seen him in such an emotional state and it frightened her a little.

Francis gave his sister an encouraging smile and asked, "So what *did* happen here? We were led to believe that you were executed."

Tonia remembered the first time she had seen Sandor with his long black cape and his face hidden by his hooded mask. Though she had trembled at his approach, she had also been drawn to his power and the gentle nature that he hid. *Jel sa' Duvvel. Go with God, my beloved, and come back soon to me.*

Aloud she replied, "'Tis a long story best told when accompanied by good wine and food. Do you have any such provender with you, perchance?" She was giddy from both hunger and joy.

Kitt snorted with a grin. "Now I am sure that 'tis Tonia in the flesh. Always thinking of her stomach."

And with my heart.

The Cavendishes spent the rest of the day outside while the sun warmed the greening earth with its rays. While they enjoyed a prolonged picnic under the walls of the fortress, Tonia related her tale. Though she described Sandor's appearance and sweet nature in detail and told how they had concocted their plan to hoodwink the officers of the King, Tonia refrained from telling her father about her blood pledge. Guy's features had grown more stern the minute he learned that Sandor was a Gypsy.

"I admit that I owe a King's ransom to that man for sparing your life, and I will gladly pay him whene'er we meet, but now you must put this Sandor out of your mind and think happier thoughts," said her father at the conclusion of her recitation.

But Sandor is my happiness. Under the folds of her skirts, she rubbed the horseshoe-nail ring that he had given her. "He will return here within the fortnight, Pappa," she told him. "Then you may reward him as you see fit."

Guy shook his head. "Your lady mother weeps daily for you. We cannot allow her to continue now that you are found alive and well. Tonight we will camp here, and tomorrow we will leave at first light. We will be home within two days, if we push the horses."

Tonia's mind churned with a conflicting mix of emotions. She desperately wanted to see her mother and wipe away her tears, but at the same time, she wanted to remain at Hawksnest until Sandor's return. She couldn't wait to introduce him to her family. She frowned to herself. Then there was the ticklish matter of her marriage. Her father's strong disapproval of the Rom was obvious.

"But I gave Sandor my word that I would wait here, Pappa," she said quietly, trying not to raise her voice. "And we must guard the secret of my survival from the world. If the King learns that I still live, Sandor's life and that of his family will not be worth a farthing.''

Francis nodded. ''Tonia speaks the truth, Father,'' he said. ''We must disguise her before we leave this place, and once back at Snape Castle, we must swear the household to secrecy.''

''And you will still be a prisoner, I fear,'' added Kitt, his usually merry face now serious.

Tonia put down the capon's leg she had been about to eat. The mere mention of imprisonment sent a chill through her. ''How now, Kitt?''

Her cousin wet his lips before he continued. ''Once at home, you must stay close to your chamber. You cannot walk about the moor, nor go into the village on market day. Too many eyes would see you. And we must bind all the servants' tongues with loyalty. The lure of the King's gold and good favor will too easily tempt at least one greedy soul to betray your whereabouts.''

Tonia clasped her hands together in supplication against such a grim future. The nail head of Sandor's ring bit into her skin. ''Oh, Kitt, say that you speak in jest. You cannot begin to imagine what it is like to be denied freedom.''

Kitt reached across the blanket that they sat upon and took his cousin's hands within his. ''With all my heart, I wish 'twas not so, Tonia.''

She drew in a deep breath, then turned to her father. ''Then I may as well stay here. Once Sandor returns, we will flee this wicked clime and together seek a better fortune in Scotland.''

Guy's eyes darkened. ''Nonsense, child! I am not such a lackwit parent to allow you to go haring off in the company of a lewd barbarian. You will come home and from there we will devise a plan to circumvent this dire outlook.''

''But Sandor is no—''

Guy cut her off with a glare. ''Peace with your prattling, Tonia. I can see that this wretched affair has unhinged your mind. 'Tis no wonder! Once under your mother's tender care, you will soon return to your own sweet self.''

Tonia hated to disagree with her father, but she had to make him understand Sandor's importance to her. ''He promised to return soon and I gave him my word that I would be here, waiting for him,'' she repeated as calmly as she could.

Guy lifted one of his brows. ''A Gypsy's promise is only hot air. They are not like us and never will be. You have been too sheltered from the world and have no experience in knowing the hearts of men. I met many of these vagabonds years ago at the Field of Cloth of Gold, and they proved themselves to be nothing but a pack of ravens, stealing everything that was not tied down.''

''But, Pappa—''

Guy stood up. ''Speak no more to me of this man. If we ever meet, I will reward him. Trust me, Tonia, my gold is the *real* reason he told you to wait for him here. Peace! I'll hear no more of this matter.'' With that, her father strode down the hillside toward his retainers. Mumbling an apology, Kitt followed after him.

Tonia chewed on her lip. ''Sandor is not like that at all,'' she said under her breath.

Francis gave her a smile. ''Let us not break the good cheer of your safe recovery, Tonia. Let tomorrow take its own course when it comes. For tonight, let us be gladsome.''

Tonia nodded her head, but she did not trust herself to speak, lest the tears she held back would be discovered in her voice.

Francis touched her arm. When she looked up at him, he asked, ''Methinks you show all the signs of a woman in love. Is that the way this wind blows? Does this Sandor claim your heart?''

Relieved that someone understood her plight, Tonia returned her brother's smile. ''You were always very clever at reading other people's minds, Francis.''

He sighed. ''I only wish I could read the future as well.''

''Say nothing to Pappa or Kitt as yet. I will tell all in good time when I think Pappa will be inclined to listen.''

''That might take a year of Sundays,'' he remarked.

That night, while her family slumbered around her, Tonia lay on the cot and tried to remember exactly how to form the *patrin* that Sandor had taught her. She would leave a trail of these markers all the way to Snape Castle so that her beloved could follow after her with little trouble. At least she had one ally in Francis. He seemed open enough to accept her love for a Gypsy—a most uncommon Gypsy.

Tonia smiled in the dark as she remembered her last night with Sandor. They had lain on this same hard, narrow bed and had made such sweet love together. How could she possibly tell that to her father? Or how could she explain to Guy that she knew she would waste away if she never saw Sandor again? He had promised that he would come for her. In her very bones, Tonia knew that Sandor would keep his promise.

Three-and-a-half days after leaving Tonia alone amid the ruined fortress high in the northern mountains, Sandor led his weary horse through the jostling streets of London. After spending several weeks in the fresh country air, the fetid stench of the city's crowded byways and alleys assaulted his nostrils. He patted Baxtalo's neck as they avoided being doused with a potful of slops from a second-story window.

"'Twill be a day, no more, my friend, before we shake the mud of this place from our feet," he soothed the horse. "Then we will go to my sweet wife, and she will make us two happy fellows. You will see anon."

They climbed Tower Hill, where several lifeless bodies swung from the gibbets that were permanently erected there. Black-winged ravens circled overhead in the twilight, croaking over their grisly booty. London's justice was particularly swift and the hangman's noose rarely went unfilled for more than a day. Avoiding the unwholesome sight, Sandor elbowed his way down to the Byward Tower Gate that led into the dreaded Tower of London. He intended to make his business there as brief as possible.

When he announced himself to the guard and said he had King's business with the Constable, he was led immediately into the Middle Ward. He looped Baxtalo's reins through the ring of a nearby hitching post and promised that they would soon be gone from this evil place. The horse laid back his ears and did a little side step to show his nervousness.

"You and I are of one mind, my friend," Sandor

said, as he eyed the forbidding walls of mottled gray stone that hemmed them in on all sides. "I only hope that Demeo has not caught a fever in this pesthole."

After cooling his heels on the damp cobblestones for a quarter of an hour by the clock tower's bells, Sandor was conducted to the office of the Constable of the Tower of London, a man whom Sandor had never personally met.

Sir Archibald Brackenbury looked up from a mound of papers on his polished desk. When he saw the box in Sandor's hand, he smiled with a reptile's warmth. "'Tis high time you have shown your face, Gypsy."

Sandor had prepared himself for just this rebuke. "The weather in the mountains turned bad, my lord."

The officer pointed to the brassbound casket. "Open it," he commanded.

Though Sandor's heart pounded in his chest, he kept his expression bland. He placed the box on the desk before the Constable, then lifted the lid. The pig's heart, now over a week old, stank.

Sir Archibald lifted his clove-studded pomander to his nose. "'Tis the wench's?" he asked.

Sandor inclined his head. "Aye, my lord."

A gleam darted into the other man's eyes. "Did she bleed much?" He almost salivated.

Sandor's empty stomach rolled over with disgust. "I shed no drop of her living blood, as I was commanded, my lord, and the dead never bleed."

Looking a little disappointed, the Constable prodded the inside of the box with the tip of his letter opener. He lifted a strip of gray woolen cloth with the point. "This does not look like something that a noble lady would wear. Explain, Gypsy. What thieving trick is this?''

Sandor's blood drummed against his temples. He drew in a deep breath slowly. ''The woman at Hawksnest was dressed in plain garb and wore a wooden cross about her neck. I know not if she was a gentlewoman, but she spoke in the accents of one. She said her name was Lady Gastonia Cavendish, my lord.''

''Just so,'' the other remarked. He dropped the cloth, then lifted the lock of Tonia's hair. ''And this?'' Sir Archibald asked.

He is testing me, but why? Aloud, Sandor replied, ''I was ordered to cut some of her hair and bring it with the heart. I took that piece from the nape of her neck,'' he added truthfully.

The Constable leered at him. ''And was she a sweet piece to bed?''

Hot anger boiled in Sandor's veins at this slur against his wife. He schooled his features to remain unchanged. ''I am a Rom, my lord. I do not pleasure myself with *gadji* women.''

Sir Archibald sniffed. ''I have heard of this strange philosophy of your kind. Pity. I should have liked to hear the details of that encounter.'' He returned Tonia's hair and gown snippet to the box, then closed the lid with a snap. He leaned against the back of his padded barrel chair.

''You have done right well, Gypsy.''

''Thank you, my lord. And my cousin Demeo Lalow? Does he also fare well?''

The Constable sneered. ''As well as any who inhabit the lower depths of my prison.''

''Now you may release him,'' said Sandor, hoping

he did not sound too demanding. This *gadjo* was one who enjoyed cruelty.

Sir Archibald cocked his head. "Indeed, for I understand the boy is an excellent gamester at cards and dice. My guards are much the poorer for his visit here."

Sandor hid his grin. "Then I will relieve you of his company."

The Constable rang a little silver bell that sat on his desk. The door opened behind Sandor and two guards entered. "The boy will be sent on his way, but *you* will take his place," Brackenbury said with an evil smile.

"How now?" Sandor erupted, lunging forward. The guards grabbed his elbows and pulled him back.

The Constable patted the casket. "'Tis a neat piece of work, but how do I know that these…objects are genuine? Lord Cavendish is a very wealthy man. Mayhap you were bribed by his gold?"

Sandor tasted bile on the back of his tongue. "I have never met this lord, and I own no gold but the other half that you owe me for my services."

Brackenbury raised an eyebrow. "Time will tell the truth of your tale. Until then, you are my newest guest." To the guards, he said, "Take this man to the Salt Tower." Then he turned to Sandor. "It has a fine view of the river and a great deal of fresh air blows through it at all hours. I trust you will be comfortable there while I make my inquiries."

Sandor tried to pull away, but the guards held him tighter. "I have promises to keep," he protested, thinking of the sweet lady who waited for him in her lonely eyrie.

"Ah, so do all of us." The Constable snapped his

fingers. "Away with this refuse. Release the brat, then send for my supper." He shuffled among his papers.

The guards dragged Sandor to the door. Just before they quit the chamber, he looked over his shoulder and spat at the floor in front of the Constable's desk. Then Sandor muttered a Romany curse in an undertone.

May the devil dine upon your heart!

Chapter Seventeen

Snape Castle, Northumberland
July 1553

Lady Celeste Cavendish's usually cheerful disposition had turned sad, despite the glorious days of midsummer. Seated on a stone bench in the most beautiful spot of her rose garden, she abandoned her embroidery in favor of her thoughts. Not even the heady fragrance of her favorite flowers could lift her heavy spirits.

When Tonia had first returned to Snape, her eldest child had been full of joy and expectation for a merry life in the future, now that she had been delivered from the King's wicked sense of justice. Celeste sighed as she recalled those happy first days. But as the weeks went by, Tonia grew more distant. Dark circles hovered under the girl's pretty eyes, making her look older and more haggard. She glided along the galleries as silent as a ghost. Lately, Tonia's once-healthy appetite had not only disappeared, but Celeste had noticed that she was ill in her chamber pot almost daily.

Celeste's younger unmarried daughter, Alyssa, had quickly grown weary of her sister's moody silence and had sought happier pastimes at Wolf Hall, the nearby home of Guy's brother, the Earl of Thornbury. Not even Kitt, the extended family's master entertainer, could entice many smiles from Tonia. Only Francis and his wife Jessica had been able to penetrate the barrier that she had built around her. In desperation, Celeste had sent to York for a doctor. The learned man had arrived yesterday and had spent many hours in Tonia's company. This morning, he related to Celeste the most distressing news.

"Your young lady is deep in a fit of melancholy," Dr. Pincher began. "Her humors are muddled. She should be dosed with a spring tonic and mayhap bled to correct her balance. But, my Lady Cavendish, the seat of her distress is not in her heart, nor her blood, but in her womb."

Celeste cringed. "How now?" she whispered.

The doctor nodded. "Exactly so. Lady Gastonia is with child, nearly three months gone, I wager." He gave Celeste a piercing look that screamed his disapproval of unwed motherhood. "'Tis little wonder she is out of sorts. Methinks she would be best treated with the procurement of a husband as soon as possible. In the meantime, rest and a diet of good broth made from young chickens will suit her well."

Celeste felt stricken by the doctor's blunt diagnosis. No wonder Tonia had been so withdrawn! How many soldiers had raped her while she was in their clutches? Why hadn't Celeste even suspected the truth before now? Poor, poor Tonia! How frightened she must be!

How could she tell Guy this latest development? He would ride down to London, search out those wicked men and kill them in cold blood without a blink of an eyelash. And what were they going to do about Tonia's advancing condition? It had been difficult enough to keep her return a secret from all but the closest servants. But how would Celeste explain a new baby in the household? And would Tonia want to keep it, considering how it was conceived? Best to foster the child as soon as it was born. Mayhap, Tonia need never see it.

"By the by," Dr. Pincher added as he prepared to ride back to York. "Did you know that there is a rumor going about the city that Lady Gastonia is dead?"

"Dead?" Celeste repeated, still reeling from the news of Tonia's pregnancy.

The doctor tied his travel cloak about his shoulders. "Just so. I hear that soldiers of the King have been asking about the marketplace if the Cavendish servants were wearing mourning bands for the young lady. Most perplexing," he concluded.

Celeste thought quickly. This prattling fool must be kept silent. "*Oui,* but I beg you, good doctor, say nothing at all to anyone about Tonia or her…delicate condition. The scandal of wagging tongues would surely kill her and you do not want her real death on your hands, *non?*"

He tapped the side of his nose. "Fear not, good lady. Her health and well-being are of the uppermost importance to me." Pocketing the heavy pouch of coin that Guy had paid him, the doctor took his leave.

While Celeste mulled over these unsettling developments, one of the footmen appeared on the garden path. "Yer pardon, m'lady, but m'lord requires yer presence in the great chamber. There's a visitor from Londontown."

"Very well," Celeste replied in an even tone that belied the sudden stab of fear in her heart. "Tell my lord that I will join him forthwith."

The footman hurried away on his mission.

Celeste's hands turned cold and damp. Visitors from London were rare enough at Snape since Guy and Celeste had chosen to live in the quiet countryside and eschew the dour pleasures of the Tudor courts. But this stranger may be the dreaded one that Tonia had warned her parents about when she had related to them the hideous details of the brassbound casket. Why else would those monstrous men of the little King's court have demanded her heart if not to taunt Tonia's parents? Thank *le bon Dieu* that the Cavendishes knew the truth of the substitution.

After gathering up her embroidery hoop, as well as all the courage she could muster, Celeste left her temporary retreat. Before she joined her husband and their mysterious guest, she dabbed her flushed face with lavender water. Hesitating outside Tonia's closed door, Celeste was tempted to tell her daughter about the visitor. But that talk might lead to the greater matter of Tonia's unwanted pregnancy and Celeste did not have the time now to give Tonia her full attention and comfort. They would speak in private later this evening.

Two men rose when Celeste entered the hall. She could tell by the fire in Guy's eyes that her suspicions had been correct. Their uninvited guests were here on King's business.

"This is Sir Roderick Caitland, secretary to the

Duke of Northumberland,'' Guy growled, waving at the somberly dressed courtier.

Lord Caitland bowed. The servant behind his master's chair was not introduced. With a start, Celeste noticed that he held a wooden, brassbound casket under his arm. It fit exactly the description that Tonia had given them.

Celeste pasted a false smile on her trembling lips. ''Be seated, my lord,'' she said. ''Welcome to Snape. Have you taken refreshment?'' She glanced at the empty table. Guy gave her a little frown. He had no intention of showing hospitality to this man, no matter how long a journey the gentleman must have had.

Sir Roderick perched on the edge of the wide armchair much like a crow on a stile. He clutched his deerskin gloves in one hand as if he sought to strangle the life out of them. ''No need, my lady,'' he replied in a high-pitched voice. ''My business will not take long. I must return to York by nightfall.''

Celeste cast a quick look at her husband before she said, ''And what is this business of yours, may I ask?'' She avoided looking at the box.

Sir Roderick tapped his foot on the floor. ''My…um…my lord, the duke, sends you his compliments and he has asked me to inquire after your daughter, the Lady Gastonia.''

''What about her?'' snapped Guy.

Celeste placed her hand over her bodice, where her heart beat against her breastbone. *Play the role as we have planned,* mon cher. *Pretend to know nothing.*

Lord Caitland dabbed a silken handkerchief at the corner of his mouth. ''Have you heard from her recently?''

''Our daughter has renounced the pleasures of the

world, my lord. She lives in a simple house some distance from here together with a small coterie of like-minded friends. We last received a letter from her some months ago, did we not, my dear?''

Guy's question jolted Celeste. ''Indeed, my lord,'' she answered in turn. ''Tonia wrote that she enjoyed most excellent health.''

The visitor shifted in his chair. ''Alas, I fear 'tis not so, my lord, my lady.''

''How now?'' Guy asked, his tone becoming more velvet. ''What news is this?''

Celeste did not trust her tongue to speak. She steeled herself for what she knew was to come. The man with the box stepped a little closer to Caitland.

Sir Roderick ran a finger under his plain, pointed collar. He cleared his throat. ''On April the fifth of this year, the Lady Gastonia, along with her companions, was arrested in the name of the King for crimes against His Majesty.''

Guy pretended to laugh. ''''Tis a jest! My daughter is the most retiring and modest of women. How could she possibly have offended the King? She has never met him. And by what right do you come here to distress my lady wife with this falsehood?'' he added.

Tread very carefully, mon cher. Celeste gnawed the inside of her cheek.

Caitland dabbed his mouth again. ''This visit is none of my liking, I assure you, my lord. I am merely a messenger from my master, the duke, who speaks in the King's name.''

''Then say your message and be brief.''

The visitor twitched. ''The Lady Gastonia was taken to York, together with her friends, where they were brought before an *ad hoc* Star Chamber—''

"Mon Dieu," Celeste murmured under her breath. She lifted her fan from her girdle and waved it before her face. *This mummery is worse that I had expected.* She felt very warm.

Caitland hurried on. "—where they were accused of treason—"

Guy leaned over the man. "Treason?" he hissed. "Are you addlepated?"

Caitland swallowed then wiped his forehead again. "I pray you, my lord, this message is as much an agony to me as 'twill be for you. Give me time and space to conclude it."

Guy held him in a withering glare before he nodded. "Go on."

"Treason by practicing heretical, popish rituals instead of the true faith as set forth by King Edward for the good of his people—"

"And for the further acquisition of power by his grasping ministers, such as your master."

Caitland whimpered under his breath. His skin had taken on an unhealthy, pasty look. "The Lady Gastonia was charged with praying in Latin—instead of English as the King has directed his subjects—for burning blessed candles, for venerating relics and painted statues of the saints and for hearing the Mass, which is expressly forbidden."

"The Princess Mary also hears Mass—in Latin—and burns blessed candles, whyfore is she not arrested?"

"Because she is...a royal lady," squeaked the agitated man. "The King's true sister of the blood. She is the undoubted daughter of our late King Henry—"

"And so your master seeks to punish the princess by persecuting members of the nobility who might practice the same old faith in the privacy of their homes?'' Guy whispered. "The same faith that Great Harry himself followed? Remember, messenger, I knew the old King well.''

Celeste shivered to hear the threatening note in her husband's voice. She prayed that he would keep the Cavendish temper in check, at least until after this horrible man had left their home.

Sir Roderick slunk lower in his chair as if he sought to escape the tempest that was brewing. "My Lord Cavendish, the duke has sent me to tell you that he knows of your daughter's whereabouts and to bear a warning to you and your whole family, most particularly to your brother, the Earl of Thornbury. Lady Gastonia was convicted of all the charges and was sentenced to immediate execution—''

"Oh!" Celeste gripped the arms of the chair. Though she had heard this tale before, first from Tonia's friend, Lucy, then from Tonia herself, hearing it a third time from the lips of this royal official made it seem even more cold-blooded. She did not have to pretend her distress. It was real enough.

"And was this sentence carried out?" Guy asked, still whispering.

Caitland plastered himself against the back of his chair. "I...I regret to inform you that the Lady Gastonia was executed by the King's headsman on or about the twentieth of April. I know not where, my lord. 'Twas done in secret.''

Guy pushed his face close to the perspiring Caitland's. "I don't believe this lie. You were sent here to test our loyalty with this vile tale. Is that how your master rules the King? With intimidation? Is this how the people of England will be ruled? By fear and hatred instead of love and loyalty?''

Celeste fanned harder. A low humming sounded in her ears, a warning signal that she was close to swooning.

''My lord, I did not wish to come here this day— nor any day. I am bound to obey the duke.'' Caitland turned his head away. ''Look inside yon casket for your proof of my news.''

Celeste drew in several deep breaths in quick succession but her giddiness refused to leave her. *I will not look at it.*

Caitland's servant stepped between his master and Guy. Then he lifted the lid. Celeste shut her eyes as a foul, sickening stench wafted on the air. The silence in the room was more deafening than a thunderbolt at close range.

'' 'Tis…'tis her heart,'' mumbled the courtier, holding his handkerchief over his nose and mouth. ''Your daughter's. May God forgive me for bringing it to you. I had no choice.''

Guy slammed down the lid, catching the thumb of Caitland's servant, who howled with the unexpected pain. Celeste placed a hand over her heaving stomach while she fanned herself even harder with the other. Her head swam.

''My daughter's heart?'' Guy shouted. ''What manner of churl is it who would conceive of such a knavish, horn-mad, brazen trick as this to play upon a gentle mother and a loving father? Weep, England, for you are ruled by monsters!''

''Pea…peace, my lord,'' jabbered Caitland. ''Your own words could condemn you as well. 'Tis treason, methinks, to call the King a monster.''

"I doubt young Edward had anything to do with this perfidy!" Guy ranted to the rafters. "I understand that he is not well, indeed he is very ill. Some say 'tis fatal."

"Peace, my lord," Caitland babbled. "I pray you. 'Tis also treason to speak of the King's death."

"Then speak to me of mine," said a low feminine voice from the far end of the hall.

Opening her eyes, Celeste beheld Tonia, looking like a wraith with her hair unbound and her eyes darkened by the smudges of worry under them. The visitor's servant dropped the grisly box. Mercifully the latch did not come undone. The man cowered behind the table and hid his face in the crook of his arm. Lord Caitland slid out of his chair onto the floor. His red-veined eyes nearly popped out of their sockets.

A grim smile wreathed Tonia's lips. "Look at me, my lord," she continued in honeyed tones. "And behold a woman most unmercifully wronged. I am the spirit of Lady Gastonia Cavendish."

Sir Roderick Caitland wet his tights before he fainted in a heap.

For the first time in over a week, Tonia joined her parents for the evening supper. Following her surprise appearance in the great hall, her sister Alyssa had been hurriedly dispatched across the fields to Wolf Hall, where Guy had instructed her to remain indefinitely. Alyssa was only too happy to be perpetually entertained by Kitt's merry company.

After Tonia had withdrawn, Guy revived Lord Caitland and his terrified servant. Both men could not wait to flee the house and were astride their mounts within a quarter of an hour. Now at the end of that disquieting day, the Cavendishes enjoyed a quiet meal together.

Guy drained the malmsey wine from the bottom of his goblet, then he gave his eldest daughter a wry look. "Well, sweetling, I must commend you. Your sense of timing was exquisite."

Celeste, looking much healthier since she had changed from her tight bodice to her loose dressing gown, patted Tonia's hand. "*Mais oui, ma chère,* the expression on that little man's face was like choice wine to me after what he had said and done to us."

Tonia smiled at her mother. It was the first time in weeks that she did not have to force a smile. "When I heard Pappa's shouting, I knew who was here. 'Twas time that I did something for myself. The revenge was sweet, even if he was only a lackey of the true evildoer."

Guy rubbed the back of his neck. "Northumberland, he is the wicked mind behind this evil plot. I have known of John Dudley for many years past, but I never suspected that his ambition had so blinded him that he would commit murder. This affront needs to be addressed."

Celeste put her hand on her husband's arm. "But not tonight, nor this week, *mon cher.* You hit a sore spot with Lord Caitland when you mentioned the King's health. Mayhap Edward is closer to death than we suspect. Once the Princess Mary is secure on the throne, the wind will blow from a different direction throughout this land. I counsel patience."

Guy covered her hand with his. "As always, you are the voice of moderation. We will wait and see what develops—for a while."

Tonia placed her hand over her stomach wherein

lodged Sandor's child. Would their babe ever see its father? She could not believe that Sandor had deliberately seduced and abandoned her. His love had been too intense and real. The appearance of the King's minion armed with the dreadful box was proof that Sandor had arrived safely in London some weeks ago. Tonia could not bear to think that he might have been executed to keep the secret of her death forever in a grave. Fate could not be that cruel.

"How now, Tonia?" Celeste leaned toward her daughter with a look of concern in her violet eyes. "Feeling unwell again?"

Shaking her head, Tonia looked away. Would her mother tell Pappa of her pregnancy here and now? Tonia braced herself for the verbal whirlwind that would erupt.

Guy lifted her chin with his forefinger. "Tears. Tonia?" he asked with deep concern.

She bit her lip. She could not break his heart just yet—at least not until she had mended her own. She glanced down at her palm and traced the hairline scar there. *Blood of my blood, where are you?*

"Aye, Pappa, a drop or two," she confessed aloud. "You have no idea how good 'tis to be home."

Chapter Eighteen

The Tower of London
Mid-August 1553

For the third time within a month, the cannons on the walls of the Tower fircd a ceremonial salute. Pressing his face against the stout bar of his window, Sandor strained to catch the shouts he heard coming from the Thames River boatmen. Though great events were happening beyond his cell's door, Sandor learned little from his guard, other than the fact that young King Edward had finally succumbed to his wasting illness and had died on July 6. The first round of the Tower's cannon fire marked the boy-king's passing. Church bells all over London tolled the death knell and counted out Edward VI's scant fifteen years of age.

Even before the King's death had been announced to the populace, the Tower had turned into a hive of activity, though why, Sandor could not glean from Stipe, his dour jailer.

"Eat yer victuals and pray," was all that the bald-headed man said.

"Pray for what, friend?" Sandor asked, half-afraid to learn the answer.

"Fer salvation," Stipe replied as he locked the door behind him. When the cannons boomed again a few days later, Sandor heard a few voices below his window shouting "God save the Queen." When he asked Stipe for details, all he got was a sneer in return.

"Ye think 'tis Mary Tudor on the throne, does ye? Ha, not so! We are ruled by another wench."

Sandor chewed on this piece of news while he gnawed on the hard rye bread that was his breakfast. He could not think who this new Queen could be unless the Lady Elizabeth, Mary's half sister, had finally been legitimized by Parliament. He shook his head. Kings, queens—what did these *gadje* rulers matter to him except as a possible release from this windy prison? Sandor could think of no woman, except his beloved Tonia.

He prayed that she had not starved to death at Hawksnest, waiting in vain for his return. Worse, he feared for her safety. He begged Black Sara to protect Tonia from the King's men who searched for her. What must his beloved think of him? Did she believe that he had left her to her fate? Sandor gritted his teeth. Nay, Tonia loved him with her life's blood. She would never doubt his fidelity.

"Minek mange kado trajo kana naj man bold og-sago?" he sang an old Rom lament under his breath to soothe his troubled soul. "What is my life when I have no joy?" *When I have no sweet Tonia to hold*

in my arms at sunset? "I shed bloody tears and I am homesick for you, my beloved."

The week passed by as the previous weeks had passed, with no news, no release and little hope. Sandor's lifelong training had taught him to take each day as it came, without expectations or anticipation. Worry about the future was wasted energy. Tomorrow would come soon enough, with its own worries.

Since meeting Tonia, Sandor had undergone a complete change in his philosophy. He had begun to dream of the future, with Tonia by his side. He could not imagine the two of them riding down unknown country roads, seeking nightly shelter on the wayside. His childhood fantasies resurfaced—dreams of living in a real cottage with a permanent roof over their heads and a stoutly built fireplace to warm them in winter. Sitting alone in his cheerless prison, Sandor allowed his mind to touch upon all sorts of *gadje* ideas. At least, thinking of them kept his mind alert.

When the cannons boomed for a third time, Sandor did not give his jailer a chance to escape without answering his questions. When Stipe brought Sandor's dinner of thin pottage and more stale bread, the Gypsy backed the man into a corner.

"Whyfore the cannon? Who has died? What news, *gadjo,* or I will put a curse upon you that will wither your manly parts."

Sandor had no idea what sort of a curse could do such a dire thing, since only women dealt with magic as a general rule, but this simpleton didn't know that. Like most *gadje,* he thought all Gypsies were witches and wizards.

Beads of sweat popped out on Stipe's brow. He made the sign against the evil eye. "'Tis no matter to ye or me,'' he blathered. ''Tis only that the new Queen Jane 'as been sent down, and now we 'ave Queen Mary, God bless 'er. She should 'ave been queen in the first place, seeing that she is old 'Arry's true daughter.''

Sandor had never heard of this Queen Jane, but her fate was no concern of his. He wondered what the much-oppressed Mary Tudor would be like now that she finally held power in her hands. More to the point, what would Her Majesty do with him? He turned away from the nervous jailer and stared out of the window that overlooked the river.

Stipe backed toward the door. ''Ye best keep yer spells to yerself, Gypsy scum. The new Queen is a pious lady and methinks she will frown on such witchcraft.''

Still staring out the window, Sandor waved him away as if the man were nothing but an annoying fly. The jailer slammed the door to show his displeasure.

Miraculously Sandor's release came a few days later with no advance warning. Stipe merely flung open the door, jerked his thumb toward the stairwell beyond, and growled, ''Yer free, and good riddance to ye, says I.''

Sandor blinked at him. ''Tell me true, Stipe, is this some trick to lead me to the gallows?''

The jailer curled his lip. ''If'n the choice was mine, I'd of 'ung ye two months ago and thrown yer body on the refuse 'eap fer the dogs to eat.'' He shrugged. ''But now 'is 'igh and mighty lordship, the Duke of bloody Northumberland, is 'isself fast locked in the Tower, and faces his death this very day. Yer released by order of the Queen. If'n I was ye, I'd be on the first fast boat back to froggy France, and I'd count meself lucky.'' It was the longest speech Sandor had ever heard Stipe utter.

He grinned at his jailer. ''My thanks, friend.'' Before Stipe could change his slow-moving mind, Sandor snatched up his cap and cloak, then followed him through the door and down the narrow spiral stairway to freedom. Only one thought drummed on Sandor's mind—Hawksnest and sweet Tonia.

''Oy,'' said Stipe, stopping before the final gate into the Tower's Middle Ward. ''About me privates— ye didn't…do anything, did ye?''

It took Sandor a moment to realize that the jailer still worried over his alleged power to curse him. He gave Stipe a broad grin. ''Nay, friend, for your good service this day, I promise you *years* of vigor. Enjoy it well!''

Stipe grinned for the first time. Only then did Sandor realize that the man had barely a tooth in his head. ''Ah well, then, that's that,'' he gloated with obvious pleasure.

Sandor left him quickly and strode toward the stable by the Byward Tower. His heart nearly stopped when he did not find Baxtalo there. One of the tack lads informed him that young Demeo had taken the horse away with him when he had been released.

Hurrying through London's crowded thoroughfares, Sandor hoped that his family had not left the heath for their summer swing through the countryside. The Springtime Feast of the Kettles was three months past when Rom families traditionally decamped from their winter's lodgings. Summer market days and village fairs brought out many people who sought the Gypsies' skills with horses, blacksmithing and fortune-telling. Sandor shouted his relief when he climbed Hampstead Hill and saw the Lalow family's *vardo* still under a copse of trees. The wagon sported a new coat of red paint and fanciful decorations.

In answer to Sandor's call, Baxtalo jerked on his loose tether and dashed to meet his master. Sandor embraced his horse with soul-satisfying joy. "I find you with God, my good friend, and tomorrow we will go to find our Tonia."

Uncle Gheorghe limped around the side of the *vardo.* To Sandor, the old man looked pinched and drawn. *So the hand of sickness still lies on his shoulder.* Sandor lifted his cap in greeting. "I find you with God, my uncle!"

He covered the ground between them in several easy strides, then embraced the man who had been a second father to him. Gheorghe felt like a sack of loose bones in Sandor's arms. His uncle settled himself on the wagon's top step. He gave his nephew a hard stare with his watery eyes.

"So the *gadje* finally grew tired of feeding you?"

Sandor seated himself on the lower step. "Aye, Uncle, it seems the new Queen had no further need of me in her Tower."

Gheorghe muttered a curse under his breath. "This Mary Tudor is surrounded by many priests," he observed. "She is said to be very holy and strong-minded, like her father before her. 'Twill not bode well for the likes of us."

Sandor nodded. Like his uncle, he realized that the new Queen would seek to cleanse England of her late brother's religion and return the people to the teachings of Rome. Any purge of heretics would naturally include the Rom, who lived under sufferance on the fringes of English society, with a blind eye toward the old Act of 1530 against the ''outlandish people calling themselves Egyptians.'' Once again, the wind would change. Sandor felt it in his bones—bad times were coming.

He changed the subject. ''I am surprised that you are not already on the road, Uncle.'' *And thankful that Baxtalo is still here and looking so well.*

Gheorghe shrugged. ''My fever comes and goes. Old Towla was determined that we remain after the others left. Methinks she knew you would return soon.''

''Aunt Mindra? Demeo? They are well?''

His uncle gave a quick nod. ''They are down at Covent Garden Market today. Demeo is a-scrumping among the vendors for our supper, while Mindra reads palms and tells the *gadje* a pack of lies for coppers and silver.'' He chuckled as he contemplated the cleverness of his wife and son.

''But you, Sandor—'' he stabbed the air with a bone-thin finger ''—you have done nothing. Instead, you send the King's soldiers here to badger me with questions. All you had to do was strangle the woman up north and cut out her heart. How was that so hard?''

Sandor guarded his tongue. He had spent the past two months practicing how he would explain Tonia to his family. He could not lie to his uncle as he could to a *gadjo.* The Rom never lied or stole from each other under the pain of banishment from the clan.

''The woman is dead to the world,'' Sandor hedged, choosing his words with care. ''I delivered the heart to the Constable, as you told me to do. Beyond that, I know nothing.'' He plucked a blade of the bright green grass growing at his feet, and chewed on it. Its bitter taste reminded him of his blessed freedom.

Gheorghe grunted. "Let destruction eat that pack of Englishmen! Tonight we will sing and feast on whatever odds and ends Demeo finds at the marketplace. Tomorrow, we will travel south to Dover. 'Tis high time we returned to France." He spat on the ground. "Pah! I have never much liked these English. No joy thrives in their cold blood."

Sandor cleared his throat. He had never before seen his life's path so clearly as now. "Then I wish you *baxtalo drom*—a lucky road, my uncle. For my part, I will stay here."

Gheorghe narrowed his eyes at him. "Did they drop you on your head while you were in the Tower? Have all your brains dribbled out of your ears?"

Sandor took a deep breath. There was no way to escape his uncle's prodding except to tell the whole truth, no matter how much it would cost Sandor. As his foster father, Gheorghe deserved to know. Perhaps he would understand Sandor's decision. After all, his uncle had once been young and in love.

"I am married again, Uncle." He showed the stunned man the thin scar on his palm. "We have mixed our blood together. We are one."

Gheorghe whistled through his chipped teeth. "Have you been a-wooing one of the Buckland girls this past winter, or did this lightning strike recently?"

"I married while in the north…to a *gadji*." Sandor held his breath and waited for the ax to fall.

Gheorghe looked as if he had been thunderstruck. Then he stood, turned his back on Sandor and entered the *vardo*. He shut the lower half of the door before turning to look at the man he once called son as well as son-in-law. With painful difficulty, Gheorghe drew himself upright and pulled back his shoulders.

"You know the law of the *kris,*" he told Sandor in a cold, hollow tone. "You have defiled yourself beyond all reckoning. Begone from my fireside so that you do not taint my family."

Though he had expected this reaction, its reality stung Sandor to his core. "She is a good woman, Uncle."

Gheorghe sliced the air with the flat of his hand. "Enough! Your words hurt my ears. Take what is yours and leave before my family returns. I do not wish my son to witness your shame. My sister would weep if she saw her son now. Your name will never be spoken again. You are dead to us." He spat on the ground at Sandor's feet, then slammed shut the top half of the double door.

Sandor hung his head. "The dice are cast," he murmured to himself.

"And the cards told the truth," said his grandmother behind him.

Sandor spun on his heel to see the tiny woman with her bright-colored striped shawl covering her snow-white hair. She sat on a low stool before her bender tent. "Do you also shun me, Towla? I am now unclean."

She chuckled. "Come inside, my *tarno shushi,*" she said, calling Sandor by her pet name for him since his childhood. "We will drink some elderberry wine and talk before you go down your road. I have a tale that will interest you."

Her kind words and loving smile nearly unmanned him, even if she had called him a little bunny rabbit in broad daylight. Sandor swallowed down the knot that had risen in his throat. He ducked under the bent hickory poles that supported the tent's buckram skin. Inside, Towla settled herself on the tight-woven colorful blanket that covered the ground. Beside her lay a wineskin with two salt-ware cups on a wooden tray.

"Close the flap," she instructed him, as she arranged her colorful red and yellow skirts around her. "I have been waiting a long time for you."

Sandor released the leather thong that held back the front panel of the tent. In the semidarkness, Towla lit the candle in her lantern. Then she took out her velvet bag. Sandor immediately recognized his grandmother's *tarocchi* pouch.

She tapped the wineskin. "Pour us some wine, Sandor, and we will talk."

Sandor uncorked the skin and filled both cups. He offered one to his grandmother.

With a merry glint in her black eyes, she took it and toasted him. "*Te xav to biav*. May I dance at your wedding."

Sipping his wine, Sandor gave her a rueful look. "I have already performed that ceremony, *puridai*."

Towla nodded. "With the one you were sent to kill."

Sandor almost choked. "Did your cards tell you that?" he asked, pointing to the worn deck that she shuffled as she spoke.

Towla turned up the Lovers card and laid it on the blanket between them. "Aye, though it did not take any special skill to see the truth of the matter. You went north to execute a *gadji*. Three weeks later, you return married to a *gadji*. 'Twas not much time to find *two* women in the north, methinks."

She turned up the Hermit card and laid it across

the Lovers. "Besides that, you went on a journey to find your inner self. Methinks you have done so."

He nodded. "I have found great happiness with Tonia," he confessed.

Towla cocked her head. "Pretty name. It has a nice feel on the tongue."

Sandor thought of the other places that Tonia felt nice and his cheeks warmed.

His grandmother chuckled. "I see she pleases you. That pleases me." She tapped the deck, then spread the cards faceup on the blanket. "Do you know where these *tarocchi* came from?"

Sandor pinched the bridge of his nose in thought. "I was told that they were given to you by a very rich man." He shrugged. He had heard a story something like that when he was much younger. To him, it meant little. Grandmother and her cards were one and the same to him.

Towla took another sip of wine. "A rich man." She chuckled. "Aye, he was the Duke of Milan once, a very long time ago." Her expression grew soft as her mind slipped into the distant past. "I was barely sixteen and quite beautiful, they said."

Sandor agreed. Even though the decades had incised wrinkles in her skin, and years of living outdoors had roughened her complexion, the fine bones of Towla's face still held the hint of her great beauty.

"I had been married to your grandfather when I was fourteen and had already borne him a son. But my body was young and supple. I danced for the duke and his court. He liked my dancing. I saw much coin at my feet, so I danced into the night for him."

"He was a kind man," she continued. "Tall, like you, with very broad shoulders, also like you."

Sandor felt an odd tickling sensation at the back of his neck. He put down his cup and leaned closer to catch every word of Towla's story.

"His eyes were the deepest turquoise I had ever seen," she mused with a smile. "And his hair was the color of honey. He was very handsome to look upon. And when I danced my last dance for him, he invited me to his inner apartments where we supped together."

"And where was Grandfather?"

"He was also very young, and the thrill of wagering on the cards filled his head that night—that and a good deal of thick red wine. He thought I had returned to camp with the others."

"But you stayed with the duke."

Nodding, she resumed her tale. "I had never eaten such rich food. A pie of larks' tongues, roasted venison in a wine sauce, plump olives and pastries made of nuts and honey." She sighed at the remembrance. "I confess that my stomach was not used to such fine fare, and it gave me grief later, but ah! Such a feast!"

Sandor moistened his lips. "And then?" Did she, a married woman, actually bed with a *gadjo?*

Towla skimmed her fingers over the cards. "Then he opened his chest and took out these. Take one, Sandor." She gave him the Fool card. "Even after all these years, they still feel magnificent."

Sandor gingerly picked up the Fool and ran his finger along the still-gilt edge. Towla had never before allowed anyone touch her cards, saying that the good luck would rub off.

She smiled. "Real vellum and painted with rare inks made from powdered jewels, methinks. The colors have not faded over time."

Sandor replaced the Fool with the others. "And so you told the duke's fortune?"

"Aye, though not all of it." Towla sighed. "I saw his death from the plague in the coming year, but I could not tell him that. Why make such a kind man sad? I told him only the good things in the cards. He would learn the bad in time." Her voice trailed away.

Though he was itching to know what happened next, Sandor sipped his wine and said nothing. Good manners dictated his silence. His grandmother would resume her story when she was ready.

"Aye, Sandor, we spent the whole night together in his large gilded bed that was shaped like a swan. Most wondrous! In the early morning, he kissed me farewell and he gave me three things—a bag heavy with ducats and these cards that I have cherished since that night."

Sandor held his breath. He sensed there was something more to come.

"The duke's third gift was your mother."

Chapter Nineteen

Sandor expelled his breath in a rush. "So my mother was half *gadji?*"

Old Towla nodded. "Your grandfather never even suspected that his favorite child was not his blood. I prayed when she was born that she would not inherit the duke's eyes or light-colored hair."

"Her hair was black as a raven, as I remember," said Sandor, conjuring up a dim memory of his long-dead mother. "And I was the one who received the *gadjo's* eyes." Then he stared at his grandmother. "*Puridai,* I do not understand how you could betray your husband—even for a bag of gold." The mere thought of Tonia lying in another man's arms set his blood boiling.

Towla sighed again. "Your grandfather was not a cruel man—merely an absent one. Even when we made love, his mind was elsewhere—on his horses, on his gambling, on his schemes against the *gadje.* I was only the one who washed his clothes, made his bread and bore his children—nothing more. The duke was...so very tender to me. Kind. Loving, if only for a night." She smiled to herself. "But that one night was enough for me."

She returned her attention to the present. "I never told your mother that she was *poshrat,* a half-blood. I didn't want her to feel ashamed or to be shunned by our family. She would have never gotten herself a good husband if anyone knew that she was part *gadje.*"

"Then my real grandfather was a duke?" Sandor whispered in awe.

Towla reached over her cards and patted his hand. "To the Rom, a *gadjo* is only a *gadjo,* no matter how noble he is, or how rich."

For the next few minutes, they sat together, sharing the silence. With a sweet, sad smile on her lips, Towla relived her memories, while Sandor attempted to grasp all the implications of his grandmother's startling revelation. No wonder he had always felt a little different from his cousins and friends! Somewhere deep in his soul was a yearning for permanence, a place to settle down. The eternal open road held no allure for him, though he would have died before admitting such a heresy to his family.

The more Sandor accepted his astonishing background, the more he understood himself. In sharing her great secret with him, his grandmother had soothed the sting of his banishment from the Rom. Now he knew for certain that his home and his destiny were where his heart lay—with Tonia in the north.

Towla gathered up her *tarocchi* and shuffled them again. Then she fanned the deck toward Sandor. "Choose three," she commanded.

Sandor contemplated the cards—the beautiful cards

that were his grandfather's parting gift—knowing in his soul that this would be the last time that Towla would ever read his future.

He gave her a sidelong glance. "Would you tell *me* if I am to die of the plague?" he asked in a half-teasing manner.

Lifting one gray brow, she returned his smile. "May I die if I lie."

Sandor pointed to three cards. Towla laid them facedown on the blanket. Sandor touched the design of three golden coins that graced the cards' backs. Several words, written in red ink on an ivory scroll, wove among the coins.

Towla tapped the middle card. "'Tis the duke's family motto. The words are Latin and I cannot read it, but he told me that they meant 'Love conquers all.' I have never forgotten that. I whisper those words over the cards each time before I shuffle them. It has always brought good luck."

Sandor stared at the scroll, burning into his memory the letters inscribed on it. "'Tis *my* family's motto now."

"Si kovel ajaw," said his grandmother. "This thing is so. You *are* the duke's grandson." She cocked her head. "Are you ready to see your fortune?"

His pulse quickening, Sandor nodded. Once again the first card was the Fool. Towla chuckled. The second card was again Death. Sandor grimaced but did not look away. The third was the Sun. His grandmother clapped her hands with satisfaction. "Good, good," she muttered.

"Once again, you are Prosto, the Fool on the hill," she told him. "You have taken the first step into the unknown, but you must go all the way to reach your journey's end. Death does not frighten you so much this time?''

He gave her a long look. ''I have stared death in the face. I am ready.''

''Good, for there will be yet another change and another beginning…ah!'' She rocked with silent laughter.

Sandor knotted his brows. ''What do you see?'' There was nothing at all amusing in the skeleton's face.

'''Tis a new birth!'' she chortled. ''Mayhap one with turquoise eyes.''

Sandor had no idea why this was so funny. Instead of explaining herself, Towla moved to the third card.

''The Sun shines his warm rays upon you, my Fool. You are promised prosperity, joy, a great celebration, contentment and liberation once you have passed through the final trial.''

''I will have all that and more when I am reunited with my Tonia,'' he replied.

''Aye,'' she agreed. She gathered all the cards except one and returned them to her pouch. Then she handed the Fool to Sandor. ''Take this one for luck. 'Tis you.''

Surprised, Sandor protested, ''But your *tarocchi* is incomplete without it.''

She shook her head. ''Nay, *tarno shushi,* 'tis yours. You are the only Fool in this pack. 'Tis right that the card goes with you. Think of it as your legacy from your grandfather.'' She touched the motto on the back. ''Remember these words. They are yours now.''

In reply, he kissed the Latin inscription. ''They are upon my lips and in my heart.'' Then he carefully placed the card in the pouch that hung from his belt. "Thank you, my grandmother."

She gave him a heartfelt smile. "The light wanes. 'Tis time to begin your most important journey."

Sandor lifted the tent flap and was surprised to discover how late the day had advanced. He glanced toward his uncle's wagon but the *vardo*'s door was still shut. "Give Gheorghe my thanks for taking me into his family, *puridai*. I am sorry to have caused him such shame."

Towla lifted the lid from a small black kettle that hung over her slow-burning fire next to her tent. She stirred the contents. The delicious aroma of hedgehog stew filled Sandor's nostrils.

"Hotchiwitchi," he murmured, his mouth watering.

"Eat before you go," she offered. "I made it especially for you. 'Twould be a shame to waste it." She ladled out a large bowl full of the savory dish and handed it to him.

With several incoherent words of thanks and appreciation, he ate his favorite meal. In the back of his mind, he wondered if he could teach Tonia how to make this delicious concoction. While he ate, Towla slipped a few golden angels into his pouch. When Sandor protested, she crossed his lips with her finger and shook her head.

"'Tis a wedding present, to 'give a push to the new wagon,' as they say."

When Sandor hugged his grandmother for the last time, his heart grew heavy within his chest. "I do not know if our paths will ever cross again, *sukar puridai,*" he murmured, kissing her forehead.

"In the spring in France, I will light a candle for

you at Black Sara's shrine. When you next go there, you will see it and know that I love you,'' she said. Her black eyes misted.

"And I love you,'' he replied with heartfelt tenderness.

"As you love another, who has more need of you now than I. Go, Sandor Matskella, son of Milan. My blessing accompanies you.'' She handed him a wrapped packet of bread and cheese that she had prepared while he ate. *Jal 'sa Duvvel.*''

"Go with God,'' he answered.

Before he made more of a fool of himself by crying like a child, Sandor turned away and strode across the field of daisies and cornflowers to where Baxtalo waited for him. He quickly saddled and bridled his horse. He stuffed his few personal belongings into a single sack, much like the one the *tarocchi* Fool carried. Sandor armed himself with a set of his spare knives, then rolled up a blanket and tied it to his saddle. After one final wave to the distant figure of his beloved grandmother, he swung himself onto Baxtalo's back.

"Hi-up, my friend,'' he said to his horse. "We head for the north once more, this time on lighter feet. Let us go down the road! *Jallin a drom!*''

Tonia tugged on her bodice, not laced as tightly as it had been only a few weeks earlier. She smoothed her skirts over the little curve of her stomach then adjusted her headdress. This was the first time she would speak to her father since her mother had told him of her pregnancy. She had no idea how Guy had taken the news. She chewed some fresh mint leaves both to sweeten her breath and to aid her continued indigestion. Mamma had promised her that the nausea would pass soon. Tonia certainly hoped so. She had not been able to keep down much food and she worried that the babe in her womb would suffer from the lack of nourishment.

Squaring her shoulders and lifting her chin, she knocked on the door of her father's counting room. Because of its privacy, the counting room had always been Pappa's lair, especially when it came to serious discussions with one of the four women in his family. Tonia highly doubted that the walls of this chamber had ever heard anything like what would be said within the next few minutes.

"Enter," growled Guy.

Tonia's hand shook a little as she lifted the latch. Pappa sat behind his imposing, carved desk—not a good sign. He looked up when she entered, the pain in his blue eyes was heartrending.

Assuming that this interview was a formal one, Tonia dropped a deep curtsy as befitted a dutiful daughter to her father. "Pappa," she said softly.

Would he unleash the infamous Cavendish temper? Call her a slut and a whore? Of all the men in the family, Guy was usually the most controlled, which made his rare outbursts all the more frightening.

He rose and came around the desk. "Sweet Tonia," he said in a low, gruff tone. He took her hand in his and raised her to a standing position. Then he enfolded her in his arms.

"How you must have suffered," he murmured against her cheek.

Tonia drew in her breath. Making love to Sandor had been ecstasy, not painful. It was his continued absence that had driven a great thorn into her heart.

Until Tonia understood her father's sympathy, she would play the role of a simple maiden.

"I am feeling much improved, Pappa," she replied brightly. "I am able to eat more these past few days."

Guy led her to his padded chair and held it for her as she took her seat. "That is good news, indeed, but 'tis…ahem…I was speaking of your time at Hawksnest. I know that you would prefer to put the entire matter of your arrest and imprisonment behind you, but I must ask you to bear the pain of memory a little longer. I must bring those dogs to justice."

Tonia folded her hands over her stomach, very conscious of its slight rise under her gown and petticoats. "I fear that my judges are too close to the throne for punishment, Pappa. I pray you, leave them be. 'Tis past and done. I am dead in their minds, and I prefer to stay that way."

He dropped to one knee beside her chair. "I did not mean those men, Tonia," he said. His eyes searched hers. "'Tis your guards that I speak of, the ones who violated your person and stole your… honor. Do you remember any of their names? Or can you describe what they looked like? Any scars or moles? I vow that they will swing in chains for your injury."

Tonia swallowed. She twirled the horseshoe-nail ring around her finger. *He thinks I was raped!* She bent her head, allowing her hair to slide over her ears and hide her face, while her brain spun like a whirligig in a high wind. If she told the truth of her marriage to Sandor, she knew that her father would not understand. He would say that a honey-tongued knave whose daily pastime was deceit had duped her. Pappa would think that she had bought her life with her body.

And had Tonia done just that? She squeezed shut her eyes. Is that why Sandor had not followed the trail of *patrin* she had laid from Hawksnest to Snape Castle's very door? She bit her lower lip until she tasted blood.

Guy rubbed her shoulder. "Tonia?" he whispered. "It cuts me to the quick to see your distress. 'Twill be soon over and done. We will find a good family to take the babe and—"

"Nay," she cried, opening her eyes. "The child is mine. I will keep it." Sandor might never reappear in her life, but Tonia would never give up the child that their love had formed. The baby would be the lasting reminder of the only man Tonia would ever love.

Sitting back on his heels, Guy stared at her, completely baffled. "I applaud your maternal instincts, sweetling, but in this case there is no need. The child will only be a reminder of a time best forgotten."

But I want to remember every detail about my baby's father. Aloud, Tonia replied, "Pappa, I thank you for your love and your concern for me, but I assure you that I am of sound mind when I say I want to keep the babe. It is mine—as well as *your* grandchild. He is a Cavendish, no matter who his father is, just as I am. And as you are. My child deserves the best we can give him in this life, and I intend to see to it."

Guy stood, then crossed around to the far side of his desk, putting a distance between them. Tonia clasped her hands tightly in her lap. She had not realized until this very moment how much this child meant to her. Five more months and a bit, she calculated, before she could hold him in her arms.

Guy drummed his fingers on the smooth-polished surface of his desk while he immersed himself in thought. Tonia found that she felt more tranquil now than she had been a quarter hour earlier. She knew what she would do with her future, even if her father didn't. Mamma, with her notorious love of any baby, be it human or animal, would certainly agree with Tonia's point of view.

Guy cleared his throat. "Methinks 'tis best if you left here before you begin to show your condition. 'Twould be easier traveling now than later."

Tonia gaped at him. "You are sending me away when I sorely need you and Mamma? Have I disgraced you so much that you would turn your back on me?"

Guy's face softened, and he returned to her side. "You mistake my meaning, sweetling," he said, holding her cold hand. "Forgive me, for I can be abrupt upon occasion. My concern is that your whereabouts and identity must remain a secret for your safety's sake—and that of the child." He gave her a lopsided grin. "I imagine that I must sound like the father of the Virgin Mary when he was faced with somewhat the same situation."

Tonia relaxed against him and kissed his cheek. "'Tis good to know that there is precedence."

Guy nodded. "Ideally, we should find you a complacent husband."

Tonia frowned. "Nay, Pappa. I want no husband." *Except the one that I have lost.*

"Methought you would say something like that. Therefore, I propose that we take you to your sister's home in Scotland. There you may live openly and freely, without constraint, while you await the babe's birth. You know that Gillian and her husband will surround you with love and cater to your every whim. Indeed, you will become quite spoiled, methinks. What month is the child due?''

''December or early January.''

Guy smiled again. ''Better and better. We have just received word that Gillian is also expecting about that same time. You two will have much to talk about while you wait. When your joint times draw near, no one at Snape will be surprised when Celeste and I leave to attend Gillie's laying-in. That way, we will be at your side when your time comes.''

''Oh, Pappa!'' Tonia slid out of her chair and wrapped her arms around her father's neck. '''Tis a most excellent plan! When will we leave?''

Guy hugged her close to his chest. ''As soon as possible. You will travel disguised as Mamma's serving maid, at least until we are well clear of Northumberland, where you are known. If the good weather holds, the trip will take us no more than three or four days to reach Bannock.''

''I have known you to make the journey in two.''

Guy tapped her on the chin. ''Aye, but not in the company of an expectant mother.''

Four-and-a-half days after he had left London, Sandor rode up the rocky trail to Hawksnest. The land had changed greatly since the snowy day when he had left his beloved wife alone in this stone fortress. Bare trees were now clothed in thick green foliage. Birds that had been silent during the colder months sang and called to each other across the mountainsides. As he drew nearer to Hawksnest's crumbling walls, Sandor admired the lush greenery of the once-brown meadow before the castle. Lavender springs vied for space with meadow grass that had grown so tall and thick, Sandor almost missed the spot where he had dug Tonia's grave. When he spied it, he reined his horse to a sudden halt. Startled, Baxtalo reared on his hind legs.

Sandor slid off his back and raced through the grass to the site. Instead of the rain-filled hole that he had expected, he saw that the grave had been filled in and was gently mounded. Ice ran through his veins instead of warm blood. He sank to his knees and threw himself across the grave. His tears flowed without shame.

"Is this your idea of a jest, *Duvvel?*" he cried up to God. "Why have you plucked away my happiness the instant I had found it?" He dug his fingers into the mound of earth as if he sought to touch Tonia's cold hand.

Those King's men he had misdirected must have found a better guide. Seven of them against a single woman! Though Tonia had the heart of a lioness, she could not have withstood such odds.

"I am truly fortune's fool," he sobbed. "I should have taken you with me. You would have been safer in London with my grandmother than here. Forgive me, *sukar luludi*. I am the world's worst husband."

Sandor hoped that the men had killed her quickly. He could not bear the thought of the soldiers torturing her or, worse, using her sweet body for their amusement. "Is this the death your *tarocchi* foretold, Grandmother?" he called to the sky. "You should have warned me. You should have…" His grief choked off further words.

As the summer's lingering sun began to slant westward, Sandor collected himself and pondered what course he should take now. Since Uncle Gheorghe had banished him, he would not be welcome in any Rom camp. News of this nature spread like wildfire throughout the Gypsy community, no matter where the Rom were. Nor did Sandor really want to return to a wandering way of life. In truth, he did not want to live at all, but instead remain on this hillside, lying forever beside his love. Yet, his zest for living overrode this macabre idea. Sandor did not possess the temperament to stab himself in the heart.

While he thought, he occupied his hands with cleaning the gravesite—pulling up irreverent weeds that had dared to sprout from Tonia's body. He would fashion the cross she had once told him that she wanted to stand at her head. He cleared the ground around that spot. Sandor was so intent upon his sad duty that he nearly overlooked an arrangement of brown leaves held down by two stones, one on top of the other.

A *patrin?* Blood thudded against Sandor's temples so that he felt momentarily giddy. Half in awe, half in disbelief, he touched the rocks. He had taught Tonia this exact signal. Kneeling, he whispered a pleading prayer to the deity he had just shouted at. "Forgive me, *Duvvel.* You know what a fool I am. Tell me that she lives. Let me find a second sign, I beg you. Is one life too much to ask? May she live awhile longer upon this earth before you call her to heaven? Saint Sara, help me and I will light a hundred candles in your honor!"

Having said all that he could think of, Sandor closed with a whispered *"Ajaw."* Then he pulled himself to his feet and studied the terrain, searching for the logical spot that Tonia would have laid a second marker. What a clever woman she was to have thought to leave a mark by her grave! She knew he would see it first.

While Baxtalo cropped the lush mountainside grass, Sandor wove back and forth through the meadow up to the turning of the trail that led across the ramshackle drawbridge. On the right side of the path he found what he had hoped to see—a second *patrin* that clearly pointed down the hillside, away from Hawksnest.

Sandor touched his fingers to his lips and blew a kiss heavenward. "*Parika tut,* Black Sara!" he shouted with a joy-filled voice that echoed around the steep ravine below. "Thank you! A hundred candles, I swear it!"

As he turned, he looked again upon the mute grave. Mayhap one of the guards was buried under the lavender. Sandor shrugged. The unknown dead was no matter to him now that he knew Tonia still lived.

"*Jel 'sa Duvvel,*" he muttered under his breath as he picked up his cap from the ground beside the mound. "Go with God, whomever you are."

Sandor scanned the bowl of the sky. Purple-shadowed dusk had already filled the mountain clefts and distant valleys. The last of the sun's golden rays kissed only the tall peak across the ravine from Hawksnest. Sandor decided to bed down in the ruin. Tonia's signs had lasted this long. What was one more night?

I am coming, my beloved. I will hold you in my arms and kiss away this loathsome separation. Never will we be parted again, I swear it!

Chapter Twenty

The next morning dawned cloudy with rain on the horizon. Sandor took little notice of the weather. After a hasty breakfast for himself and Baxtalo, he rode down the mountain, marveling how well Tonia had laid the *patrin* considering that her trail was now several months old. By late afternoon, it was obvious that she and the large party who traveled with her had headed north, bypassing York.

She must have gone back to her home. Though he was glad that Tonia appeared to be in safe hands, Sandor's heart grew uneasier as he rode farther into the wild Northumberland countryside. If his beloved had indeed returned to her family, Sandor knew he would have to do a great deal of explaining to her *gadje* relatives, who no doubt would frown upon their union. In particular, he would have to win Tonia's formidable father to his suit. While he rode across the moorlands, Sandor half considered the option of kidnapping Tonia, then afterward explaining himself.

Sandor followed the signs until the last bit of the gray daylight dissolved into dusk. He and Baxtalo spent the night on the side of the road, as they had done so often in the past. Though he had been in the saddle all day, Sandor could not sleep. He knew without the aid of map or guide that he was near Snape Castle. The emotional pull to Tonia had grown very strong over the last five miles.

As soon as the predawn light streaked the eastern sky, Sandor saddled his faithful horse. The aroma of smoke from many cooking fires wafted on the morning's fresh breeze. "'Tis Snape," Sandor told Baxtalo. "I know it."

A mile or two later, he saw the old castle crowning a low rise with a swath of forest on one side and a good-sized village nestled around the base. Tonia had told him that her home had originally been built as a fortress against the plunder-seeking Vikings, as well as the reivers from Scotland. Since Lord Cavendish had acquired the castle some twenty-five years earlier, he had made a number of modern improvements, including glass in all the windows of the domestic wings, chimneys constructed of fanciful brickwork and an improved drainage system.

Deciding that prudence and caution were the best courses of action, Sandor skirted around the village and entered the wood. He left Baxtalo cropping amid the underbrush while he reconnoitered the castle on foot. Though the hour was still very early, the entire place was alive with many flaming torches and a bustle of activity. Sandor crept nearer, though he dared not attempt to blend in with the castle's population. His southern features, darker skin and gold earring would mark him instantly as a stranger.

Sandor climbed a stout oak tree at the near edge of the forest. Nearing the top, he found a thick branch from where he could see into the castle's courtyard.

Boxes and canvas bags were being loaded onto the rear of a closed carriage and into a baggage cart. From the look of the preparations, a lengthy journey was about to commence.

Just as Sandor had deduced this fact, he saw several women come out of the castle's front doors. Attended by two very tall men, they descended the stairs and walked toward the carriage. Even though the distance was too great to discern facial features, Sandor's heart leaped for joy. The second woman, dressed as a maid, moved with a most familiar manner. He knew beyond a shade of doubt that he looked upon his beloved wife. "Tonia!" he whispered under his breath. "I am here."

As if she had heard his voice, the maid paused and looked around, almost as if she were searching for him. Even with her midnight tresses gathered primly under her servant's cap, Tonia's fine-chiseled beauty could not be hidden. Sandor's excitement was so great that he nearly fell from his precarious perch. As soon as she had stepped inside the coach, Sandor scrambled down to the ground. A plan quickly formed in his mind. He would follow the travelers at a distance. He knew that, with ladies among the party, the progress would be slow, with a number of pauses along the way. He would attract Tonia's attention at one of these rest stops. What happened after that would be in God's hands.

The first pause in the journey came just after the carriage had passed through the village. With a flurry of skirts, Tonia alighted and stepped to the side of the road. At first, it appeared that she was ill. Sandor controlled his initial impulse to dash from his hiding place to comfort her. Then he grinned. The sly minx laid yet another *patrin* on the verge of the road while she shielded her actions with her body. As soon as she had completed the trail marker, she hurried back into the carriage. The two noblemen riding beside the vehicle, as well as the coterie of men-at-arms accompanying them, took no notice of Tonia's actions. In fact, they all modestly looked away.

Sandor's attention fastened upon the large charcoal-gray stallion that the taller man rode. With a jolt, he remembered where he had seen that particular horse and its larger-than-life rider—back in April on the road toward Harewold. He scrutinized the second gentleman and his mount. Though the man had been swathed in a long cape and winter hood, Sandor felt sure that he had been the silent third gentleman of that party. His horse was the same.

"*Jaj,*" he whispered to himself. "I am twice again the fool! These men are Tonia's family and I sent them on a merry chase. Methinks they will not thank me for it."

Now that Sandor had deduced the men's identities, he observed Tonia's father more closely before the travelers disappeared down the northern road. The nobleman sat astride his horse as if he had been born in the saddle. Without the muffling cape and low-slung hood, Sandor noted that Lord Cavendish was indeed a handsome man, just as Tonia had described him. In his youth, Sir Guy had been called angelic, she had told Sandor, but now that he was in his middle life, people said he was merely godly. No matter. Lord Cavendish was definitely a man to be respected.

As soon as the party had gone over the rise, Sandor mounted Baxtalo. As long as the road wound through the wood, he had no trouble keeping a parallel course with the carriage. Once out on the open moor, following them secretly would become trickier but not beyond Sandor's skills. A couple of heavy carriages and a dozen horsemen were child's play to track, especially on a little-traveled byway.

An hour later, Sandor almost blundered onto the Cavendishes at the crossroads where once again, Tonia had stopped the coach. Pulling Baxtalo off to the side behind a large growth of brambles, he watched her lay yet another sign, pointing their direction. Once again she covered her actions with a counterfeit of nausea. As soon as Tonia had returned to the carriage, the travelers continued on their way.

Sandor waited until they were out of sight before he checked the *patrin*. "She is a true wife and my beloved!" he said to Baxtalo. The thought warmed his blood. He could not wait to hold her in his embrace. Examining the ground around the marker, Sandor noted with relief that there was no sign of true illness.

Once again, he followed them at a distance. The sun eventually burned through the gray cloak of clouds. By its height in the sky, Sandor concluded that it would soon be midday. He presumed that the Cavendishes would soon stop at some obvious spot ahead for their dinner. Instead of continuing to follow them and risking detection on this open ground, he decided to circle around the travelers and meet them from the front.

He turned Baxtalo off the road. They cantered a half mile out onto the wasteland before Sandor thought they were far enough away not to be seen from the road. Then he steered Baxtalo north again.

Touching his horse lightly on the flanks with his heels, Sandor raced ahead. He prayed to Black Sara to keep their path smooth and free from unseen rabbit holes or hidden bog patches.

When he calculated that he had covered several miles beyond the carriages, Sandor slowed Baxtalo and turned him again toward the road. Once back on the beaten track, Sandor alighted and checked the markings on the ground. The carriages had not yet come this far. After he remounted, he stood in his stirrups and scanned down the byway. A thin cloud of dust on the horizon pinpointed Tonia's position. He watched their progress for a quarter of an hour until he perceived that they had stopped. He nodded to himself in satisfaction.

"'Tis dinner." He patted Baxtalo's neck. "Methinks now is the time to join the family—but softly, very softly."

Once again, they left the track and retraced their steps until they drew closer to where Sandor estimated the carriages had halted. A roadside copse of trees offered shade and cool respite to the travelers. Sandor dropped Baxtalo's reins to the ground. The well-trained horse knew he was to stay until summoned. Then Sandor crept closer until he could hear voices. He flattened himself behind a large growth of prickly thistles.

"Now that your stomach is full, you will feel better," the older woman remarked.

Sandor tensed. The Cavendishes were much closer to him than he had suspected. He glanced in both directions to see if the men-at-arms kept a vigilant watch, but thankfully, they were not in sight. *They look for large bears and do not expect an adder among the thistles.*

"Aye, Mamma," Tonia replied clearly. "I do hope so."

The sound of her voice gave wings to Sandor's spirits. He wanted to leap over the brambles and claim her as his own there and then. Instead, he held himself in check. He knew that if he suddenly stood up, he would be readily mistaken for a highwayman. Instead, he would wait until Tonia withdrew to take her ease. Then he could catch her alone. It would be best if Tonia was by his side when he introduced himself to her family.

He heard the two women move closer to his hiding place. Their voluminous skirts made a great deal of noise swishing through the underbrush.

"Watch out for the thistles, Tonia," her mother warned. "*Ma foi!* They surround us. Pah! I dare not lift my skirts just yet."

With a shock, Sandor realized that both women were searching for a place to relieve themselves. No wonder there weren't any guards on this side of the trees! If he didn't reveal himself quickly, he would meet his unsuspecting mother-in-law under very embarrassing circumstances.

Thinking on the fly, Sandor whistled for Baxtalo. He hoped that Tonia would recognize the horse and thereby know that Sandor was close at hand.

At the sound of his call, the ladies stopped. "What was that?" Lady Cavendish asked in a wary tone.

At the same time, Tonia shouted, "Sandor!" Then, "Oh, Mamma, look there. See the horse? 'Tis Baxtalo! Oh, Sandor! Where are you?"

Needing no further reassurance of his welcome,

Sandor rose from behind the thistles. Tonia and her mother were less than six feet away from him. Her mother screamed in fright and stumbled backward. Holding her skirts above her ankles, Tonia half ran, half leapt through the thistle patch to his side.

"'Tis Sandor!" she cried again. Then she threw herself into his arms. "Oh, my love, you came back!" she said through her tears that fell freely.

"Sukar luludi," he murmured. "How could I stay away? Forgive me for taking so long." He hugged her to his chest, covering her cheek, ear and neck with his kisses.

Before Sandor had the time to explain the reason for his extended absence, Lady Cavendish's cry alerted the rest of the party. Meanwhile Baxtalo thundered to a stop behind his master. He whinnied when he saw Tonia. Sir Guy, the other nobleman and the men-at-arms burst through the trees. The two gentlemen unsheathed their swords while several of the men-at-arms notched arrows in their bowstrings.

"Unhand my daughter, you varlet!" Sir Guy shouted, shielding his wide-eyed wife with his body.

Spinning around in Sandor's arms, Tonia faced down her outraged family. "Nay, Pappa! You cannot harm him! 'Tis Sandor—the father of my babe!"

Her announcement brought the Cavendishes to a sudden halt amid the thistles. Sandor exhaled as if someone had gut-punched him. His pounding heart sent a sudden rush of blood to his head. Giddy joy welled up inside him. "You carry our child under your heart?" he asked her in wonder.

Tonia dimpled. "Aye, I hope you are pleased." She laid her head on his chest. "Oh, Sandor, I am *so glad* you have come back. I have missed you terribly.''

He gathered her closer to him with a protective gentleness. ''And I have longed for you, best beloved. I vow I will never leave you again.''

Momentarily stunned by Tonia's unexpected announcement, Guy finally found his voice. ''What tale is this? Lies from beginning to end! Has your melancholy snapped your wits, Tonia? 'Tis a highwayman who holds you. Unhand her, I say!'' He pricked Sandor's bare forearm with the point of his blade. A small trickle of blood rolled down his flesh.

Sandor flinched but did not release Tonia. ''You mistake me, my lord. I mean no harm to this sweet lady. How could I? She is my wife.''

''Mon Dieu!'' Celeste stared at the couple in open astonishment.

At the sight of Sandor's blood, Tonia pulled her handkerchief from her sleeve and bound up the wound. ''Fie, Pappa! Put up your sword. You too, Francis! I will not have you skewer my husband and make our child an orphan even before he is born.''

Her words swelled Sandor's pride. Fate had sent him a most magnificent woman. He silently thanked God for giving him the good sense to marry her. ''My lord,'' he began again. ''I am no brigand, nor outlaw. I ask only for your ear, not your fortune. I pray that you give me your leave to relate our full story.''

Francis drew abreast of Sir Guy, his sword still pointed at Sandor. ''I recognize this knave, Father, and his horse yonder. You are the rogue we met near Harewold, the one who sent us far out of our way.''

More anger darkened Lord Cavendish's eyes. ''You! Aye, now I remember! Did you lie to us to give yourself more time to ravish my daughter? Twice-double villain! A quick death is too kind for you.''

Tonia's body shook with her frustration. ''Pappa! Unstop your ears and listen to me! If Sandor misguided you, 'twas for my safety.''

''Aye, my lord,'' Sandor added, stepping around Tonia. He refused to cower behind her skirts—he would fight his own battle. Taking her hand, he entwined his fingers through hers and gave her a little squeeze for encouragement. ''Methought that you were the King's men come to ascertain Tonia's death. Though she had described her family to me, on that day, we were all well wrapped against the cold and I did not recognize you.''

Francis lowered his sword. ''I perceive that you have lost your northern accent,'' he remarked with a small trace of humor.

''Indeed, my lord. That too was a ruse.''

Sir Guy cocked his head. ''How did *you* know that she was to die?'' he asked, drawing out each word.

Sandor steeled himself for the answer. ''Because, my lord, I was the late King's executioner. I was sent to kill her.''

''*Le Monsieur de Mort* that Tonia spoke of,'' breathed Celeste. Her countenance softened when she looked at him.

Sandor flashed a warm smile at the petite gentlewoman. Now he knew where Tonia had inherited her dark hair and her beauty. *''Oui, ma dame,''* he replied in his childhood tongue, then continued in that language. ''''Twas my former office until I met your most beautiful daughter.''

Celeste clapped her hands with surprise and pleasure. "Oh la la! You are French!"

Sandor bowed to Lady Cavendish. "I was born outside of Paris, *ma dame,*" he replied in flowing French. He chose not to reveal that he had been born literally outside—in a field.

Sir Guy narrowed his eyes. "Did you say the *late* king? What news is this?"

Chapter Twenty-One

Before the Gypsy could relate the events that had rocked London for the past few months, fat raindrops suddenly splattered upon them. While the Cavendishes had given their attention to Sandor, a large black storm cloud overtook them. Tonia and her mother ran for the shelter of their carriage. Sheathing his sword, Guy shot the rogue a withering glare before he addressed his servants.

"We will return to Snape at once," he instructed his driver. To Sandor, he continued, "And once there, you will answer a great number of my questions."

The Gypsy returned Guy's steady gaze with his own. Only then did Guy notice the man's blue eyes. Most unusual for a dark-haired, swarthy Gypsy, he thought. Unsettled by the strange eye color and boldness of the man's gaze, Guy mounted his horse and spurred it into a trot, heading back down the road toward home. As he rode, his mind spun in a hundred different directions, none of them comforting. What manner of mischief had this charlatan worked upon his innocent Tonia? How had he bewitched Guy's most sensible daughter so that...

He gritted his teeth as he blotted out the mental image of his chaste daughter making love with this foreigner. No doubt the knave had employed some devilish charm to blind Tonia's mind while he had his way with her body.

Guy's blood grew hotter. Casting a quick glance over his shoulder, he was satisfied to see that Francis rode beside the man—the better to keep an eye on him. On the other hand, Francis did not show as much wariness as he should. Instead, he engaged in a lively conversation with their unwelcome guest. Guy eyed the carriage. At least, Celeste had kept the leather blinds closed. Tonia would not be able to call out to the rogue who had used her so foully and who had poisoned her mind in the bargain.

When we return to Snape, I will deal harshly with this churl. He will count himself fortunate if he ever sees daylight again.

Inside the stifling carriage, Tonia fanned herself and glared at her mother. "Cannot we lower the blinds, just a little, Mamma? By my troth, I will melt ere we arrive home."

Giving her daughter a sad look, Celeste shook her head. "'Tis better this way. The rain comes in fits and starts."

Tonia snorted. "Not so! You really mean to say that you do not want me to speak with Sandor."

Celeste sighed. "Methinks that your Pappa would be most upset if you even look at that man."

Tonia curled her lip. "You mean my husband? Do not gape at me, Mamma. 'Tis true—we are married—and soon we will be the parents of *your* grandchild."

Celeste's eyes grew wistful. "Oh la la! A grandchild!'' She sighed. "I have longed to hold that little one in my arms ever since the doctor told me of your condition."

Tonia spied a small chink in her mother's defenses. "Aye, I know that you do. I have seen you sewing little gowns and wrappers."

Her mother shrugged. "The child will need clothes no matter who its parent is."

Tonia pressed her advantage. "And the babe will be a beautiful child. You have seen his handsome father. You must agree."

Celeste cleared her throat. "*Oui,* I will confess that your Sandor makes a very good appearance despite his poor apparel, but he is a common vagabond, not a proper husband for my girl."

Tonia patted her stomach. "I am no longer a little girl in leading strings, Mamma, but a woman grown—and married."

Celeste rolled her eyes. "How so this marriage? Did you exchange vows before a priest?"

Tonia swallowed. "Nay, there was none to be had at Hawksnest, and we were pressed for time. But we did profess our love and loyalty inside a chapel."

"No banns? No witnesses? No marriage contract?" her mother asked.

Tonia shook her head in answer to each question. She showed the horseshoe-nail ring to her mother. "Sandor gave me this as his pledge, and we mingled our blood together so that now we are one forever." She leaned over and took her mother's hand in hers. "Mamma, help me. I love him so much. I will die without him."

Celeste kissed her daughter's cheek. "*Oui,* any blind fool could see that. The problem is, what does your father see? If looks could kill, your Sandor would have died back there amid the thistles.''

Francis observed the man riding beside him, and he found he liked what he saw. Like the rest of the Cavendish family, he had despaired when beautiful, gifted Tonia had chosen to shut herself away from the secular world instead of being married to some fortunate man. Only when he had seen Tonia and her lover together, did Francis realize how lonely she had been before this Gypsy had come into her life. Within Sandor's embrace, his half sister glowed like a bright sunbeam dancing on the surface of a pond.

Eyeing his father's straight back and the unyielding set of his jaw, Francis knew that Sandor's suit for Tonia would be an uphill struggle. Did the Gypsy have any idea what a dangerous road he walked?

Urging his horse closer to his companion, Francis asked, ''Tell me, Sandor. Do you love my sister? Or is it her fortune?''

The Gypsy's sun-kissed skin turned a few shades paler. ''If you were not my Tonia's beloved brother, I would split your liver for that question. To me, her fortune is herself alone. I accept no dowry like a *gadjo*.''

His answer and the emotion behind it took Francis by surprise even though he did not understand the meaning of *gadjo*.

''How can this be true? All men are in love with wealth.''

Looking down his nose at Francis, the Gypsy replied, ''Men are blind if they do not see that your sister is beyond the price of gold and silver. May I die if I lie.'' Then he added, '''Tis *I* who must pay the bride-price. I will explain this to your father—if he gives me the chance before he runs me through like a roast on a spit.'' He flashed a rueful grin at Francis.

Francis's eyebrows rose; he whistled through his teeth. "Hoy day, I have never heard of such an idea."

Sandor's smile widened. "'Tis the custom among the Rom…that is…my people. A man would be shamed—and so would the bride—if he did not pay the girl's father a goodly price for his daughter's hand. Methinks your father will see my point, once he understands that my heart is true."

Francis puffed out his cheeks. "Sir Guy Cavendish is a very reasonable man, most of the time, but in the matter of his three daughters, he tends to lose all reason. You have your work cut out for you. If it makes you feel more easy in your soul, be assured that I will add my words to yours."

Sandor stared at Francis, then he laughed. "Methinks that you speak true. My thanks. I will count you among my friends, my lord."

"Since it seems that we are already brothers-in-law, call me Francis."

Though the Cavendishes returned unexpectedly and after dark, the chamberlain of Snape Castle rose to the occasion. New fires were lit in the great hall's hearth, and fresh candles were inserted into the sockets of the chamber's large staghorn chandelier. Supper was hastily prepared for the famished travelers while clean linens were laid on the recently stripped beds. While her parents refreshed themselves after the day's journey, Tonia followed Sandor to the stables. It was her first opportunity to be alone with him since they had parted at Hawksnest. Not quite knowing how to pick up where they had left off, she watched him in silence while he prepared Baxtalo for the night.

Sandor had rarely set foot inside such a lavish abode as Snape. Most of the nobility did not allow the Rom under their roofs for fear of theft. Seeing Tonia within her own setting for the first time made him wonder if she could be happy with him, no matter what comforts he could provide for her.

"You live in a grand house," Sandor remarked as he curried his horse.

"I had rather live with you," she replied.

He glanced at her over his shoulder. "I have very little to offer you."

She cocked one of her beautiful, sweeping eyebrows. "Give me your heart and I will be happy."

He grinned. "Do you require it wrapped inside a brassbound box?"

She shuddered. "Oh, I mistook! I meant, give me your love."

He put down his brushes and took her in his arms. "You have that already, ten times over and more. But will that be enough for such a fine lady as you?"

Two red spots colored her ivory cheeks. Her eyes flashed in the lantern light. "How now, Sandor? Do you think damask gowns and ropes of pearls win me? What do you take me for?"

"I took you for my love," he answered in a quiet tone, "but at the time I forgot that you were also nobility."

She pulled away from him. "Did my brother offer to buy you off? How much did he pay for you to renounce me?"

Looking up to the stable's roof, Sandor sought

guidance from heaven. "*Jaj!* What is the matter with you *gadje?* You look at me and think that you can read my soul—that all I seek is your coin. Had that been true, I would have taken the King's gold and wrung your neck."

Tonia pressed her lips together and stared down at her feet. Sandor returned to brushing his patient horse.

Venting his frustration, he spoke to Baxtalo in Romany. "What am I to do with this pigheaded wife, eh, my friend? Doesn't she see how much I love her? I am ready to leap into the fire of her father's wrath for her, yet all she talks about is money!"

Tonia punched his arm with her fist. "If you are going to be angry, pray do it in English, or French, if you prefer. I am well-versed to argue in either language."

Relieved that she had not stalked away, Sandor hid his grin before he turned to face her. "I merely asked Baxtalo's opinion of my wife. As you can see, he is a wise horse and says nothing."

"And what is *your* opinion of your wife?" Tonia asked, tilting her chin up and staring quizzically at Sandor.

He stepped closer to her and slipped his arm around her waist. "I think that she is the most beautiful woman in this world."

"Ha!" she replied, though she blushed.

Heartened, Sandor continued. "That she is also the bravest, for she dared to challenge her executioner and so won his heart."

"Oh," she murmured, allowing her body to relax.

"And that she is most buxom in bed, though I have not tested that opinion in recent months."

"Ooh," she murmured, wrapping her arms around him. "I have missed you so much, my love."

He pulled off her maid's cap and unpinned her hair so that it cascaded over her shoulders. "You have no idea how much I have missed you, *sukar*. At night, when the wind blew cold through my little window, I would close my eyes and dream that I held you close to me. That made the weary days in prison fly faster."

"Prison?" She gasped, looking up at him.

"Aye, beloved. 'Tis why I have not returned to you until now. Under orders from some royal minister, I was kept in close confinement at the Tower of London until good Queen Mary released me."

Tonia trembled. "God save you, Sandor. You were in that dreadful place? Whyfore?"

He smoothed her satinlike cheeks with his thumbs. "Who knows? The King's pleasure? A whim of the Constable? I knew not. They said they would hold me until they were satisfied of your death."

She hugged him tight. "Forgive me, my love. I didn't know. Methought—"

"That I had abandoned you?"

She hung her head. "I prayed for your return, night and day. I worried that the *patrin* I had left at Hawksnest might have blown away. Then I wondered if I had been misled by your sweet words. Then, when I knew I was with child…"

He lifted her chin with his finger. "Peace, *sukar*. 'Tis past—bury it. Let me remind you of my great love for my wife."

He lowered his head and caressed her lips with a whispering touch as if she might melt away, as had her image when he dreamed of her. Without hesitation, Tonia returned his kiss with her own, pressing her strawberry-sweet mouth against his and twining her tongue with his. By her response, Sandor knew that his prayers had been answered. He drew deep from Tonia's bounty and she returned it to him in double measure. She tasted of warm honey and summer's clover. He fumbled to loosen her bodice.

Just then someone coughed loudly behind them. Sandor reluctantly pulled his lips from hers. Tonia straightened up then looked over her shoulder.

"What is it, Tad?" she asked.

A young turnspit boy stepped into the circle of the lantern's light. "Yer pardon, m'lady, but yer lord father awaits ye and him." He pointed to Sandor with a mixture of awe and fear. "An' yer lord father said that ye had better not be a-rollin' in the hayloft or he would flay *him* alive."

Sandor ran his fingers through his wind-snarled hair. "*Jaj,* 'twas a near thing," he muttered under his breath.

Tonia retrieved her cap from the stable floor. "Tell my father that we follow directly and that we were *not* in the hayloft doing anything. Do I make myself clear?"

Tad nodded. "Aye, m'lady, fer I found you in the stable, and ye was only a-kissin'."

"Tad!" rebuked Tonia. "You do not need to say *what* we were doing. Just say that we are coming now."

Tad touched the brim of his cap. "Aye, m'lady." With another swift glance at Sandor, the child ran out the door. His footsteps echoed on the courtyard's cobblestones.

Tonia slipped her hand into Sandor's. "Pappa is

really a very kind man,'' she assured him, though her kiss-swollen lips wobbled a little.

Sandor kissed the tip of her nose. ''Aye, and pigs with wings fly around Snape Castle.'' He lifted the lantern from its nail. ''Fare thee well, Baxtalo. I trust that we shall meet again in the morning, provided that my lady's father does not fry my liver before then.''

As they wended their way to the yawning door of the castle, the image of the *tarocchi* Fool flashed through Sandor's mind. Tapping his pouch at his belt, he felt the stiff vellum card.

This is the moment when I will jump off the cliff with both feet and my eyes open.

In the great hall of Snape Castle, Guy and Celeste sat upon their padded armchairs before the fire, and drank warmed wine from glazed pottery cups. Francis occupied a smaller chair at his father's left hand. His Venetian wife, Jessica, sat on a footstool beside him. A large gray wolfhound snoozed on top of Guy's feet. Otherwise, the large chamber was empty, though Tonia suspected that the family's servants were hiding in nearby nooks and crannies, eager to catch every word that was spoken. She tightened her grip on Sandor's arm.

''Do not be afraid,'' she whispered to him, though her own heart beat in double time. ''Pappa's bark is much worse than his bite.''

Sandor gave her a quick sideways glance. ''I will remind you of that jest at a later date. For now, let us render proper courtesies so that your parents will see that I am not a barbarian.''

Together, Sandor and Tonia bowed and curtsied in a courtly manner to the Cavendish family. When Sandor stood, he rolled back his shoulders and faced Sir

Guy. Tonia squeezed his arm to give him silent encouragement.

Guy sipped his wine. He did not offer any to Tonia or Sandor. Instead, he asked, "Before we discuss your ravishment of my daughter, tell me the news from London. You said King Edward is dead?"

Sandor tensed. Then he replied, "His Majesty died in early July, though what date I cannot say. My jailer did not confide that information to me."

"Jailer?" echoed Celeste.

"Aye, Mamma," Tonia answered before Sandor could. "'Twas the reason he did not come to me sooner. One of the King's minions had Sandor imprisoned in the Tower."

"'Tis a hellish place," Francis told his wife.

Sandor nodded to him. "Aye, my lord, you speak the truth. Within the week after the King's death, a young girl named Jane Gray was proclaimed Queen by the Duke of Northumberland."

Guy slammed his fist down on the arm of the chair, waking the hound. "The very villain who ordered Tonia to be executed for her religion. I see now why he did it. I will wring his life from him, drop by drop."

Sandor shook his head. "You are too late, my lord," he told him. "On the day that I was released from my cell, the great duke was released from his life. He was executed for treason on the twentieth of August." He turned to Tonia. "And so the wheel of fate has come full circle."

Francis glanced at his silent father, then asked, "On the road, you told me that Queen *Mary,* not Jane, gave you freedom. Which one rules our fair land?"

Sandor smiled. "Mary, King Henry's elder daughter, is now the rightful Queen. They say she will be crowned in London come November.''

"And Jane Gray?'' Francis asked.

Sandor sighed. ''She too is now a prisoner behind the Tower's rough walls. I never saw the lady myself, but they said she was very young and did not want the crown in the first place. 'Twas all Northumberland's idea. His son was married to her.''

"And so the duke would have been a kingmaker,'' Francis murmured to his wife.

Celeste lifted her wine cup. "And there's an end to it. A health unto Her Majesty, Queen Mary!''

Guy, Francis and Jessica raised their cups. "And so say all of us.'' The four drank in silence.

Sandor glanced at Tonia.

She nodded. "Speak now while Pappa has his mouth full,'' she whispered.

Taking advantage of the momentary lull, Sandor cleared his voice. "My lord and lady, 'tis time to discuss the bride-price.''

Guy blinked, then a sneer crossed his lips. "I see that you are not shy, knave, but a hardheaded businessman. Therefore, I, too, will come straight to the point. There is no dowry for the likes of you. Begone by morning's light.''

Tonia gulped. This interview was much worse than she had anticipated.

Sandor did not show the slightest distress. Instead, he said, "My lord, you misunderstand me. I do not ask a payment *from* you. I ask you to tell me how much you want for your daughter's hand in marriage.''

Both of Tonia's parents gaped at him. Francis quickly added, "'Tis true, Father. 'Tis a custom among the Egyptians to *pay* the father of the bride. A most interesting idea, don't you agree?''

"Oh la la!'' Celeste laughed, breaking the tension. "How marvelous! Just think of it!'' She poked her husband playfully in his ribs. "Tell me, Guy, my love, how much would you have offered for *my* hand, eh?''

Tonia's father colored from the neck up and cleared his throat several times. A grin hovered on Tonia's lips, but she bit them to suppress it.

"I...I would have paid a great deal, sweetling,'' Guy stammered.

Celeste's violet eyes danced with wicked delight. "*Oui,* but *how* much? In round figures?''

Guy twitched in his chair. Francis covered his smile by drinking deeply from his cup. Jessica giggled behind her fan. Only Sandor remained serious.

Guy coughed. "A hundred gold sovereigns! Nay, five hundred! By the stars, my love, you are priceless. I cannot put a value upon you.''

Celeste clapped her hands. "You have all heard my husband. Five hundred gold sovereigns! Oh la la! What grand shopping I will do when we go to London in November for the coronation!''

Guy turned redder. "'Twas a sum for your father, not for you to spend, my sweet. What of it? I have been married to you for years—and with only a dozen silver spoons as a dowry, if you recall.''

Sandor frowned. "Mere silver for this great lady? My Lord Cavendish, your good wife is worth a thousand times that amount.''

Celeste grinned broadly at him. "See? That is how a Frenchman speaks.''

Sandor inclined his head to her. "*Merci, ma dame.*

I am grateful for your support, but I must confess that I am also part Italian. I am the grandson of the Duke of Milan.''

Tonia stared up at him. ''You never told me this,'' she whispered.

Sandor smiled at her. ''I never knew myself until my grandmother revealed it, after I had been released from the Tower.''

Guy leaned forward in his chair. The sleeping wolf-hound twitched one ear. ''How now? This is a new tale. Now you pretend to be of noble birth so that you can claim my daughter?''

'''Tis no lie, my lord. The duke wooed my grand-mother when she was young and very beautiful. The child of their love was my mother, born on the outside of the blanket, of course, but still the daughter of a duke.''

''A pack of lies,'' Guy muttered to Celeste. ''The Gypsy's stock and trade.''

Sandor's ears burned at the tips but he held his temper. Opening his pouch, he withdrew the *tarocchi* card. ''The duke gave my grandmother many gifts, including a deck of beautiful cards like this one.''

Francis extended his hand and Sandor, after a mo-ment's hesitation, gave the card to him. He trusted the younger man would not destroy his precious me-mento. Sandor was not so sure of Tonia's father.

''On the face, you see the Fool. He is a traveler in search of new horizons. On the back is the duke's coat of arms and his motto.''

''Amor vincit omnia,'' Francis read aloud. '''Love conquers all' and I recognize the arms as belonging to the Visconti family. I once lived in Italy for several

years and had the honor to meet your cousin, the present Duke of Milan.''

His wife Jessica nodded. ''*Si,* my lòrd,'' she said to Guy. ''Even in Venice we knew of the Viscontis. They are a very noble family and great patrons of the arts.''

An unexpected sense of pride washed over Sandor. Francis had called the present duke his cousin. ''‘Love conquers all’ is the motto that I have adopted as my own.''

Guy drummed his fingers on the arm of his chair. ''You are overbold, Gypsy,'' he remarked in a soft voice.

Sandor looked Lord Cavendish straight in the eye. ''I am of the Visconti blood, my lord, and I dare to love your daughter, Tonia, with every sinew of my being.''

''And I love Sandor, Pappa. We are married and I carry our child. We are one blood, and there's an end to the matter.'' Her eyes flashed with blue fire.

Guy sat back in his chair and folded his hands together. ''Is that so, Tonia? You would forsake this warm, safe home to wander up and down the byways with this man?''

Before Sandor could protest that he planned to build them a cottage, Tonia replied, ''I do. Sandor risked his life for me, and I am proud to be his wife. Like Ruth in the Bible, I will go where'er he goes.''

Sandor kissed her hand before he returned his attention to the business at hand. ''The bride-price, my lord. I wish I could offer a hundred sovereigns for Tonia, though she is worth her weight in gold. Alas, I do not possess that much. However I am willing to work—''

Guy signaled for silence. "Cease this haggling. You have already paid the price."

Sandor glanced at Tonia, who shrugged. "How so, my lord?"

For the first time since the nerve-wracking interview began, Guy permitted the corners of his mouth to turn upward with the barest hint of a smile. "You saved Tonia from a miscarriage of justice. Her life and well-being are all I have ever wanted."

"And I agree," added Celeste.

Sandor was not sure that his ears had heard correctly. "You *accept* my service to Tonia as the bride-price, my lord?"

Guy nodded. "I do."

Sandor was almost afraid to breathe, let alone ask one more question. "And if you accept this price, then you agree that I am worthy of Tonia?"

Guy glanced at Celeste, who gave him a little nod. He sighed. "I do."

Tonia broke from Sandor's handhold and dashed for her father. Wrapping her arms around him, she kissed him on the cheek. "Oh, Pappa! Mamma! You have made me the happiest woman in England."

Sandor heard music in his ears. He felt like dancing around the chamber, but he feared that his exuberance might confound the Cavendishes. Instead he struck his chest with his fist. "I will be an honor to Tonia and to your family, my lord. You will see anon."

Celeste rose from her chair, drawing all attention to her petite form. "Mark me, my children, I have one condition to make—now that a Catholic queen rules England, you two must repeat your vows before a priest in our chapel." She gave Sandor a look of concern. "Are you Catholic, perchance?"

Sandor relaxed his shoulders. "*Oui, ma dame,* I was baptized—" He was about to say that he had been drenched with holy water seven times, but Tonia cut him off.

"—in a cathedral in Paris, Mamma. Sandor is most Catholic." She cast him a look that he did not dare to challenge.

Celeste clapped her hands. "*Très bien!* Then 'tis done. In one swoop, we have regained our daughter, who in turn has regained her mirth. We have a new son to add to our family, and in the wintertime, we shall greet our grandchild. I am most pleased. What say you, my love?" she asked her husband.

Guy finally smiled. "Your mother has spoken, Tonia. I am a wise man—I know when I have been vanquished."

Francis poured wine into two more cups. Then he handed them to Tonia and Sandor. Lifting his own cup, he said, "Drink with me to the happy couple."

Laughing, Tonia looked up at Sandor. "And what is the toast?" she asked.

With a wry grin, Guy raised his cup. "Love conquers all!"

"And so say all of us," Tonia and Sandor cried, before they kissed.

Epilogue

Mid-December 1553

Guy was enjoying a quiet doze in front of the fire-place in the upstairs solar when Celeste burst into the room waving a piece of paper. "How now?" he grumbled.

"*Ma foi!* They did not wait for us!" Celeste pointed to the paper.

Guy pulled himself upright and rubbed his head to clear away the cobwebs of sleep. "No one waits for us, my love, least of all time. Who has left us now? Did Alyssa elope?" he added hopefully. His last un-married daughter had been giving them a great deal of worry lately.

Celeste laughed as she settled herself on his lap. "Nay, 'tis a letter from Sandor. I must congratulate him. His writing has much improved."

Guy became instantly alert. "What's the news?" he asked, thinking of the young couple now settled on a modest farm at the far side of the moorlands where Sandor bred and trained horses. A very easy dowry to pay, Guy thought, and the only one that his stubborn son-in-law would accept. "Are they coming sooner for the Christmas revels?"

Celeste giggled. "Nay, they will not come for Christmas at all."

"What?" Guy roared. He looked forward to having all his children around him during the holiday season. "Doesn't that Gypsy celebrate Yuletide?"

Celeste kissed him on his nose. "*Oui,* he does, but they will keep closer to home this year. Their babe has come—a month before its time."

"What?" Guy clutched her arm. "Is Tonia well? Is the child healthy?"

Celeste laughed again. "Oh la la! My husband is such a brave knight, yet he turns into a cream pastry when he—"

"Peace, peace, woman! You are killing me with suspense. Is it a boy?"

She eyed him over the top of the letter. "So what is wrong with girls?"

Guy snorted. "Nothing! I have three of them! Is it a girl? Do not tease me, Celeste! What is it?"

"Hold your tongue, *mon cher,* or else you will never hear the news. Sandor writes, 'In the early hours of the seventh of December…'" Celeste paused. "Why do babies always come before breakfast, I wonder?"

Guy snapped his fingers. "Ask God, not me. Read on, I beg you."

"Let me see, ah…'Tonia was safely delivered of a…'" Pausing again, she giggled.

Guy blew out his cheeks. "Of a *what?* I am a dying man, sweetling. What did Tonia have?"

"'Of a *boy*—'"

"A boy," Guy mused under his breath. "Thanks be to God and all his angels." Having never had the pleasure of spoiling a baby boy, Guy thought himself in paradise.

"Sandor goes on to say that…hmm. Methinks he says that he wrapped his son in red flannel—"

Guy nodded. "A wise precaution against fever. My mother always did that."

"And laid him within a…a *horse's* collar?"

Guy snatched the letter from her hands. "Did you read that aright? Did Sandor misspell 'cradle'?" He reread the letter with particular care. "'Tis true—a horse collar, for Sandor writes that all Gypsy children sleep their first nap in this fashion. He says 'tis for good luck."

Celeste smoothed her hand over her husband's silver and golden hair. "'Tis a novel idea to be sure, but not a dangerous one. You did not give me time to finish the letter. Does the child have a name yet?"

Mumbling "horse collar" under his breath, Guy scanned down the ink-blotted sheet. When he spied what he was looking for, he grinned broadly. "Aye, they have named the little one Thomas—for my father, God rest his soul—Cavendish Visconti Matskella. 'Tis a mouthful to pronounce, methinks. But, Sandor goes on to say that they will call the child Cavi. Sandor ends by promising to have our grandson baptized 'seven times over.'"

Guy glanced up at his wife. "Now what do you suppose he means by that?"

* * * * *

Author Note

If you refer to your father as "dad," if your good friend is your "pal," if you protect yourself on the streets by carrying a "shiv" ("chiv"), if something is sweet as "sukar" (sugar), if you call a wild dog a "jakel" (jackal) or if you knock someone over the head with a "kosh"—you are speaking in the tongue of the Gypsies.

The Romany language has its origins in ancient Sanskrit, though it was not a written language until the mid-twentieth century. Today, the same Romany word is often spelled in several different ways. Scholars now believe that the original Gypsies came from northern India and not Egypt, as was commonly thought in the sixteenth century. In fact, the term "Gypsy" is an abbreviated word meaning "Egyptians." The Gypsies themselves much prefer to call themselves the Rom, meaning "the People." While the majority of modern-day Rom live in Eastern Europe, over a million reside in the United States, mostly in the warmer climes of California and Florida.

Tarot cards have long been associated with Gypsy

fortune-telling since both tarot and the Rom appeared in Western Europe at nearly the same time in the early fifteenth century. Tarot cards were originally used to play a game akin to modern-day bridge, a game that is still played in northern Italy. Fortune-telling with the cards became very popular throughout Europe before the 1500s. A tarot deck consists of seventy-eight cards. They are divided into the Major Arcana of twenty-two face cards depicting allegorical figures, and the Minor Arcana of fifty-six cards divided into four suits: cups, wands/staffs, pentacles/coins and swords. Modern playing cards are an outgrowth of the tarot deck. The cups become hearts, the wands are clubs, the pentacles are diamonds and the swords are spades. The original court cards were four: king, queen, knight and page. Modern decks have only the king, queen and the jack who replaced the knight. The page disappeared.

The Fool card that is featured in my story is the only one of the Major Arcana to be found in modern playing cards. He has become the Joker—and the Joker is always unpredictable.

Do Westerns drive you wild?
Then partake of the passion and adventure
that unfold in these brand-new stories from
Harlequin Historicals

On sale July 2002

THE TEXAN by Carolyn Davidson
(Texas, 1880s)
*A U.S. Marshal and an innocent spinster
embark on the rocky road to wedded bliss!*

THE BRIDE'S REVENGE by Anne Avery
(Colorado, 1898)
*An overbearing husband gets more than he bargained
for when his feisty bride demands her independence!*

On sale August 2002

BADLANDS LAW by Ruth Langan
(Dakota Territory, 1885)
*Will an honor-bound sheriff be able to choose
between his job and his devotion for a woman
accused of murder?*

MARRIED BY MIDNIGHT by Judith Stacy
(Los Angeles, 1896)
*In order to win a wager, a roguish businessman
weds a love-smitten family friend!*

 Harlequin Historicals®
Historical Romantic Adventure!

Visit us at www.eHarlequin.com   HHWEST20

New York Times Bestselling Author

Stephanie Laurens

Four in Hand

The Ton's most hardened rogues could not resist the
remarkable Twinning sisters. And the Duke of Twyford
was no exception! For when it came to his eldest ward,
the exquisite Caroline Twinning, London's most
notorious rake was falling victim to love!

On sale July 2002

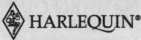

Visit us at www.eHarlequin.com

PHFIH

You are cordially invited to join the festivities as
national bestselling authors

Cathy Maxwell

Ruth Langan
Carolyn Davidson

bring you

Wild West
Brides

You won't want to miss this captivating collection with
three feisty heroines who conquer the West and the
heart-stoppingly handsome men who love them.

Available June 2002!

HARLEQUIN®
Makes any time special ®

Visit us at www.eHarlequin.com

PHWWB

Is he tall, dark
and handsome...
Or tall, dark
and *dangerous*?

Men of Mystery

Three full-length novels of romantic suspense
from reader favorite

GAYLE
WILSON

Gayle Wilson "has a good ear for dialogue and
a knack for characterization that draws
the reader into the story."
—*New York Times* bestselling author Linda Howard

**Look for it in June 2002—
wherever books are sold.**

HARLEQUIN®
Makes any time special ®

Visit us at www.eHarlequin.com

BR3MOM

If you enjoyed what you just read,
then we've got an offer you can't resist!

Take 2 bestselling love stories FREE!

Plus get a FREE surprise gift!

Clip this page and mail it to Harlequin Reader Service®

IN U.S.A.
3010 Walden Ave.
P.O. Box 1867
Buffalo, N.Y. 14240-1867

IN CANADA
P.O. Box 609
Fort Erie, Ontario
L2A 5X3

YES! Please send me 2 free Harlequin Historical® novels and my free surprise gift. After receiving them, if I don't wish to receive anymore, I can return the shipping statement marked cancel. If I don't cancel, I will receive 6 brand-new novels every month, before they're available in stores! In the U.S.A., bill me at the bargain price of $4.05 plus 25¢ shipping and handling per book and applicable sales tax, if any*. In Canada, bill me at the bargain price of $4.46 plus 25¢ shipping and handling per book and applicable taxes**. That's the complete price and a savings of over 10% off the cover prices—what a great deal! I understand that accepting the 2 free books and gift places me under no obligation ever to buy any books. I can always return a shipment and cancel at any time. Even if I never buy another book from Harlequin, the 2 free books and gift are mine to keep forever.

246 HEN DC7M
349 HEN DC7N

Name	(PLEASE PRINT)	
Address	Apt.#	
City	State/Prov.	Zip/Postal Code

* Terms and prices subject to change without notice. Sales tax applicable in N.Y.
** Canadian residents will be charged applicable provincial taxes and GST.
   All orders subject to approval. Offer limited to one per household and not valid to
   current Harlequin Historical® subscribers.
   ® are registered trademarks of Harlequin Enterprises Limited.

HIST01   ©1998 Harlequin Enterprises Limited

eHARLEQUIN.com

community | membership

buy books | authors | online reads | magazine | learn to write

Visit eHarlequin.com to discover your one-stop
shop for romance:

buy books

💛 **Choose from an extensive selection** of Harlequin,
Silhouette, MIRA and Steeple Hill books.

💛 **Enjoy top Harlequin authors** and *New York Times*
bestselling authors in Other Romances: Nora Roberts,
Jayne Ann Krentz, Danielle Steel and more!

💛 **Check out our deal-of-the-week** specially discounted
books at up to 30% off!

💛 **Save in our Bargain Outlet:** hard-to-find books at great
prices! Get 35% off your favorite books!

💛 **Take advantage of our low-cost flat-rate shipping** on all
the books you want.

💛 **Learn how to get FREE Internet-exclusive books.**

💛 **In our Authors area** find the currently available titles of
all the best writers.

💛 **Get a sneak peek** at the great reads for the next
three months.

💛 **Post your personal book recommendation online!**

💛 **Keep up with all your favorite miniseries.**

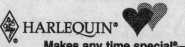

HARLEQUIN®

Makes any time special®—online...

Visit us at
www.eHarlequin.com

HINTBB

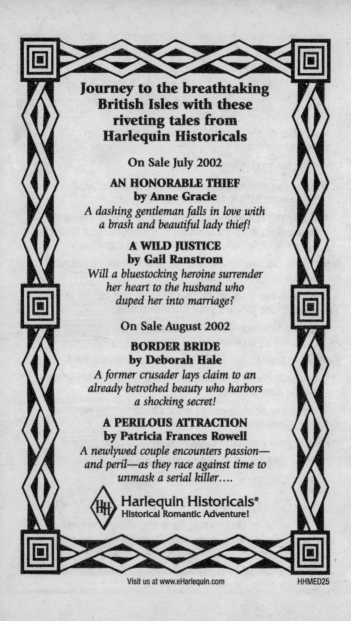

Journey to the breathtaking
British Isles with these
riveting tales from
Harlequin Historicals

On Sale July 2002

AN HONORABLE THIEF
by Anne Gracie
*A dashing gentleman falls in love with
a brash and beautiful lady thief!*

A WILD JUSTICE
by Gail Ranstrom
*Will a bluestocking heroine surrender
her heart to the husband who
duped her into marriage?*

On Sale August 2002

BORDER BRIDE
by Deborah Hale
*A former crusader lays claim to an
already betrothed beauty who harbors
a shocking secret!*

A PERILOUS ATTRACTION
by Patricia Frances Rowell
*A newlywed couple encounters passion—
and peril—as they race against time to
unmask a serial killer....*

Harlequin Historicals®
Historical Romantic Adventure!

Visit us at www.eHarlequin.com

HHMED25